CAGE (
& OTHER DEADLY OBSESSIONS

A SHORT STORY COLLECTION BY

JOHN EVERSON

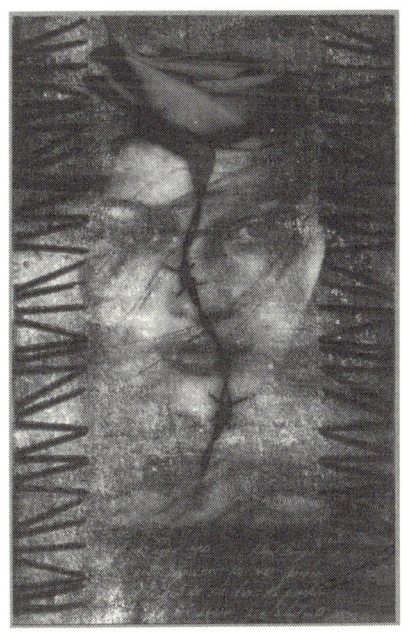

Introduction by P. D. Cacek
Artwork by Andrew Shorrock
Cover design by Colleen Crary

Also by **John Everson**

NOVELS:
Covenant
Sacrifice
The 13th
Siren
The Pumpkin Man
NightWhere
Violet Eyes

NOVELETTES:
Failure
Violet Lagoon

SHORT FICTION COLLECTIONS:
Cage of Bones & Other Deadly Obsessions
Vigilantes of Love
Needles & Sins
Creeptych
Deadly Nightlusts: A Collection of Forbidden Magic
Christmas Tales

FOR CHILDREN:
Peteyboo and the Worm

AS EDITOR:
Spooks!
In Delirium II
Sins of the Sirens
Swallowed By The Cracks

For More Information Visit:
www.johneverson.com

Cage of Bones
& Other Deadly Obsessions

A SHORT STORY COLLECTION BY

JOHN EVERSON

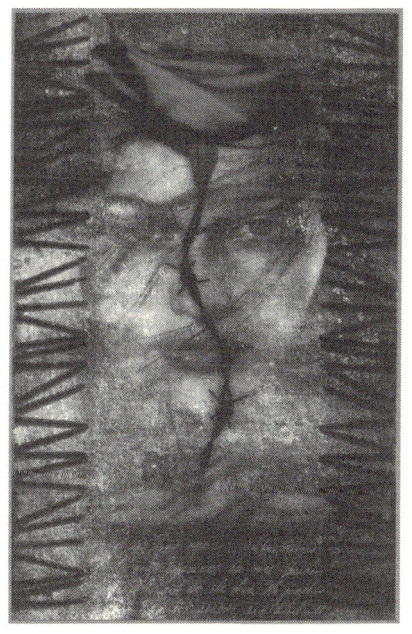

NAPERVILLE, ILLINOIS

~2013~

CAGE OF BONES & Other Deadly Obsessions

Dark Arts Edition copyright © 2013 by John Everson.
Cover art copyright © 2000 by Andrew Shorrock.
Hardcover edition foil stamp design copyright © 2000 by Colleen Crary.

"Introduction" copyright © 2000 by P.D. Cacek.
"Yellow" copyright © 2000 by John Everson.
"Long Distance Call" copyright © 2000 by John Everson.
"Cage of Bones" copyright © 1994 by John Everson. Originally appeared in *Into The Darkness* #2.
"Dead Girl on the Side of the Road" copyright © 2000 by John Everson.
"Pumpkin Head" copyright ©1999 by John Everson. Originally appeared in *Grue* #19.
"Direkit Seed" copyright © 2000 by John Everson.
"Every Last Drop" copyright © 1998 by John Everson. Originally appeared in *Bloodsongs* #10.
"When Barrettes Brought Justice to a Burning Heart" copyright © 2000 by John Everson.
"The Mouth" copyright © 2000 by John Everson. Originally appeared in *Delirium Magazine* #1.
"Creaks" copyright © 1994 by John Everson. Originally appeared in *Crossroads* #9.
"Remember Me, My Husband" copyright © 1994 by John Everson. Originally appeared in *Terminal Fright* #6.
"Anniversary" copyright © 1995 by John Everson. Originally appeared in *Dead of Night* #13.
"Wooden" copyright © 2000 by John Everson.
"Swallowing the Pill" copyright © 2000 by John Everson.
"Broken Window" copyright © 1998 by John Everson. Originally appeared in *Xoddity* #3.
"Tomorrow" copyright © 1998 by John Everson. Originally appeared in *Shadowland* #7.
"Mirror Image" copyright © 1999 by John Everson. Originally appeared in the British anthology *Nasty Snips*.
"Murdering the Language" copyright © 1995 by John Everson. Originally appeared in *Outer Darkness* #2.
"The Last Plague" copyright © 1996 by John Everson. Originally appeared in *Outer Darkness* #8.
"Bloodroses" copyright © 2000 by John Everson.
Afterword copyright ©2013 by John Everson.

All Rights Reserved. No part of this book may be used or reproduced in any manner whatsoever without written permission except in the case of brief quotations embodied in critical articles or reviews. This book contains works of fiction. Names, characters, places and incidents either are the products of the authors' imaginations or are used fictitiously and any resemblance to actual persons, living or dead, business establishments, events or locales is entirely coincidental.

For more information on this and other Dark Arts Books titles,
visit www.darkartsbooks.com or e-mail sales@darkartsbooks.com.

Printed in the United States of America.
First Delirium Books Printing, October 2000
First Dark Arts Books Printing, September 2013
ISBN-13: 978-1492-20804-4
ISBN-10: 1-492-20804-3

www.darkartsbooks.com

Dedication

For Geri, who taught me
about fighting for love.

Acknowledgments

Many of these stories would never have seen print but for the encouragement of some very special editors, and I want to thank Marybeth O'Halloran, Pat Nielsen, Shane Ryan Staley, Dave Barnett, Tina Jens and many more for their critiques and encouragement over the years.
Whatever seeds I planted, they helped grow.
I've been richer for the nurturing.

Table of Contents

Introduction 11

Yellow 17

Long Distance Call 33

Cage of Bones 49

Dead Girl on the Side of the Road 57

Pumpkin Head 65

Direkit Seed 73

Every Last Drop 95

When Barrettes Brought Justice to a Burning Heart 115

The Mouth 135

Creaks 149

Remember Me, My Husband 153

Wooden 163

Swallowing The Pill 169

Broken Window 181

Tomorrow 185

Mirror Image 193

Murdering the Language 197

Anniversary 205

The Last Plague 217

Bloodroses 231

Afterword 245

About the Author 249

*"It is always by way of pain
one arrives at pleasure."*

—Marquis de Sade

Introduction

I. Guilty Pleasures

Ah, that got your attention, didn't it?

Well, it was supposed to.

Given the thrust (no pun intended) of the stories in this collection – "mature content" and deadly obsessions – I wondered how the heck my poor little introduction would stand a chance. I mean, let's be honest... why would anyone want to take the time to read my mental meanderings when the lure of sexual misconduct with vegetables and unbridled passions beckons just a few pages further on?

Answer is no one would... unless they were tricked into it. Hence the *Guilty Pleasures* tag. Of course, now that you know the trick, there's nothing to keep you here... or is there? I was going to explain how reading this book is a guilty pleasure, but you it's your choice if you want to know or not.

Take your time, I'll wait.

You decided to stay.

Cool.

Now about that guilty pleasure – As I mentioned before, the book you're holding if filled with stories about things most of us would never attempt in real life (and which will, forever more, make you look at carving Halloween pumpkins in a *whole* new light)... but that's not going to keep us from reading about it. In fact, we might very well go out of our way to read about it even though we might suddenly blush and snap the book closed should a minor or less liberal thinker walk by. Why? I mean, all we were doing was reading, we weren't actually doing anything (at least *I* wasn't!), but we still may feel a little guilty if anyone knew we *liked* this kind of thing.

Not that we going to stop, mind you. One of the true joys of giving into a guilty pleasure is that no one, including you, gets hurt. Because guilty pleasures, like truth, beauty, and sex, are only in the minds of the beholder.

Huh? What part of that last statement didn't you understand? Oh, that sex is only in the mind. Yeah, I can see where this might be confusing, but the truth of the matter is that no matter where the actual act takes place (and you might want to take notes while you're reading the stories that follow), sexual urge begins in the mind. The mind sees or reads something provocative and the procreative juices begin to flow. We might feel a bit guilty about it… but you have to admit it's a pleasurable sensation, right?

Guilt + Pleasure = You get it.

Lucky you!

II. Erotica vs. Pornography
Well, there *is* a difference, trust me.

I know. If you listen to the "Moral Majority" in this and other countries, you might be under the impression that the words are only different terms for the same thing: *Nasty things*, i.e. dirty pictures and bad words. But the truth of the matter is that even though both pornography and erotica strive toward the same goal, that being sexual arousal in the viewer/reader, the methods are different.

Let me try to demonstrate with two descriptive passages:

I. The two dogs boinked each other senseless on the front lawn.

II. The great golden mutt lifted his head and sniffed the warm summer wind. He could smell her scent long before he saw her – the rich, moist musk permeating his senses

Introduction

with desire. And then he saw her, his goddess. She was all beauty, her long, silky hair shimmering in the bright light, the wanton glint beckoning in her luminous brown eyes. A moment's pause and he rushed at her, leaping high as they came together, his hot, throbbing...

Okay, you get the idea. Besides, who knows the kind of trouble I could get into with *PETA* if I continued. So... which of the above is pornography and which is erotica?

I know, it's not really a fair question, I doubt if anyone could get sexual aroused by either (and if you did, I don't want to know about it). What I was attempting to do, in a round about, but highly entertaining way, was show the basic difference between pornography and erotica.

Still don't get it, huh? Okay, let's try this... pornography is intended to sexually arouse without artistic merit. Erotica arouses from the mind down (remember my earlier statement) by using as many of the senses as possible. Erotica is tactile. Erotica is sensual. Touch, taste, smell... those are the things that qualify erotica and those are the things you'll find in John Everson's stories. These are stories that are not so much read as experienced.

Granted, some of the experiences won't be very pleasant, but you'll feel them and I guarantee you'll not soon forget them.

Please return your seats and tray tables to their upright and locked positions.

It may be a bumpy ride.

III. Obsessions, Deadly and Otherwise

Romantically inclined gourds, genetically created love machines, see-through chests, succubus roadkill, self imposed moralists, killer television, real "boners," demonic possessions, freaks, geeks and forlorn rotting vampires seeking revenge. Looking at the stories like this, it'd be hard to come up with a connective tie... but if there wasn't, would I be writing anything right now? No.

Regardless of the diverse (and remarkable) settings, these are stories of obsession, the kind that will crawl under your skin and make themselves at home. Obsession, like sexual arousal, is one of those things that we humans are pre-programmed for... and John Everson not only knows that, but plays with it. Of course, because this is a collection of horrific tales, the obsessions don't turn out well. But do they ever?

And there, my friends, is the hook. We *know* that what the probably outcome of these stories will be and yet does that stop us or even slow us down? Nope. If anything, we grip the pages a little tighter, look over our shoulders a little more often to make sure no one is watching, and (again, pardon the pun) plunge in deeper. Have we ourselves become "obsessers?"

I'll let you answer that yourselves.

You may not find yourself agreeing with or even sympathizing with the characters in these stories, but more times than not, there will be a tiny spark that'll recognize. And once you do, there's no getting away.

When you finish this collection, you may hate the stories or love them... but like I said before, you won't forget them.

IV. Conclusion and Other Sins

Yes, I've come to the end of my introduction, and hopefully, I've, dare I say it, aroused your curiosity about the stories in this book.

Hope so.

In *Cage of Bones and Other Deadly Obsessions* John Everson shows us a world that exists, or could exist, just beyond the one we're comfortable with.

INTRODUCTION

We're lucky to have him as our Tour Guide.

Please have your tickets ready.

But, if you're still having a hard time swallowing the things I've written about John and this book, don't worry. You're not the only one... as you'll find out when you read "Swallowing the Pill."

Enjoy!

– P. D. Cacek
Arvada, Colorado
January 2000

I've always been fascinated with caves – the dark hidden spaces of the earth where the buried and forgotten successes and excesses of the past lie hidden. Caves are treasure trove and crypt combined. In "Yellow," the hidden lore of the earth's interior counterpoints a couple's interior quest to save their marriage. Relationships are tricky balancing acts at best, and so often weighted down not by the visible disagreements in taste and style (I hate Chinese, couldn't we eat Italian tonight?), but with unseen and unspoken baggage. By private obsessions. And by unconquered cowardice that doesn't allow both to face the dark together.

Yellow

In the cool kiss of a sun-drenched dawn, so much can be dismissed, so much forgotten. But it's hard to dismiss the empty space in the bed beside me last night.

It's hard to ignore the brick-red stains that mar the otherwise bleached pebbles on the dry stream bed down the hill.

And it's impossible to still the voice behind my eyes that screams "yellow, yellow, yellow" without pause or compassion. The voice names me truly. I can brook no argument.

\/\/\/\/\\/\/\\/\/\\/\/\\/\/\

Ostensibly it was solitude for my writing which brought Rachel and me to this backwoods cabin two months ago, but there was an underlying agenda to our relocation as well. We hoped that – no, we wondered if – spending time together could pump vigor back into our flagging marriage. I can't say that we both wished that our life together could be saved. Call it wistful curiosity. We treated it more as some kind of psychological experiment in human emotion. Consign the two rats to an otherwise rat-free cage and what will they do? Reproduce, or consume each other. It was a move of joint desperation, not hope.

Perhaps it was that lack of hope that ultimately caused Rachel's doom. If we had acted together, as one, so many things might have been different. But the two rats found a third alternative. They neither mated nor chewed each other. Instead, amid the lazy bird songs of the forest, we simply retreated to our own corners of the cabin. She withdrew into a correspondence course on computer languages, and I, as many "retreat" writers may admit, did not write. Instead, I spent an increasing amount of time away from the cabin, exploring the miles of hilly wooded trees around us.

The upshot of all this is, when I discovered the cave during one of my daily walks along the dry stream bed, I didn't, as many a mate would, run back to drag Rachel out to the spot.

I held it to myself jealously.

It seemed a small cave, when I first pushed the cascade of weedy leaves aside and peered within. My stomach trembled, as I expected at any moment to hear the growl and meet the unforgiving jaws of a black bear or some similarly unfriendly animal. But I could smell no spoor as my head hung just inside the lip of the opening. I ducked and slowly poked my body in, now adding snakes and scorpions to my "to be worried about" list.

"Hello?" I called, and then listened intently for any telltale movements. There were none.

I couldn't see how far the cavern extended to the sides, but I could, from the dim light the cleared entrance allowed in, see that the front cavern of the cave narrowed to a tunnel that continued into the mountainside. It took every bit of restraint I owned to not barrel into that corridor right then. I was a child again, and I had found a secret place to call mine.

"I'll be back tomorrow," I called out loud, and smiled as my voice vaguely echoed in the hidden recesses of the cave.

I don't know what Rachel thought when I got home that evening. I'm sure my face beamed with secret pride at my discovery. She glanced at me oddly a couple times over dinner.

"What is with you tonight?" she asked at one point.

"Just a beautiful day, I guess," was my empty reply.

That night as she lay beside me in bed, I reached out to massage her chest, but she pushed my hand away.

"No," she whispered. A while later as I fumed in unfulfilled lust beside her, I felt the bed shake in a rhythm I recognized. It was not erotic. She was crying.

The cave had once been inhabited by something. Stacks of dried brush lay where the front cavern ceiling diminished to meld with the silty floor. The former bed of bear and 'coon, I thought, and flashlight in hand, I pushed my way deeper into the cave, to begin the exploration of the tunnel beyond that first small cavern. Would it only peter out to an impassable crack in the mountain, or lead to more geological treasure rooms within? I ached to find out.

I had come prepared. My backpack held spare flashlight batteries, a canteen, a hammer and a variety of snacks. After hearing horror stories all my life of unlucky and unprepared spelunkers, I had attached an end of twine to a tree just outside the cave lip. The spool hung from my belt, unwinding a guideline back to daylight with every hesitant step I strode.

As I moved into the murky recesses of the earth, my mind kept returning to Rachel. This should have been a shared excursion, I growled to myself, blaming her for our current lack of connection. Never mind that I hadn't asked her to come with me.

I found a bitter laugh in the memory of the two of us bicycling down the slope of a volcano on Maui so many years before. In the pregnant predawn gray, we'd weaved back and forth on the descending slope, pedaling close enough for me to reach out and hold her hand – a romantic and foolhardy thing to do when whizzing with almost no control down the slope of a mountain. My situation now was so completely opposite. I thought.

The tunnel did not, as I'd feared, taper off to a dead end, but instead, angled slowly upwards. Its sides were nearly smooth, completely unlike the haphazard crash of rock and boulder on the outside of this mountain. They glistened wetly in the yellow light of the flash. The air seemed humid and strangely warm, not at all the clammy cool of deep earth I'd expected and dressed for. Soon I was tying my jacket around my waist by its arms, and sweat was running freely down my cheeks and neck. And the tunnel continued, slowly but inexorably sloping upwards, toward what pinnacle I could not guess.

I stopped and wolfed down a bag of Doritos, then emptied half the canteen at the thirst they brought. Not, perhaps, the wisest choice in snacks. Still, refreshed and having caught my breath, I continued forward then. How long was this tunnel? Would I simply exit halfway up the mountain and then have to stumble my way home back down the outer face of the rock? Or would the trail end and leave me forced to retrace my seemingly endless steps straight back down? The sense of adventure in exploring an underground labyrinth was giving way to boredom and exhaustion. And the deep blackness which the light of my flash couldn't completely disrupt was giving me a slight case of claustrophobia.

After walking a little while, I was strongly considering giving up and turning around. This was no doubt a sluice tunnel from the spring thaws that simply had burrowed into the outer skin of the mountain and wended its way down to the valley, never branching, never creating any of the stalactite wonder I was hoping to find.

But then I heard the rush of water. It was faint, just a whisper, but unmistakable. My goal couldn't be too far away! I redoubled my steps and the trickle grew in my ears until the tunnel abruptly ended in a cavern 10 times the size of the one at the cave's entrance.

The flashlight only barely cut the gloom to trace out the slick gray face of the opposite end of the cavern. A few feet below me flowed the source of the sound. Crystal clear water. It looked to be only a few feet deep; I could see the white and pink pebbles that lined its bed. Carefully I eased my way down the smooth slope from the tunnel mouth to the creek bed. It seemed warmer here than it had in the tunnel. Hot springs?

I leaned over and dunked my hands into the deceptively still water and confirmed my suspicion. The water was warm, almost bath-hot. I dunked my face to wash off the sweat, and the effect after my exertion was heavenly. All I wanted to do was crawl into a warm tub and relax my aching feet.

And why not? It wasn't as if anyone was going to disturb me here. Setting the flash between two rocks to aim its light to reflect off the wall and onto the water, I stripped off my sweaty clothes and gingerly stepped into the spring water. As I felt the hidden current ripple between my legs, I also felt an embarrassing stirring. It wasn't as if this were a public pool, I chided myself, and then slid all the way into the water.

I'd been wrong about the depth. My feet couldn't touch the ground unless I dove deep. I soon found myself paddling against the current to remain near my clothes and light, but it was a joyous exertion. I flipped my feet up into the air and slalomed under the water, kicking myself lower and lower until I could grab handfuls of the glittering rock bottom. I soon felt a rash of tickles on my thighs and belly, and had a moment of bladder-voiding fright when I realized there were things in this water with me. What if they were snakes? Poisonous ones?

Trying to control my fright, I eased my way to the bank, all the while feeling the groping of smooth, slippery kisses on my exposed body. I stifled the urge to cry out. At last reaching the light, I directed its beam into the water to discover the source of my discomfort.

They were yellow. About the size of my fist. And apparently, harmless.

Darting in and about my privates were a school of what looked like giant tadpoles. Pale citrus-colored tadpoles with no obvious mouths or eyes. They were flesh with tails.

Keeping hold of the light, I let the current take me again. The creatures followed, bobbing and bumping against my butt and belly. It was a pleasant feeling, their smooth caress, and I found myself relaxing and enjoying their strange attention. In moments I drifted from one end of the cavern to the next, and was faced with the question of whether to duck my head under a rock overhang and follow the stream to its next destination, or to fight the current and go back.

The tadpoles zipped past my legs and disappeared into the under-ledge tunnel. It looked like there might be enough space for my head to surface and breathe between the water and the ceiling, but I opted for safety and turned around.

As I climbed out of the water near my clothes, relishing the steamy humidity of the cavern and the tingle of the foreign water dripping from my pores, I knew I would be back. I wanted to see where the stream – and the tadpole creatures – went.

I returned to the underground creek the very next day, better prepared and even more glad to have kept the place secret. I'd felt unusually lustful and amorous after my furtive adventure the day before and had once again tried unsuccessfully to make love to my wife. This time however, it didn't result in quiet fuming, but in a heart-squeezing torrent of bile and bitterness. As we hissed and spat at each other, I could literally feel my love for her distilling into hate.

Later, in the oppressive shadows of the bedroom, I stared at her silken dark hair tangled amidst the sheets. I'd once found it an erotic accoutrement. Now I only longed to yank it, hard, for the feelings its owner had exhumed in my heart. Rolling from the bed, I left the cabin without my clothes, eventually coming to stand naked in a moon-drenched clearing. Despite – or perhaps because of – the bitter fight, I was as aroused as I could remember, and sought to still that hunger on my own. As the cool air of the night moved against me in its own secret rhythm, I tried to picture Rachel stretched taut between the pillows of our bed back home. But the only picture that came to mind was of darting, twisting tadpoles.

It was enough.

When I returned to the cave I carried two flashlights and an old oil lamp I'd found tucked away in the cabin's cupboards. This time, I entered the water without hesitation, almost anxiously anticipating the touch of the school of lemon tadpoles. They did not disappoint.

Within seconds I felt their nibbles and slickly smooth caresses around my thighs. I'd brought more twine, and sealed my best flash in a Ziploc freezer bag to keep it dry. Letting out the rope from where it was anchored near the exit of the watery cavern, I let the current steal me down, down to where the tadpole creatures had passed me the day before. I sucked in a breath and submerged my head beneath the rock ledge.

The current was swift, and a pang of fear ripped my gut as I considered the consequences of cracking my head against an outcrop of rock, or of this watery tunnel ending in a sheer waterfall.

My light did little to show me where I was going, its beam dissipating before it reached the sides of the sluice way. I slowed my passage by letting out the twine slower than the current moved. But my need to breathe wouldn't allow me to limit my progress by much. My heart was soon hammering in my head, my lungs screaming for my mouth to open.

And I was through.

My head broke out of the water at the same moment as my mouth wrenched itself open to breathe, regardless of my mental instructions not to. I brought up the light as I gasped in the cool fresh air and saw that I was in a cavern similar to the one I'd been in before.

But not quite the same.

At the far end, next to where the river disappeared beneath another shelf of slate, was the most blatantly erotic sculpture I had ever seen. I felt myself growing beneath the water as I stared. It was like the fertility sculptures I'd seen pictures of from ancient cultures. This one was created on an enormous scale. She must have been at least 20 feet tall, and every detail lovingly carved. Rock rivulets of hair cascaded from her forehead to her shoulders and chest. Her lips were heavy and parted, her breasts erect and melonous. But the part that struck me at the start was her sex. She sat at the edge of the water, her legs spread apart, feet submerged. A pile of rocks and mud blocked the current's passage to the open cavern between her thighs, but the original purpose of the V of her stance was obvious.

It wasn't a conscious decision that led to my action. I was suddenly just doing it. Removing the smaller rocks between her calves, digging my fingernails into the packed muck that glued the dam together. Within minutes the water was seeping into crevices that my fingers also worked at. I beat at the stubborn wall using the earliest dislodged stones, and within minutes I was sweating and streaked with black slime. But I was excited. I know now, that feeling must have stemmed from her. With each stone I moved, I felt a surge in my loins, an electric reward. I became a reverse beaver, thrusting against it with unexplainable passion, until all at once, the current sloshed over the top of the splintering dam. I lay down on the long-dry tunnel between her legs and with my feet, kicked to loosen the base of the dam. With water pooled on both sides now, it began to give. Then a splash, a slow sucking sound, and the last of the rocks twisted and sunk out of sight. A warm wave passed over my body. As it kissed my face and disappeared into the hole behind my head, I think I had an orgasm.

And then the tickling began.

I hadn't noticed the tadpoles in a while, but the water around me was suddenly thick with them, all surging to dive into the channel I'd just reinvented. I moved out of their way, and the water churned with lemon creatures diving into the statue's sexual abyss. Was this some natural spawning waterway that I had reopened, that some strange artist had commemorated with this statue? I backed up into the central channel again and surveyed my handiwork. The water had risen to kiss the very tops of her thighs, just missed the mark where it would begin dribbling over them. A steady stream of lemon tadpoles disappeared up the tunnel of her exaggerated vagina. None seemed to reappear, and I wondered how far that passage continued into the rock.

I was tired, and felt odd – disconnected – after my exertions so I decided to head back. At first I tried pulling myself along the twine hand over hand, but I soon realized that it was just as easy to swim against the current – it wasn't as strong as it seemed when you just let yourself glide against it. I came up gasping but triumphant in the first cavern, and soon levered myself up on the bank at my backpack. I wolfed down the lunch I'd packed (no Doritos this time) and considered heading home.

The thought of reentering the cabin and sitting across from a sullen Rachel dissuaded that idea quickly. The lunch seemed to instantly restore my strength, and I felt almost an erotic need to plunge into the watery mouth at the opposite end of the pool – to see where the current originated from.

The water was bereft of tads as I kicked my legs and arrowed under a new ledge. Again the light failed to show my way, but I wasn't worried this time. I was unlikely to swim my way into a rock hard enough to knock myself out, and I surely wasn't going to go over a fall with water rushing opposite my chosen course.

This tunnel seemed shorter than the southern passage, and within seconds I popped my head up in a new pool, in a new cavern.

This was the place I'd searched for.

I shone my light on the walls and laughed out loud.

"Holy shit," I said to no one.

The place was beautiful; a magical mouth of rocky teeth. Stretching many feet from the ceiling were tiers of blue-green and blushing stalactites, and rising from the floor on the sides of the pool were an equally dizzying number of multicolored stalagmites. It was like swimming in the midst of a shark's mouth.

I swam to a bank and ran my hand up and down one of the glossy rock needles. It was smooth and cool. Like a marble column shellacked in varnish. I longed to break it off, but didn't want to mar the beauty of the place by destruction.

Perhaps I could find one that had fallen from the roof?

I climbed the bank and walked gingerly along the shore, uncomfortably aware of the consequences if I slipped on the smooth stone floor and landed heavily on the points of the stone spears that were everywhere around me. I stared at the path carefully, catching sight occasionally of a darting tadpole speeding towards the entry tunnel.

At last, I came to the last turn of the cavern. I'd found no broken spears, but I nearly slipped and ate one when I saw the guardian to the end of this chamber.

A man to match the woman.

He was gargantuan, like her, and in the same posture: back to the wall, legs spread to capture the water. But there was no blockage to prevent his giant sex organ from hanging into the current. Hanging, actually is incorrect. He seemed in a state of excitement, if the sculptor was attempting to work to scale. (It's hard to tell really – should a 20-foot man have a three-foot organ, or only a foot and a half? His was at least arm's length.)

I slid back in the water, and swam to the icon's feet. Its chest was bulging, shadowed muscle, its arms were clasped behind its head. Eyes closed, it seemed wholly at peace as it let its lower body dangle in the water.

But it wasn't at peace. It was in my head.

"Bring her to me," I heard clearly, though not with my ears. Its face remained passive, but I swear to god it spoke to me, threatened me. A vision flashed in my mind of what it wanted as it spoke.

"Bring her or meet my children."

In my mind I caught a glimpse of a pulsing mountain of flesh, warted gleaming gold eyes, and teeth. Teeth everywhere. A crash came from my left. A stalactite had somehow dislodged from the ceiling to land a yard from where I stood.

"Promise to bring her, or the next one will not miss. Use it. Bring her."

I promised.

Then I grabbed the stone spear and dove back into the current. I almost forgot to pull my pants and backpack back on before running down the long slope out of the mountain.

"You have to come see this cavern," I crowed that night. Rachel looked at me with something less than boredom.

"I've never liked caves," she sighed. "And I don't think I like you anymore, either. So why would I want to go to a cave with you?"

"It'll be quick, I promise. Just humor me one more time, OK?"

"And I'll get what out of it? Claustrophobic and clammy? No thanks."

But I didn't let up. Finally she gave in, simply, I think, to shut me up. Reasons didn't matter. I smiled inwardly. And as we lay down to another sexless night, I dreamed of nuzzling citrus tadpoles and an amazon stone woman. The sheets were sticky when I woke in a warm sweat to the sound of croaking frogs.

Rachel complained the entire walk up the inside of the mountain, which only strengthened my resolve. The closer I got to the cavern, the less I heard of her. My mind began remembering the sensation of the tadpoles against my legs, of the watery extended orgasm I'd experienced in opening a channel to the statue woman's deep and thirsty tunnel. And I remembered the vision of her partner.

When we reached the cavern, Rachel looked around with her flashlight. Her face dropped.

"Where are the stalagmites?"

I was already peeling off my clothes.

"We have to swim for them."

"I'm not diving into that! You don't know what things are in there. Caves have all sorts of weird fish and things with no eyes swimming around in them. Uh. Uh.'"

"I've been in a couple times now," I said. "It's fine."

She turned her back to me and began to retrace our steps.

"Goodbye, Jim. I'm going to the cabin, packing, and leaving. You stay here in your little cave."

I threw myself at her, my shoulders connecting with the backs of her knees. She fell hard, crying out as her head cracked against the rock floor. The force knocked her out, and something inside me whispered, "it's easier this way."

I pulled her back into the cavern, and saw the swelling on her forehead already goose-egg big and blue. She was breathing fine, so I undressed her and pulled her into the water with me. Immediately a swarm of tadpoles gathered around us, but this time they concentrated, not on mine, but on Rachel's thighs. She moaned slightly, and I swam to the giant man's tunnel quickly, before she came to completely. I held her with one arm around her chest, and felt myself swelling at the feel of her familiar, yet still tantalizing, breasts. I pulled her under the water with me, and the dunking served to wake her fully. She started clawing at me, but I only gripped her harder, and pushed us against the current the short space underwater until we could surface in the stalagmite cavern.

I let her go when we broke the surface, and she immediately dove away from me, choking and crying at the same time.

"You're crazy," she yelled, and swam ahead as I chased her.

Chased her right to the statue.

She was as awed as I had been.

For a moment, she seemed to forget my coercion, as she rose from the water to stand at the feet of the giant. My flash played upon her dripping buttocks, and I was suddenly overcome. I believe it was the giant and not myself. But something happened to her too. Because when I walked up behind her and reached my hands around her waist to feel her up, she didn't push me away. And when I ran those same hands down the trail of her belly, into the light down of her pubes, she changed her stance to accommodate.

When I turned her to face me, she had a blank, lost look in her eyes. Concussion or possession, I don't know, but without any suggestion from me, she suddenly knelt and put her mouth to work. Something she'd never done for me. Ever.

I was in ecstasy, but she wasn't finished. Smiling a retarded sort of grin, she stepped into the water between the giant's legs, and got down on her hands and knees. Only her hands were clutching the giant's phallus, and her rear was waving in a gesture that not many men could ignore under any circumstance.

I took my wife for the last time there, in a cave, her hands on another's organ. A rod of stone. And as I found the best release I can ever remember having, a swarm of golden tadpoles shot from the rock between my wife's hands and darted around us slickly kissing our every pore. I almost loved her again in that moment.

And then the spell wore off.

And she screamed.

"Oh my God, what have you done!"

The tads were not letting up this time, and Rachel soon showed me why.

"I can't move my hands!" she wailed, and holding her arms up, I saw they were entwined together with hundreds of tiny lemon filaments.

In that instant, I saw again the vision I'd seen before, and again a rocky spear fell nearby to remind me of my promise.

"Come on," I said and tugged her back into the channel. "Let the current take us back."

In seconds we'd resurfaced in the main cavern. I heard it then.

The heavy thunder that rose above the sound of the gurgling river. It came from her cavern. It sounded like the croaking of a thousand bullfrogs. And as we swam to the shore, it grew louder.

I pulled her out of the water, and then reached down to pick up the twine I'd used to mark my progress. Before she knew what I intended, I looped the twine through her glued hands, and tied her fast. She could move to the water's edge and stand in the lip of the exit, but could go no farther.

"What are you doing? You can't mean to leave me here!"

I looked into her face, and tried to remember why I had once loved her. Instead a strange sensation rumbled through my stomach.

Hunger.

Insatiable, painful hunger. It grew with the sound of the now not-so-distant croaking.

"I do," I said, and like the last life-changing time I'd said it to her, I really did mean it.

Something huge and glisteningly green broke the surface of the water as I turned from her and ran to the exit.

I forgot my clothes this time, but it didn't matter anymore, did it?

\\\\/\\/\\/\\\\/\\/

I'm all packed now, and ready to leave. I want so badly to walk up that trail once more, and bathe in the waters of the lusty cavern. But I don't know if Rachel only bought me time, or bought me endless license. If the former, my meter is up.

Last night as I lay alone in bed, my belly rumbled contentedly, as my sheets became stained with uninitiated pleasure.

This morning I stood at the base of the mountain, in the dry stream bed where I'd first discovered the hidden tunnel. The otherwise white stones were marred in spots with something sticky. Something dusky red. A shred of the t-shirt I'd ripped off Rachel was caught in a bush nearby. And every few feet, glistening and shriveling in the sun, were thin, sticky threads.

Yellow threads. Like corn silk.

As I stood there contemplating the evidence of my betrayal, I felt a rumbling in my stomach. And a stirring in my loins. Suddenly I wanted to rip off my clothes, run up the hidden tunnel and plunge into the secret pool again.

But I didn't.

Sometimes being a coward has its advantages. It helped me run.

But can I stay away?

And if so, can they follow me?

\N/\N\/\N\/

As I turn the car onto the first paved road in 20 miles, I can swear I hear croaking behind me. Not too far away. And not diminishing.

I can feel their hunger.

I heard on a talk show that a huge percentage of couples have at least one partner cheat on the other, and a large proportion of that cheating happens in the workplace (makes you think about Windexing your desk each morning, doesn't it?) Sometimes the price of strangling a relationship with inattention and sexual subterfuge can lead to calls you don't want to have. The kind of call that's untraceable...

Long Distance Call

Christina twisted on Jack's lap to allow her to silence the disruptive ring. The outer office was eerily dark, back lit by the yellow glow of the elevator hallway. It was as if they were performing for an audience – the only light centered upon their bodies. Green glass softened the glare of the banker's lamp on Jack's desk. Softened but not obscured, the warm light threw shadows across the filing cabinets, projected the tawdry silhouette of their two bodies in motion across the side wall – bigger than life and twice as tantalizing to would-be peeps.

"It's your wife," Christina harrumphed breathlessly. She twined the phone cord around her middle, forcing him to pull her closer if he wanted to stretch the receiver to his ear. With one thick, hair-camouflaged paw, he pulled her in close, and while still subtly moving inside Christina, Jack greeted his wife.

"Hi honey, what have you been doing all day? I tried to get through and the line was always busy."

"Jack, I'm so alone." Her voice trembled, seemed to come from miles and miles away. Christina thrust a blushing nipple between the phone and his lips but he only frowned and shook his head. He still cared for his Angela, even if she'd been living in another world these past months.

"I'll be home soon," he promised, eliciting an exaggerated pout from Christina's cherry lips.

"Why is Christina there so late, Jack? It's after 7 o'clock. What are you doing with her?"

He answered too fast. Scared now.

"Nothing honey. I mean, she's helping me with this project, that's all. I've got to get it finished by Friday."

Angela's voice seemed to be drifting. Its normally full, throaty rasp was reedy, insubstantial.

"I've known, Jack. Always."

"Known what, hon? Angie, you're not taking too many of those Valium, are you? You sound funny."

Christina was rocking, ignored on his lap. She could feel him slipping steadily out of her, no longer keeping it up. Her face fell in disappointment.

"Ooooh. Uh. Uh. Uh." Angela had begun groaning and grunting on the other end of the line! Sounding like she had when they'd first gotten married, and had enjoyed the wanton push of each other's fleshy bodies. Like she hadn't sounded in months.

"Ohhhh Jack. Is this what you want? I know how to do it *gooooood* for you, baby. I'll be your little slut, Jack. That's what you want, isn't it? A slut? Maybe some phone sex? *Oooooh* Jack. Go ahead now. Finish what you started."

Jack's desire dove rapidly into the impotent range. Something was majorly wrong. Somehow she must know about Christina – and the way she'd been lately…

"I'll be right home, honey. Hold on."

"Known," Angela whispered.

Jack thought maybe she was crying. "I'm ready now. I'm waiting for you Jack. Me and Eddie. *We'll* be waiting for you."

The line went dead.

Jack handed the phone back to Christina, who cradled it absently behind her, not taking her eyes off the man beneath her.

"How does she do it?" she railed, blue eyes flashing in frustration. The past five times they had managed to get the office to themselves to make love, the phone had rung just prior to completion of the act.

"I don't know," Jack shook his head and gently helped Christina up from her complicated squat through the arms of the chair. "But something's wrong. She sounded really strange, and she…"

His voice trailed off, eyes clouded in confusion.

"What? What did she say?"

"She said she'd known, and then started making sex noises. I don't know what's come over her. It's been eight months since she made love to me, and then it was like she was doing me a favor."

He smiled lopsidedly at her, a puppy dog's look after tracking muck from the yard across white carpeting. "I'm sorry. I promise I'll make it up to you." He hesitated, about to say more, then shook his head. "I better get home."

The house was dark when Jack's headlights swung into the driveway. He was genuinely concerned now. He loved Angela; had never dreamed he'd cheat on her. But then, last year, she had started to change. He blamed the books. After her brother Ed had driven off Hwy. 32 and into a tree, killing both himself and some woman he'd picked up in a club earlier that night, Angela had started checking out occult texts from the library. She couldn't accept her brother's death. But the books were only the beginning. Hunting for a way to contact her Eddie, Angela had begun frequenting a New Age bookstore downtown that sold crystals and incense and all sorts of gimmickry.

Jack had kept this quiet at first, assuming wrongly that time would heal – that she would see that this hocus pocus crap was just that – crap. Eddie was dead and was going to stay that way.

But she didn't see. Instead, she delved deeper and deeper, attending seances, bringing home all manner of creepy, spaced out weirdos. Jack had tried to put an end to it, but by then it was too late. He'd lost her long before. The final blow came when one night, as he'd crept up behind her at the sink to cup a breast in each hand and blow in her ear (always a sure bet to have them both naked and coupling within five minutes) she'd swatted his hands away. Turning to look into his eyes, she'd calmly announced: "No more of that, Jack."

He'd stepped back, staring at the freckles on her cheeks, hungry for those black ringlets across her forehead to brush his belly.

"Huh?" was the most intelligent answer he'd managed.

"No more sex. I think I've been unable to reach Eddie because I'm not pure. I have to be… white, clean in body and soul to reach the other side."

That had been it. That was the last night Jack considered that he had a wife – since then his house had been filled with herbal scents and empty words. A woman lived with him, but she was not Angela.

Jack turned off the car, grabbed his briefcase and stepped into the garage.

Everything was still. The reverberation of the car door slamming seemed to echo forever in his head. He stood a moment in the inky black of the garage, smelling the cold musty scents of dust and mildew. He needed to fix that fracture in the east wall, he thought absently. Leaking again.

Jack fumbled for the knob, and pulled open the door to the house. It was even more quiet inside. She must have gone out somewhere, he thought, and swatted his hand up the wall for the switch. The light at the top of the stairs blazed to life, revealing the five steps up to the front door foyer, the black and white pattern tile there, the spider plant hanging from a long macrame sling near the door.

"Honey? Angela? You home?" he called. His voice fell flat in the darkness, seemed swallowed up by the night. No answer. Shaking his head in consternation, Jack mounted the stairs to the foyer.

Something squeaked.

He paused, listening, his heart pounding loud in his chest. It had just occurred to him that someone could have broken in to the house – and hurt or killed Angela. Someone could still be here!

The squeak continued, a steady sound, like a tree limb sawing back and forth against a window in the wind. It hadn't been there when he'd stepped into the house. Slowly, trying not to make a sound, he placed a foot on the next stair of the landing. Ten stairs up to the front room/dining room/kitchen. The sound grew louder, more frenzied. Another stair. And another. He held his breath.

"Screeuuken screeeeeeuuken," the noise accelerated.

Jack closed his eyes; took a deep breath. Steeling his nerve, he ran up the next six steps. And stopped.

The noise was Angela. She was dangling several feet in the air, held to the decorative ceiling beam by a taut length of phone cord. The receiver hung at her breast, still attached to the cord looped several times around her neck. The phone base anchored the noose up around the beam. Angela was naked, and looked quite dead. The hall light reflected off something wet on the floor beneath her. Angela's eyes bugged in Jack's direction, but her lips were pulled back tight. If she hadn't been dead, Jack would have said she was smiling.

Jack felt numb; his mind refused to function. He was simply too astounded to absorb this. He walked like a zombie to where she hung, and reached out to grab one white, naked leg to still her pendulum motion. He withdrew his hand suddenly, in overwhelming disgust. She was cold. And damp.

He sat on the floor, staring at the lifeless corpse that had so recently been his wife. And hated himself for his first thought: "Well, at least Christina and I won't have to sneak around anymore."

He felt like a pupil at the feet of some philosopher. *Only her feet were not on the ground*, he thought, and suddenly began to laugh. *It's not funny*, his mind screamed at himself and he only laughed louder. And then the tears came, and he cradled his face in his hands.

Something dropped with a dull slap to the floor and Jack snapped to attention. Whoever had done this to her was still here, he thought, as something nudged his knee. He almost wet his suit pants then and there. Jack reached shakily to the floor by his leg, and quickly found the object. It was cool, smooth, tubular. And sticky at its end. He lifted it from the ground, and stared at Angela's vibrator in disbelief. It had rolled from across the room. The phone end table, he thought. It must have fallen from there. There was still a sheet of paper curled on top of it. He got up to see what it was, knowing before he got there that it would be a last note from Angela.

He guessed right.

Dear Jack,
I've gone to find Eddie. Hope you'll be happy with Christina. Give this to her for me?
Love, Angela

He stuffed the note and sex toy into his pocket.

Why had it fallen just then? he wondered, a strong case of the creeps stealing over him. Why had she begun swinging AFTER he'd started up the stairs. Goosebumps poked through the hair on his arms and he realized it was time to take action. 911. That's what he had to do. Call 911.

The line was busy. He picked up the kitchen extension and got a steady beeping tone. He'd have to go next door to call. Nodding at this sage decision he stepped back into the front room and looked at Angela again. She was ghastly. White as milk, except for the purpling at her feet and neck. Then he noticed the phone was still plugged into the wall. That's why the line had been busy all day! She'd left it plugged in. He didn't have to go next door. He bent over and unplugged the line from the wall socket, went back to the kitchen, and made the call.

But as he waited for the police and ambulance to arrive, one thought nagged at him. *If she'd killed herself this morning, and tied up the line all day, how had she called him an hour ago?*

\/\/∧\ΛΛ\/\/∧

"She was awake when you left this morning, Mr. Trenton?" the policeman asked, cocking an eyebrow that seemed more than willing to expand into a hairpiece if allowed.

"Yes," Jack replied softly. "She seemed fine."

"And what time did you go to work?"

"7:30, same as always."

"Did you talk to her at all during the day?"

"Well, I tried calling her at lunch, and then later in the afternoon – I had to work late."

"But did you reach her?"

"No. But she called me."

"When?"

"Around seven tonight?"

The officer stopped writing and looked up slow and intently at Jack. The coroner had already guessed Mrs. Trenton's death as occurring between 8 a.m. and noon, give or take an hour."

"Tonight you say?"

Jack noted the tone. Officer Starley had suddenly become very interested.

"Yeah, she called to see when I'd be home."

"You were working later than usual?"

"Yeah."

"Did she ever give you any indication that she would try to kill herself?

"No. She was getting more into occult stuff lately, but… no."

"And had you had a fight recently?"

Jack pictured the cold quiet life that had become his over the past few months. No fights. No speaking, really. "No."

Starley scribbled in his book. When he looked up he was smiling.

"That's all for now, Mr. Trenton. I'm truly sorry about your loss."

Starley shook Jack's hand and left the kitchen, pausing momentarily to look up at the high beam Angela Trenton had so recently been umbilicaled to. It was likely that she'd used the chair by the wall to climb up, wrap the phone around the beam and her head, and jumped. But then again, her husband was hiding something. Murder? He didn't know. But he always got an itch when someone was concealing. And right now his body was itching all over.

"Ohhh yeah, c'mon baby, ride me!"

Christina's nails scraped against Jack's naked back as he thrust and moaned with her exhortations. "We're gonna get there this time," she almost screamed.

And then the phone rang.

And rang.

They tried to ignore it, but the precipice grew farther away with every ring. Finally Christina pushed against his chest with her palms.

"Answer it or they won't give up."

He grudgingly agreed and rolled off of her.

"Hello?"

"Jack. You can't even lie alone for one night? I'm hurt."

It sounded like Angela's voice.

"Who the hell is this?" he yelled.

"Forgotten me so soon, Jack? After all those years of marriage? I found Eddie, Jack. He still remembers you. He says he wouldn't mind handling Christina for you if you'll come back to me. Will you, Jack?"

He slammed the receiver down.

"Who was it, Jack?" Christina cooed.

"Someone pretending to be Angela," he snarled. "Pretty mean joke."

"How many people even know she's dead?" she asked, stroking the back of his head.

"I don't know."

They slept the rest of the night. Or tried to.

\\/\\/\\/\\/\\/\\/\\/\\/

The wake was a long and tiresome affair. Chirsten's Funeral Home filled with an amazing assortment of humanity, from the hairy, odd-smelling space cadets of Angela's recent acquaintance to the mannikin-sharp models of her older relatives.

Jack smiled diligently at the kind words and kisses of the assemblage, but in his heart, he was feeling relief – the recent memories of the silent hell his home had been were still too fresh in his mind to allow the fireplace-cozy visions of his life before Eddie's death to push their way forward. He cried, but he did not feel devastated. He felt freed.

He said as much to Christina later that night, as she kissed his eyelids and began sliding lips down his cheek and neck, her tongue leaving snail's trails of wetness behind.

"I always wished she'd just disappear," Christina admitted, looking up from her ministrations at his sternum. "But I never wanted it to be like this."

For a fleeting moment, Jack saw the mixture of joy and regret in his mistress' face and wondered if this woman was responsible for Angela's death. Had this sweet-faced fountain of love turned vinegar for an hour and shoved his wife to her death, guaranteeing that at last, Jack could satisfy her needs?

He shrugged the thought away, giving in to the sweet temptation she administered. She probed and massaged and sucked him to full excitement, then rose and impaled herself upon him, allowing him only the sight of her rounded rear bobbing at his waist. And the phone rang.

She froze in mid-squat, while Jack's heart suddenly beat in double time. He shriveled instantly.

"Why???" Christina screamed, and snatched at the phone. It toppled off the nightstand, the receiver bouncing to rest on the carpet. Christina bent over the edge of the mattress to recover it, only to stop as she heard Angela's voice.

"Don't touch it, whore," Angela's normally sweet alto growled. Jack's face was pinched and white. They could both hear the voice as clearly as if she were in the room with them.

"Eddie and I are waiting for you, Jack," Angela continued, her tone again sweet and complacent. "We miss you. All of that stuff I haven't done for you these past months – I will now. But first we need to get your little tramp out of your way. It was purity that was needed, Jack. Remember how I said? No sex, no distractions. Pure thoughts of mind and spirit and you can join me. Christina, pick up the phone. Dear."

Christina's eyes looked ready to pop from her head. Her hand remained halfway between the bed and the floor.

"I said, *Pick up the phone, slut!*"

Christina grabbed for the mouthpiece and moved to slam it down on the receiver. But as she stepped on the carpet, the taut phone cord seemed to twitch at her foot, wrenching her off balance. Christina fell to the floor as the tight loops of the phone cord snaked around her neck.

Christina screamed and jumped to her feet, the ringer of the phone box banging on the floor as she stumbled to run from the room. Jack, still stunned at hearing the voice from the grave, was slow to react, not realizing the animation his phone cord suddenly possessed. Christina made it as far as the stairwell before the line went taut and jerked her neck backwards. For a brief second, her frightened eyes met Jack's as he belatedly barreled out of the bedroom after her, and then she twisted over the railing. He heard the snap as her neck broke, but threw himself down the stairs anyway, hoping against the odds that somehow, Christina could be saved.

She could not be.

He found himself again at the naked feet of a woman he loved, as she slowly spun like a silent, ghastly pinata. *Poke her hard enough and her entrails will rain to the foyer,* a voice in his head taunted.

Jack screamed in impotent rage. Not pausing to dress properly, he pulled on a pair of pants, slid bare feet into his shoes and went to his car. He no longer functioned rationally, his sole thought was to put an end to what Angela was doing to him. And there was only one way he could think of to do that: kill her. That she was already dead didn't register.

Chirsten's was cloaked in darkness as Jack used a crowbar from the trunk to force the lock on a window. He tried to muffle the sound of the window as it protested the upward force he exerted, but it still let go a loud "eeeeerrrrraahh" as it crept up in its frame. Holding fast to the iron rod, Jack flipped his feet over the window jam and pressed close to the wall once inside. He was in one of the many waiting areas strewn throughout the funeral parlor for the bereavers. After waiting long minutes listening for the telltale sound of investigative steps, he disconnected his body from the wall, and crept forward. Angela's body should still be in the waking room in anticipation of tomorrow's funeral, Jack thought, as he tiptoed past a number of closed doors. At last he came to the sign reading ANGELA TRENTON – white letters against a field of black. Even in the murky twilight of the hall he could make out her name. It angered him further just to see it, and he abruptly grabbed the doorknob to open the door. It didn't budge.

His anger only grew at the realization that, while she was apparently capable of striking out at him from behind the doors of this locked room, *he* couldn't get within 10 feet of her. He wrenched and twisted the handle, trying to force the lock, but to no avail. At last, knowing that only a scrap of steel separated him from his troublesome dead wife, he wedged the crowbar in the crack of the door and pushed. It gave a little, and he tried again, harder. Something began to splinter, but he ignored the noise. Giving it a third shot, he threw all of his weight into it, and with a sharp crack, the hollow wood around the lock gave.

Angela lay displayed in an icy glare of moonlight which stole in through a crack in the venetian blinds. Jack marched up the center aisle of the room. His eyes glinted with mad purpose as he came to a halt before her casket. She looked good in the purple turtleneck dress he'd given her last Christmas, he noted absently, though he'd seen her in it all day. Her eyes were shut primly, her mouth a vacant closed line of blush. Raising the crowbar, he smashed those innocent features, releasing a puff of makeup and a stream of liquid onto the satin pillows of the casket.

"How could you?" was his only articulate cry as he raised the dripping bar again and again before resorting to more personal attacks.

The flashlight caught him in macabre silhouette, hands squeezing and shaking the flopping neck of a corpse.

\/\/\/\\/\\\/\/\\\\/\/\\

Officer Starley spent the rest of the night in Jack's house, picking the place apart. It was with a grim but victorious smile that he faced the disheveled prisoner the following morning.

"Quite a little death circus you've been running, eh?" Starley snarled, pacing the length of the table at which Jack sat cuffed. "Killing the wife wasn't enough, huh – got a thing for phones Jack? A little sex, a little strangulation? And we found another interesting piece of evidence up there at the sex n' death cottage, Jack. Maybe we'll be reopening investigation on the sudden demise of your brother-in-law."

Jack's eyes at last flashed with a vestige of intelligence at the mention of Eddie.

"Didn't think we'd find out about that little perversion did you?"

Jack frowned in confusion. "What are you talking about?"

Starley pivoted fast, slapped his hands down on the table. "We found Eddie Perfit's hand under the mattress of your bed, creep! Did you use it in place of your own on Christina and Angela when you couldn't get it up? Or did you just like knowing ol' bro Eddie was *close at hand?*"

Jack's eyes bugged. He began to stutter. "Angela... must have dug up... she wanted to be with him..."

"Save it for the jury," Starley cut in and then stalked from the room.

The trial went quickly – Jack refused to speak on his own behalf and the evidence seemed overwhelming. He was sentenced to life, and many reporters noted the vacant stare in his eyes as they led him from the courtroom after a 20-minute verdict delivery. They put him in solitary, and assigned him a shrink. But he had retreated fully. They stuck him with needles and prodded him with batons, but he didn't speak. The shrink gently cajoled him with soft words and easy questions, but to no avail. During his second week in solitary, he was led to his daily appointment with the shrink. The guard patted his ass with the baton and whispered a crude proposition in Jack's ear, but he didn't break stride. Failing to get the rise he'd intended from the prisoner, the guard pushed him into a chair, shrugged at the doctor, and left.

At that moment, the phone ran. The prison psychiatrist noted with interest that Jack's normally blank expression had been quickly replaced by one of alarm at the sound of the phone. The shrink answered the ring, and a smile wrinkled the corner of his lips. He offered Jack the earpiece over the desk.

"It's for you," the shrink said, closely gauging his patient's response. Jack shakily held the receiver to his ear.

"Hi honey, it's me, Angela," a familiar, raspy voice

cooed. "I thought this would be a good place for you to get pure so we can bring you over to us. Eddie and I are waiting for you, Jack. Eddie says now he can understand why you were doing Christina. He says she's pretty good. I think so too. Say hi, honey."

The voice changed to a younger, more sultry tone. "Jack, it's me, Christina. We're waiting for you, baby. We'll get you out of there soon, huh? Stay near a phone."

Jack dropped the receiver and cupped his palms over his ears, letting loose a single, tortured, shriek.

"Nooooooooo!"

*I've always been fascinated with obsessions, maybe in part because my own nature is often to focus on a project, worry or desire to the exclusion of all else. The obsessive mind, depending on its direction, can as easily produce an Einstein as a Dahmer. Intellectual obsession can lead to brilliance or insanity. Erotic obsession can lead to ecstasy, but in the unending pursuit of pleasure, sooner or later, the limitations of the flesh must come into play.
How do you thrust beyond this cage of bones?*

Cage of Bones

It was beautiful. A painstaking work of genius. And after weeks of preparation, hours upon hours of slow polishing, careful craftsmanship, it was finished. A full body restraint table. Made out of steel. Wood. Leather.

And bones.

"Art for the whole family," Dan snickered.

"Think it'll hold?" Melissa asked, arching a hairless eyebrow at him. She had shaved, plucked, and depilated every lustrous shaft of black hair on her body last month as her birthday present to him. Their conjugal love fluids had subsequently made contact with most of the surfaces in the house during the following days.

"Think? I know it will. Look."

He turned the giant skeletal wheel next to the cage. It twisted a chain wound beneath the black wooden frame and the cage began to elevate from horizontal table to upright. It reached its peak position and stopped with a shudder, bones rattling against bones with the clinking sound of muted wind chimes. Dan reached for an arm restraint. Two humerus bones jutted in stark relief from the black wood. A third rested between the two held firmly in place at its joint ends by steel pins. The ends of the pins were kept from slipping out by a short length of silver chain and clip hooks. Dan grabbed the middle restraining bone and yanked. The table jostled slightly on its axis, but the bone did not break, the pins did not slip, the bolts holding the humerus bases to the wood did not give way.

"No baby, when you clamp me in this thing, I'm yours."

Melissa glided slowly across the room to stand in front of the cage. Her eyes came alight with erotic designs. She reached out a thin white arm to touch the ribs of the cage. It was like the skeleton of some mythic beast: two skulls propped beyond the lip of the wood for the living head to rest upon. Another three-bone restraint jutted just below these to clamp the captive's head to the table beneath the jaw. On the outer right and left ends of the wooden base were two sets of bone arm clamps: one for the elbow and one for the wrist. Down the center of the wood ran a series of ribs. These were attached to the table on one side with steel pins that worked like hinges. The other ends were fastened to hooks on the table with leather belts to allow adjustment for the restrainee's girth. There were two three-bone restraints for each leg, and a skull at the foot of each. The skull could be moved up and down a small groove in the wood, to assure that the restrainee's feet rested on them. Melissa rubbed her palm on the brain pan of one of the foot skulls. Her other hand snuck under her loose white cotton t-shirt. Dan could see the nipple she was not already massaging begging for attention through the thin material.

"Now?" he asked, as a glazed look stole over her face and her bottom lip hung heavy, pouty.

"Get me my fur," she breathed, never taking her hands from skull or breast. Her fingers had slipped inside the eye sockets while her thumb slid repeatedly across the top of the yellow-mottled cranium. Dan left the basement almost running.

When he returned, Melissa was naked. Her clothes lay forgotten in the middle of the green-tiled floor. She was rubbing her crotch against one of the skulls and talking softly.

"...always wanted to get between my legs, didn't you? Ahh, Mr. Bernie, yes. You always wanted my snatch in your teeth, didn't you?"

She turned then, and held out her arms to him.

He set his pile of furs on the floor beside her, and began fastening them. Squirrels which he'd killed for her with a slingshot in the back yard laced across her arms. The raccoon they'd seen in the forest preserve while picnicking he stretched over her tiny belly, laced it up across her back. The bullet holes in its head hardly showed at all. The rabbit skins fastened around her thighs, one of them covering the body of the blue and green snake tattoo that wound up and around her left thigh. The snake's neck and head crossed her pelvic skin, its eyes stared centimeters from the bare cleft between her legs. Its thin pink tongue disappeared into her own private salmon folds.

Dan considered joining his own tongue with the snake's, but knew he'd never be able to stop. He wanted to do this right for her. Picking up the last of his carcass coverings, he fastened wreaths of sparrow feathers around her calves. Then he stood, staring into her shiny black eyes as he hastily unbuttoned his shirt and pants, letting them fall to the floor. The ritual inflamed them both.

"Are you animal enough for me, now?" he asked.

Her bald white head peered down at her body. Only her breasts and vulva remained fully exposed from the covering of furs.

"No. Still I feel exposed. Offer me more," she said in a familiar response.

Dan walked across the room to an aquarium on the floor and removed the lid. When he returned, a small gray mouse clawed the air beneath his hand. She accepted the tail from him, and smiled in anticipation. Her breathing grew louder as Dan held his palms to either side of his body as though in benediction. Then he brought them around with a slap, crushing the struggling rodent. He unclenched his hands then, streaked with the gore of the exploded mouse. Tenderly savage, he streaked her cheeks, her scalp, her breasts with blood. Then he took the dead creature from her hand and again walked across the room. This time when he returned, the mouse had a silver ring through its hind end. He clipped it to the matching ring on Melissa's left nipple. The weight of the mouse pulled the breast lower. Melissa licked her lower lip and groaned.

At last, it was time. Dan backed against their newest toy, feeling the cold uneven surfaces of bones against his back, his buttocks. He stepped up on the foot skulls, and placed his arms in position. Melissa, blood shining brightly on her baby smooth ceramic skin, moved to lock his arms into place.

She undid one chain, then the other, letting both of the pinning bones dangle from the goalpost bones they fastened across. With the silky touch of a gentle lover she lifted and set his arm in place. Then she pushed the middle bones into place, clicked the pins through the holes drilled in the middle of them, and locked the chains. She repeated the process with his other arm and his legs. Dan could feel his muscles stretching as she pushed each restraint to its tightest position. She locked down an altered pubis over his cock, which grew stiff as the dead bones. It felt as though his balls were being crushed as she levered it down on him, but his cock stood tall and proud through the hole in the bone. At last, she levered the clavicle across his neck and battened his head down. As she completed chaining the last pin, Dan blew at her bloodied head to get her attention. She looked up and smiled.

"Happy birthday, babe," he said.

"Yeah," she agreed. "I think it's going to be."

She stepped back to observe her handiwork. Dan was deliciously naked, almost as hairless as she was herself. He'd refused to shave his head, but had gone along with the rest of the Nair treatment. His legs gleamed a mahogany brown beneath the white of the bones which bound them to the table. He liked the sun, she liked the moon. He was tan and muscular, she was wan, elfin. They really were night and day to each other, she thought. But when they came together...

"I have a surprise," she said, and flounced up the stairs. He heard rustling in the kitchen, drawers opening and closing, the clink of metal on the counter.

She came back down the stairs with her hand behind her back. Dan held his breath as she reached the foot of the cage and brought the hand around. Then he released his lungs with a smile. She was holding a bottle of champagne!

"I thought we should christen it," she giggled. Placing the stem of the open bottle against her bare, already glistening vagina, she jumped up and down. Foam leaked out of her crack and across her hand to drip like whipped cum on the floor. Then she released the bulk of the pressure and the froth spurted over her face and across Dan's bones. She held the bottle to his lips and he gulped, but still it dribbled down his cheeks. Then she took a swig and set the bottle on the floor. Taking his cock into her mouth still cold from champagne, she quickly fellated his waning muscle to full erection. Then with a twist of the wheel, she had him lying on his back. In a second she was straddling him, gripping the ribs holding him down for balance.

Dan was awash with sensation; the thrill of being held prisoner, the depravity of being touched by bones, the wash of liquor and sex through his body. Melissa was in ecstasy too; she banged her crotch up and down on his pubis prison like a piston. Then she leaned and licked the champagne tears from his cheeks and laughed.

"You like your cage of bones, don't you Danny?"

He groaned in answer.

"You know you're a sick fuckin' bastard."

He laughed. "You helped."

"You liked slicing open mommy and daddy for me, didn't you, Danny?"

"Yeah."

She moaned pornographically at his reply.

"You got off on it when you put their bodies in the acid, didn't you?"

Dan laughed as Melissa moaned again at the recollection. "I wasn't the only one who couldn't stop cumming that night."

She was whispering and breathing almost frantically. The mouse carcass seemed to jiggle with life independent of her breast, stretching her nipple, clawing its way to and fro across her chest as she moved atop him.

"You always said they held you back, but now they're *really* holding you back, Danny. I could climb off you right now and you couldn't do a thing but wait for me to come back. And maybe I wouldn't."

She lifted her vaginal lips from his cock in tease.

"No. Don't go," he begged. "Fuck me good."

"Yeah, you deserve it," she agreed, lowering herself once more. "You got hard good when you decided to put your mom's pussy bone between us there didn't you? I'm surprised you didn't jizz as soon as you stuck your foot on old daddy Bernie's head there."

"I almost did," he gasped. "I'm gonna cum."

She increased her pumping, and with mutual wails, they spent themselves. She rolled off him, and then lay in 69 position over the ribs so they could lick each other clean.

They finished the bottle of champagne, and his head was spinning when the buzz began in his ears. It took him a moment to realize the sound was an electric razor. She was standing behind him, and he had a sudden premonition of what was to come.

"No," he begged. "I told you, not the hair on my head!"

"Sorry Danny," she said. The mutilated mouse dangled with her breast over his face as she buzzed the hair from the top of his head. Ten minutes later he was staring at his bald head in the mirror she held before him.

It made him hard. She climbed on the table again, rubbing clumps of his thick brown hair over her breasts and between her legs before mounting him. The hair stuck to the sticky mouse blood on her body, covered Dan's helplessly prone body. They lay together again, a cushion of his detritus between them.

"I don't know if I like your brother seeing me like this," she whispered evilly as she began slowly to grind.

"Like what?" he huffed.

"All naked and fffffucking," she hissed, the words themselves driving her into a frenzy. Her hands gripped the ribs as if she was rattling a chain link fence looking for escape.

"But he's dead," Dan said.

"Yeah, but we're fucking on his mother's bones. And I don't think your brother would understand."

"Understand?"

She shifted position.

"Larry wouldn't have minded watching me fuck. But he wouldn't understand fucking the dead."

"You're fu-uh-uh-uh-king *on* the dead," Dan corrected as he approached orgasm.

"No," she said. "I'm fucking the *dead*."

She pulled the razor she had watched Dan disembowel his family with from the raccoon pelt around her middle. His eyes grew wide, but his thrusts more furious as he was both frightened and aroused by the blade.

"You've always killed for me, Danny baby, now I've got to do it for you."

"No," he moaned, pleading and cumming at once.

With each word she struggled to hold back the growing orchestra in her sex. She had a strange smile on her face as she clipped each word:

"I love my mom but if I said to, you would kill her. Oh. Oh. Anything I say, you would do, right?"

"Anything, baby," he breathed, knowing instantly it was the wrong answer.

"You'd kill rabbits and squirrels and coons and mice and mommy and daddy and sister and brother and oh God, here I cum," she screamed and brought the razor down on his neck, the blood fountaining across her face as she came in waves of ecstasy and rubbed the fluid across her body. She ripped and flung the furs from her skin and anointed herself in Dan's blood.

"Then I say *die*." She brought the razor down again and again, opened his wrists, opened his belly. His gurgling screams only drove her to another orgasm before his eyes began rolling back in his head and she leaned forward once more to kiss his lips and whisper: "thanks for the best birthday ever, baby."

It was a few days before Melissa even bothered to get dressed and go home. She'd known she wouldn't have much time with Dan and had wanted to make the most of it. As she stepped away from the stiffened mess beneath the cage of bones a final time she felt a profound sense of loss. They really had been complementary opposites, she thought.

Dan was as good in death as she was in life.

When editor Pat Nielsen announced that she was closing up shop on Crossroads, a small press magazine with which I've enjoyed a longstanding relationship, I wanted to contribute something special for that last issue. I decided the story should be set in Georgia, where the magazine began, and should deal with endings (and beginnings?) at a crossroads. While Pat loved and accepted the story, she ultimately decided not to publish that last issue of the magazine. So here, for the first time, is my "eulogy" for Crossroads.

Dead Girl on the Side of the Road

The girl was blue-faced and cool when I found her, lying there on the side of the road. She was maybe 12 years old and shaping up to be pretty in a few more years. Long auburn hair tangled in the grass where she lay; thin elfin features looked delicate as a porcelain doll's. And those same features were discolored as if the dye for her eyes had run throughout the mold to ruin the piece. Purple bled along the rim of her eyes, which, thank god, were closed.

I didn't know what to do. It was near dusk, I was traveling in a rental car on a gravel road in the middle of god-knows-where about an hour outside of Atlanta. My client, four beers happy and eager to please, had sent me down a shortcut to return to my hotel. If I'd gone the long way, I would've been there by now. I was about 45 minutes into being solidly lost.

This was only supposed to be a one-day business trip. In and out, get what you need and be back home the next day. Love 'em and leave 'em.

And now, here I was at the crossroads of a gravel intersection in the middle of the country, a dead girl lying at my feet.

I didn't want to leave her here, but given the stories told about the "hospitality" of southern police towards Yankees, I also didn't want to be the one to report her body. They'd keep me in a cell for interrogation for the next three days and if they didn't like the color of my eyes or the tilt of my chin, maybe never let me out.

I put my hand behind her head, trying to turn her face towards me to get a better look and felt something cool and sticky there. Reflexively, in disgust, I pulled my hand back and her head dropped with a soft thud back to the grass. I saw the dark crimson gel of the girl's congealed blood slicked across my fingers.

I also saw her eyes pop open. They were green, and flecked with blood. Her lips parted then and I could see a swollen purple tongue within as she started moaning. I pet her forehead with my non-blood-smeared hand and tried to calm her.

"Shhhh," I whispered. "It'll be OK."

My voice cracked on the OK part. The girl was blue and purple, not to mention cool to the touch. In fact, clammy cold. I hadn't seen her take a breath. I really didn't think anything was going to be OK for her ever again.

"It hurts," she mumbled. I could barely understand her, it sounded more like "ith errs," but I could tell that her voice was high and innocent. And afraid. Now I was really stuck. There was a dying kid at my feet and I couldn't even consider driving away to leave the body for someone else to find. Someone local.

"Water?" she whispered, her eyes staring into mine with piercing need. I wondered if her brain was hemorrhaging. Or what bones were broken.

"Can you move at all?" I asked, and slowly, carefully, she wiggled her right hand, then her left.

Her arms lifted then, and she gripped my shoulders. "Hurts."

"I know, baby, I know. We've gotta get you some help."

"Water," she said again, and then pointed into the trees off the side of the road. "Creek."

I nodded and went to the car to find something that I could put water in. I didn't know what good it would do her, but I was selfishly glad for the opportunity to step away from her and think for a minute. There was an empty Coke can in the back from my drive out to the client's this morning, and I grabbed that and went back to her.

"I don't know how good the creek water might be," I cautioned, "but if it's clear enough, I'll put some in here for you."

She smiled and closed her eyes.

I ran into the brush with my can, wondering if she'd still be alive when I got back.

She was. She even held the can herself, drinking it so greedily that some of it washed down the sides of her cheeks to dampen the grass below. When it was gone, she said, "I kin move some."

She lifted her legs, one at a time, to demonstrate. Her voice was clearer now, soft as peaches and just as southern. The last fiery glow of the sun had completely vanished, so now I could only see by the lights of the idling Ford Escort on the shoulder of the road, but her face seemed to have better color to it; the blue had diminished. I noticed she was very tan.

"My name's Heather," she said, and I told her my own. "John. Who did this to you?"

"Don't know. I was just walking by the road, on m' way home. Heard a car and then, you were here."

She said "you" like "yee-ew," a drawl that just melted my heart, and I stroked her cheeks with my hands, promising, "Well, we're gonna get you to a hospital, hon." But with my touch her eyes seemed to widen and then her arms stretched around my neck.

"Careful, careful," I said, thinking that her brain might be likely to siphon right out of whatever kind of hole she had in the back of her head, but instead she pulled herself up, fastened her lips to mine and kissed me.

Hard.

With tongue!

I broke her embrace with an explosion of air and a "hey!" and forced her back to the ground. "Whoa, honey," I said, and she laughed.

"Don't ya'll like me?" she pouted, and it occurred to me that her face no longer was discolored at all.

"Honey, I don't even know you. You're hurt, you're a kid, and I'm gonna get you some help."

"Don't ya'll like 'em young?" she asked, winking one eye at me, and suddenly I realized that she wasn't that young, she'd only looked it. Her breasts were now obviously aroused, her nipples poking through the grass-stained, white t-shirt she wore, supported by a fullness that I hadn't noticed earlier. Her lips were thick and deep blush pink, the kind that scream "passion" even when they're dictating the contents of a spreadsheet. I saw that the curve of her hips beneath her cutoff denim shorts was not the angular utilitarian architecture of a pre-teen.

"I'm legal," she declared, "and I don't need help. But you kin make me feel better."

"You're hurt," I said, becoming increasingly confused by this whole situation.

She raised herself up on arms that I swear were a good six inches longer than they'd been when I first found her, and with a quick shrug, pulled the t-shirt over her head.

"I'm not hurt, just a little hot," she purred and thrust her chest in my face. I had to admit, the view was stirring.

"Cool me off?" she asked, and suddenly her hands were undoing my buttons, and we were wrestling for balance. I don't think I made a conscious decision to allow it, but I didn't fight too hard either, and suddenly there she was, straddling me in the grass, those soft Southern belle breasts in my hungry mouth and the creamy globes of her ass cupped in my hands.

She fucked like an animal, all teeth and nails and grunting urgency, rolling me down the incline of the ditch 'til we were hidden in a thicket of weeds and sweaty as workmen on a Louisiana chain gang. At some point during the whole thing I realized that I must have completely lost my mind and tried to stop, but she silenced me with her mouth and I entered her for the third time, this time pinning her to the ground with my own need. It seemed to go on for hours, this sucking and grinding and taking and giving. And as I came for the third time, amazing myself with a stamina I'd never had before, she laughed.

It's amazing how fast a laugh can shrivel a man's privates, especially when they're busy doing what God designed them for. But when the laugh sounds more like the cackle of a devil than an angel, well, let's just say it deflated my ego, among other things.

"Who are you?" I finally asked, breathless and now suddenly a little scared, as her face sneered back at me down the naked ribs of her body, crouched like a dog's. She wiggled that shapely rear end in my face and drawled, "Just think of me as a friend of the devil."

She grinned, but there was no humor in her smile.

"Let's you and me go back up to the car. I've got something for ya'll, I left in my jeans."

"For me?" I asked, and watched as her haunches jiggled, a perfect *Penthouse* picture as she strode up the small berm to the road.

I followed her, and watched as she pulled a single sheet of folded paper from the pocket of her shorts. She held it out to me and I took it, unfolding it with a single shake.

"Give me your hand," she said, and without thinking, as I began to read the paper, I did. She immediately poked my index finger with a small piece of glass plucked from the roadside gravel and I yelled.

"Hey!" I pulled my hand back and sucked at the wound. "What the fuck?"

"Sign it with blood, please."

The paper was a contract awarding my soul to the devil in exchange for enjoying the pleasures of one Heather Collins. Her body was mine, unchanging, for 25 years to enjoy whenever I chose. At the end of that time, my soul was forfeit.

"You're Heather," I asked.

She nodded.

"You're very good," I said, "but you're not worth my soul. And anyway, I don't think my wife would approve."

She shrugged, honey curls flouncing down the sides of her beach-brown biceps.

"Your call. You've got 5 minutes to decide."

"And then?"

"And then it's midnight. And I'm just a dead girl on the side of the road."

I threw down the paper and gathered my clothes.

"Then I guess you're going to die again," I said, starting back towards the car. The moon was high overhead and so bright that I didn't need the headlights to see how beautiful the girl was that I was walking away from. She was certainly tempting.

"A dead girl with your sperm inside her," added that smooth Southern voice without expression.

My heart stopped dead.

Could they identify me that way? If they didn't know I'd been here?

I thought, police can only compare sperm DNA if they've got a suspect, right? I tried to convince myself of that, and hurried around to the driver's side of the car. They'd find a girl, they'd find she'd been raped and run over, but what would make them ever suspect a guy from 1,000 miles away?

Heather stood quietly next to her discarded clothes and

watched me back the car away from her. As I turned the wheel to return to the road, I saw the blue LED on the dash read 11:58.

I lined up with the road and threw the car into drive, stomping on the gas and kicking up gravel in a plume behind me.

And there Heather was, bare ass naked and five feet in front of my car in the middle of the road, smiling with a sad look that said, "they never learn."

I punched the brakes but it was too late. Her face disappeared beneath my hood and I felt the car shudder as I skidded over her body.

I threw the car in park and dove from the seat to see what I had done.

The body of a naked 12-year-old was bleeding all over the road behind me. She was pretty, in a beat-up way, auburn hair wet with blood from the cuts on her forehead. The stones behind her head were quickly darkening. I could see one pale pink nipple that would someday have developed into the spectacular center tease of a gorgeous breast; the other one was hidden beneath a smear of gravel-specked gore where my bumper had caught her.

I cradled her head again in my hands and cried.

"Why me? Why her?" I called out into the silent night. A breeze rippled the grass nearby, and I saw a flash of white, a bit of paper rolling end over end into the ditch to my right. From the throat of the dead girl in front of me, a thick, gurgling voice whispered in frightening monotone:

"Don't you want me, baby? Don't you want me. O-o-o-ohhhh."

I wasn't sure whether to laugh or cry. In the distance, I heard sirens approaching. I looked down the road and saw red and blue flashes swirling through a cloud of gravel dust a mile or so away.

Now her blood was on my rental car, and that was evidence that could easily be linked to me. And my sperm.

Which the police would find inside a dead girl who had never even had a period, from the looks of it. I was either giving my soul to the devil or my body to some inmates. Either way, I was about to become the property of someone else.

"Time's up," the body croaked. "Take it or leave it."

I dropped her bloodied head to the gravel and ran to retrieve the contract that would give away my soul. I could almost hear the toll of a church bell ringing in the midnight hour as I scooped up the deadly parchment from where it had lodged in a thatch of Queen Anne's Lace.

When I came back to the road, the sirens were almost upon us, and the corpse of the blue-faced young girl was still as stone. With a rock from the road, I reopened the wound on my finger, and began to slowly trace my name upon the contract in blood.

I prayed that when I finished, Heather would once again transform into the beautiful Southern belle I'd been promised. But all I really cared about was that she stood up and seemed alive before the police got here.

As I closed the loop on my last name, which closed the noose on my soul, the bruised lips of the dead girl split into a smile.

A few months after this story appeared in Grue, *a friend forwarded a news clip to me about a man who was arrested for having a public "relationship" with a gourd. Could it have been a case of life imitating art? For the record, just because I thought of it, doesn't mean I tried it!*

Pumpkin Head

Jack's hands trembled as he traced a small circle on the slick skin of the pumpkin, using a magic marker and the bottle cap he'd lifted from his mom's medicine cabinet. It looked to be about the right size.

A gibbous moon shone in garish relief off the night-polished hides of hundreds of orange globes, but Jack's chosen pumpkin was special. He'd picked it for its size as well as its seclusion. Somehow, this particular vine had crept over the irrigation ditch and nurtured its offspring well away from the others under the shade of a gnarled elm.

The tiny circle drawn, Jack opened his pocketknife and with quick, short thrusts turned his drawing into a hole. His heart began pumping with growing volume as he completed the first stage of his violation.

\/\/\/\/\\/\/\\/\\/\/\\/\\/\\/\/\\/\\/\\/\\/

"You've got to try this!" Tom had told him in a whisper the previous week after school. Exhaling a cloud of Marlboro smoke with practiced disdain for anyone who might be staring his way, Tom had laughed. "It's so twisted, it's great. You just have to make sure the hole's not too big, or it won't work."

At first, he'd figured Tom had to be making it up. *Nobody would try that! Totally gross.* But every time he thought about it, he got a funny feeling inside; the idea attracted him. And so tonight, under the chill wind of an October moon, Jack stood holding a pumpkin coring. *This was stupid,* he thought for the hundredth time. *This is warped.*

But after taking a furtive glance around the pumpkin patch behind him, silently amazed at the endless rows of orange basketball shapes stretching to the black horizon, Jack unbuckled his belt and dropped his jeans to the ground. A cold knot twisted his stomach at the realization that he was going through with this perversion, and a countering hot stab of anticipation drove through his heart and groin. With a shiver and a shrug, he shoved his underpants past his knees and, goosebumps popping out across his bare lower body, knelt next to the pumpkin.

Gripping the rough, wrinkled skin of the dead vine atop the gourd, Jack guided his straining penis into the newly sawn receptacle. He gasped aloud at its touch. He was afraid at first – would the hole be large enough to receive him? Would he be trapped inside? Would he catch some weird pumpkin disease – orange genital warts?

But none of these concerns stopped him from pressing through the gently resisting cavity. It was cold, sticky. He imagined his favorite pin-up girl lying here in the leaves and brush before him. *She'd be warmer,* he thought, *but sticky too. Would she feel like this?* He stifled a moan as he pressed into a new area of slimy seeds and pumpkin hair. Jack moved close to embrace all of the warty hide of the pumpkin as its jellied hairs tickled and caressed his member inside. It felt as if it was moving with him, pulling at him to stay as he arched away. He'd cut the hole just right. It was tight enough to grip him like a woman. Or, as good as he thought a woman might. *A woman filled with cold slime and seeds,* he laughed, the thought driving him to cleave hard to the lined sides of the gourd. He uttered one more involuntary gasp of pleasure as the tremors of release rocked him and left. And then clammy fear at the extant of his depravity gripped him. What had he done here?

Rolling away from his vegetable mate, he yanked his pants up, not even bothering to wipe off the commingled strands of orange and white mucous. It gelled in the hair on his groin and belly, a sticky accusation of his strange and darkly pleasurable fornication. He tucked two pumpkins under his arms as he stole away from the quiet field on the edge of town.

"Where'd you get those?" his mother yelled as he went dashing through the kitchen with his stolen treasures. "Don't take them upstairs, they'll rot! Jack!"

Depositing the pumpkins safely in his room, he returned to the kitchen to assuage his mother. The trick with her was to get things settled before she got talking about it. Then she wouldn't bother forcing him to change.

"I'm gonna carve them up there," he announced, staving off her objections. "Halloween's in a couple days, and they won't rot before then. If I leave them outside, kids'll kick 'em through the street."

She looked uncertain, and he pressed his advantage. "I'll clean up everything, don't worry."

\/\\//\\/\\\/\\/\\

That night, after turning out the light, Jack ran his hands lightly over the smooth, bumpy skins of his pumpkins. Their texture drove a shiver through his body. His groin jumped. Whitely naked and bent beneath the moonlight glinting through his bedroom window, Jack kissed his pumpkins good night, and then dove guiltily into bed. His saliva glittered in beads on the dark orange skins.

Jack had thought he'd share his experience with Tom if he went through with it – after all, it had been Tom who'd clued him in, right? But when he got to school the next day and saw his friend's cynical sneer as he joked about getting a piece of Mary Scott, Jack realized that he and his pumpkin queen were a private item.

That night, with the bedroom door locked, he once again traced the bottle cap on a pumpkin and punched through its pale pulpy hymen. His hips moved faster, sliding the pumpkin and himself across the floor as he fought to stay with his new lover. But as he stifled a grunt of orgasmic reaction, it was his first pumpkin that he found himself thinking of.

The next night he found himself fidgeting at the dinner table. Meatloaf and carrots with cauliflower covered his plate. The orange and white of his vegetables lay in front of him, reminding him of his new-found carnal pleasures. And it excited him. He was dying to get away from the table to lock himself away for precious moments with his pumpkin. But when he finally got there, when he'd carved a new hole and sluttishly spent himself, once again he found himself craving the attentions of his first, the monstrous pumpkin queen whose insides had seemed to suck him to ecstasy that first time. Tucking his gluey dick back in his pants, Jack quickly scooped and finished carving his first pumpkin. He had to have some evidence for his rush to get to his room.

\/\\/1\\\/\\\/\\\1

"Oh that's very, um, niiice, Jack," his mom said as he showed off his newly carved pumpkin. She looked puzzled. "I thought it was supposed to be scary though, hon."

"So, this one's a happy pumpkin," Jack shrugged and went back upstairs to clean up.

He got two more rides – one after school and one after dinner – out of the next pumpkin before carving it up into a face which his mother, in utter puzzlement, pronounced beautiful. In years past, Jack's pumpkins had always held a certain demonic terrorism in their fangs and slanted eyes. But these – she stared at the two demure smiles on the orange globes on the kitchen table – these were... coquettes.

"I'm going trick or treating for awhile," Jack announced, letting the door slam behind him before there could be protest. She thought he was too old to go, but why should the little runts get all the free candy? He'd borrowed Tom's football jersey and helmet and set off. It was a windy Halloween, and an earlier rain had set a bone-slathering chill in the air. Leaves rustled and dropped wetly all around him as he worked his way block by block to the end of town. The moon was small and piercingly white by the time he admitted where he'd been edging his way to. At last he called off the charade. Breaking into a run, Jack sprinted with a shopping bag full of candy the remaining four blocks to the pumpkin field. He'd thought about her – his first, his pumpkin queen – all through school. The gourds he'd brought home simply hadn't fulfilled him like her. He prayed she was still there. He prayed she hadn't rotted from the hole he'd gored into her side.

The pumpkin field was a dismal sight on Halloween night. Only the rejects were left here now: the misshapen, rotted, too-small pumpkins littered the field, seemingly in large numbers; but the deep, dark depressions where their brethren had but recently rested betrayed the extent of their abandonment. Jack loped through the field, heading toward the back ditch, anxious to reach the shelter of that crooked elm.

But she wasn't there. At first he thought he had the wrong tree, but then he saw the telltale deep depression she'd left, and his own rutted knee prints beside it. *Who would have taken a pumpkin with a hole right in the middle of her best side?* he wondered, and sank to the ground. *How, HOW, had he become such a perve that he was lusting after a pumpkin? But, she'd been right here, so cool, so... good!*

"Looking for someone?"

The voice at his back startled him to his feet.

"No no," he stammered, as he stared at the girl before him. She was naked, entwined in a vine that stretched from her belly to the ground beside him. She stepped closer, and his breath caught. She was orange. The deep, mottled orange of ripe pumpkin. She exuded a musky vegetable odor as she stepped closer and ran a warted finger up his face to poke into his open mouth.

"There was a pumpkin here," he said, pulling away and pointing to the hollow on the ground. The hollow near where her vine was embedded in earth.

"Yes," she answered, her voice a husky rustle of summer and seed. She touched him again, and he saw then that her skin, though smooth, was marred occasionally by dark warts and dimples. Wet-looking translucent strands of hair hung from her head and her crotch. He guessed that hair would be cool and sticky. As she wrapped her arms around him in askance, he found that he'd guessed correctly.

"You were looking for my mother," she whispered like the wind in his ear. Her tongue, cool and wet, traced designs on his neck before she said, "That means you are the man who raped her. You are my father."

At that, she dropped to his waist and began tugging at his belt. "I will be the woman my mother could never have been for you," she promised, and slowly, he began to aid her in releasing his clothes. Common sense told him this was not what it seemed; pumpkins did not have human, albeit orange and warty, children. Girls did not give blow jobs to strange boys in fields. But here she was, and her cool touch was driving him to fever. He let her crawl across his skin. Her slimy kisses stuck to his skin like fruit pulp. His cock was so erect it was painful. He'd never been so aroused. Her breasts were hard, tipped by dark brown warts the size of quarters. And her hair was entangling itself around his body, ripping loose from her in sticky heaps. He felt it on his crotch from the pressure of her own, it was hidden in the crease of his neck like chilled sauerkraut.

And then she pulled back. Stretching out across the dirt where just days before he'd had her mother, she showed him the oval valley between her smooth, lightly creased legs. "You can have this," she promised. "I'll be better than my mother. But first, you'll have to cut my cord. She held the browning vine up from her belly, and with squeamish understanding, he dug through his discarded clothes for his pocketknife. Flipping open the blade, he held it as close as he could to her belly, and began sawing. She stiffened as he did, but said nothing. A clear, sticky fluid flowed across his knife and onto his hands, and it was over.

"Now," she said, her voice a rasp of longing. "Seed me, fertilize me, water me." In her tone, those words sounded like the dirtiest night talk Jack had ever heard. Without pausing to close his knife, he tossed it away and pressed his legs to hers.

This was like the first time, he thought as he bucked on top of the cool pumpkin girl. Her eyes glittered blackly in the moonlight beneath him as he kissed her hard lips, ran his tongue along the pulp ridge of her teeth. She sucked his heat into her, her natural frigidity only driving him to a hot wash of orgasm.

"Yes," she wheezed as he came at last, panting and flopping atop her like an epileptic. And then, as Jack looked to see if his lover's eyes were as satisfied as his own, he saw that her hunger had only just begun. "We will fertilize hundreds of seeds together, my love" she promised, encircling him in a grip of orange rind as solid as wood. He struggled, kicked, screamed. But there was no escaping the grasp of the pumpkin queen as, in a flash, her arms and legs sealed around him and they began to roll as one downhill.

And who paid attention to muffled screams in the depth of night on Halloween?

\\\\/\\\\\\\\\\\\\\/\\\

They found his clothes eventually, underneath an old gnarled elm behind an empty pumpkin field. They were lying on bare earth; nearby a knife was stabbed crookedly in the dirt. As the farmer led police to the spot to search for clues of the missing boy, he spied a huge orange pumpkin peeking through the weeds at the bottom of the hill. He shook his head at having missed such a prize pumpkin the week before. It would have brought a good price.

Inside that "prize" gourd, a white-slimed shape contorted at the sound of voices. Kneading hands of pumpkin hair kept him in near-constant orgasm, and handful by handful, deposited orange-slick, newly formed white seeds into pockets on his flesh.

"We will fertilize hundreds of seeds together," she whispered, in words only he could hear.

As a music critic for a local newspaper, I've spent countless nights listening to bands play from behind sticky black tables in sticky black bars with often desperate-looking patrons (I'm not sure of their stickiness quotient) and tired black-clad waitresses. Since I married my high school sweetheart, I never had to fear going home alone when the closing call of 2 a.m. came. But I've often thought about the strange places my fellow clubgoers might have ended up.

Direkit Seed

"I'm off in an hour. Wanna screw?"

Charles couldn't answer. His mouth dried up like beef jerky in the desert. He nodded frantic agreement. Whatever she had just asked was fine with him. She accepted his proffered $5 for the drink and winked one heavily mascara-ed eye through a curtain of jet black ringlets as she pulled coins from a plastic cup.

"Keep the change," he somehow blurted out. She grinned then, and with a flip of her shoulder length black curls, she disappeared into the murky recesses of the club.

He must have misunderstood her. Maybe heard only what he wanted to hear. Something. It was almost midnight and he'd been sitting for three hours at a black round table, in a black-walled bar, watching a succession of noisy, amateur bands strut on the tiny stage as if this was a stadium rock show.

The stage was also black.

In three hours only the waitress had approached him. Most of the bar's inhabitants wore ripped black clothes; many women looked as if they'd rummaged the second hand store for lingerie and then decided putting something on over the meshed mess would be too much trouble.

In most cases, it may have been worth it, he'd long since decided. The jiggling fat that many of the bra & ripped t-shirt crowd revealed was, to him, far from intoxicating, and the midnight colors only served to accentuate the inadequacies of their bloated white flesh. Moles, fat, birthmarks, hair. They all stood out on these writhing clubbers like tattoos at a Young Republican convention.

He'd noticed the waitress an hour or so into his futile vigil. Too much mascara, too much lipstick – but the skin-tight sable mini was mucho enticing – no flab hiding there – and the lace-tipped matching midriff piece even more so. An intricate silver dragon pendant dangled from a chain between her breasts, green gem eyes sparkling as she moved. And her hair was lustrous. Kinky dark curls twisted across her forehead, crept across her cheeks like spiders, dove down the slant of her back. She was a knock-out. Just the kind of girl he'd come here to meet. And after a couple hours of staring she asks him to screw? Not fuckin' likely!

But he stayed planted at the sticky table anyway, arguing with himself over her intent. Should he say something to her the next time she came around? Should he just leave? Would this damn Funky Annihilators band quit pretending they knew what a tuned chord was and just get off the stage?

He was ready to cut his losses and sneak out of the club when he felt the vibration of the storm arriving outside. Somehow, he heard the booming report of lightning over the distorted whine of the over-amplified Annihilators, and decided it would be best to wait out the rain. A short while later there was a tickle at his earlobe.

"Can you drive me home? I don't have my car here and it's really going out there!"

No doubt this time, he thought incredulously, turning to meet the emerald gaze of the silver dragon resting in a seductive shadow of pressed white flesh. His eyes traveled upwards to meet her own, and he nodded once more. She leaned in to his ear and began singing a Barry Manilow song: "Mandy."

But he quickly realized she'd altered the words: "I'm randy, won't you fuck me and fry me like bacon, cuz I'm in a hot way, I'm randy…"

She laughed and shook her butt as she strode to the next table. Charles checked his wallet for the condom he had kept there unused for months. He hoped it was still good. He began humming an oldie of his own over the din of the band. *"Tonight's the night…"*

\/\\/\\/\\/\\/\\/\\/\\/\\/\\

She held his hand as they ran three blocks to his car through the rain. As he fumbled for the keys to unlock his peeling orange Honda, she held her arms wide and shook her head back, embracing the spit of the sky.

"It's a beautiful night, isn't it?" she said, tonguing the rain from her lips. Her mascara had begun to run. She resembled nothing so much as a wet, playful raccoon.

She held out her hand after they slid into the car. "Ceiran," she said, "with a C."

He took her tiny hand in his own and was abruptly wrenched with surprising strength across the seat. She stopped him two inches from her face, and then pecked his lips with a teasing kiss.

"Charles," he stammered, hypnotized by the light dancing in her eyes.

"With a C?" she asked, and laughed before he could answer.

"Um, where do you want to go?" he asked.

"To hell."

"Now?"

"138 Parkside. Then hell."

Charles started the car and turned the defrost up to full. The windows were opaque with the film of their breath and the cool humidity of the storm. They got worse before they got better and he was forced to sit inactive behind the wheel and wonder what the hell he was getting himself into. She broke the quiet with a slap on his thigh.

"Giddyup cowboy. Let's get moving," she giggled. Her voice sounded funny as she mouthed the phrase. Too high. Too girlish. So sexy. He stared at her again, trying to drink her in through his eyes, trying to understand who she was – why she had chosen to come with him.

"I'm not any good with mimes," she said, and poked a finger on his nose.

"Beep," she chirped. "Wanna know who my favorite singer is?"

"Barry Manilow," he stabbed. Her eyebrows crossed.

"Nope," she tossed her head in denial and pressed her palms to her chest. "Me."

She began to sing. Another Manilow song. But softly, her childish voice quivering:

> *"I've been in heat forever*
> *And I fucked the very first dong*
> *I put the cock and the va-gi-na together*
> *I am Eros and I fucked the dong."*

Her voice rose louder, surer as she drove into the chorus:

> *"He's got the dong that makes my girl hole sing*
> *he's got the dong I need with balls that will sting*
> *He's got the dong that makes my girl hole cry*
> *He's got the dong, he's got the dong…"*

Charles ignored the white streaks still receding on the front windshield and pulled out into traffic. This was going to be a night to remember.

138 Parkside was a large white two-story frame surrounded by giant spruces and wildly overgrown hedges. As Charles stepped past the front gate he felt as though he'd crossed a barrier into another world. The rain barely seemed to make it through the latticework of trees as Ceiran's spiked steps clicked against the stone walkway. The chilly October wind raised goosebumps on his arms.

She pushed open the front door without using a key and motioned him inside.

"Don't you lock up?" he asked, stepping into the gloom of a foyer. She clicked a switch and a lone bulb on the ceiling glared upon the room. Charles blinked. Both to get used to the sudden painful wash of light, and at the strangeness of the view. There was no furniture in the house! Decaying gray floor planks, dirty white walls, unadorned by anything but yellow shadows revealing where once, something had been hung…

"No," she answered his question. "I don't need to lock up. There's nothing here to steal, as you can see, and no one could get in that I didn't want here anyway."

He was about to ask what she meant when he got a poke in the ribs and she flounced down the dingy hallway.

"Want a drink?" she called over her shoulder.

"Sure," he answered, wondering if perhaps now would be a good time to duck right back out the door and head home. Still, he hadn't had even a chance at getting any in months, and while she talked and apparently lived a bit odd, she was certainly more attractive than anyone he had ever dated, let alone scored with. So he followed.

She did own a refrigerator – at least 35 years old with a pull-bar handle like the one his grandmother kept in her garage. The ceiling boasted another bare bulb ringed in cobwebs peppered with trapped gnats. Ceiran had filled two tall juice glasses with ice and was splashing a healthy dose of vodka into each. She filled the rest with orange juice and handed him one.

"Cheers," she grinned and downed hers in a gulp.

"Let's go upstairs, it's cozier there."

Grabbing him by his non-drink-holding hand, she pulled him up an ancient creaky set of stairs (even the wooden banister looked dry-rotted and ready to crumble). When they reached the top step, she flipped another switch. Another bare bulb. More rotting floorboards. The short hall ended in two rooms, both dark but apparently empty.

"Close your eyes," she demanded. When he didn't comply, she placed her forefingers on his eyebrows and delicately trailed them down, forcing him to shut his eyelids. She held her fingers splat in the middle of his eyeballs for a few seconds and then musically trilled: "now keep them closed."

She clomped a few steps down the empty hall. He heard something slide. Then she returned to take his hand once more. "Closed. Closed. Closed. Closed." she said as they walked.

"Open."

They stood in a pleasure pit.

The walls were covered in erotic paintings, nude photographs, porno movie posters, *Kama Sutra* tapestries. If there were windows, they were obscured by the tantalizing array of sex art. The floor was polished oak, and littered with vibrators, cuffs, leather garments, whips. They'd stumbled into the after-effects of an adult book store orgy. In the center of it all was an unmade king-sized bed, looking madly out-of-place with a four-poster canopy of pink and white lace. Restraining straps hung from each post. Satin-sheened rose pillows lay at the head crumpled in a heap.

She slid a door closed behind them as he stared open-mouthed at the sex palace.

"Like it?"

He nodded dumbly. *Tonight's the night,* indeed.

"It's my very special place." She whispered like a little girl revealing a deeply private secret.

Charles gulped a large dose of his drink.

"It's very um, kinky." he said.

She nipped his earlobe. "Just like me. How about you?"

"How about me what?" he asked, stalling. He was transfixed by the photographic display of writhing nudes, some bigger than life, fucking their way around the room. A hand caressed the front of his jeans.

"How kinky are you?"

He had never really thought about it before. Just getting a woman to go to bed with him had been enough of a challenge.

"Willing to learn?" he ventured. His pants unzipped.

She led him to the bed, somehow her own clothes had disappeared. She pushed the t-shirt over his head, coaxed the pants to his ankles. He pried shoes and pants off with his heels.

She took the glass from his hand and held it to his lips. The tart mix sluiced down his throat as she upended the drink and then threw the glass across the room. It shattered with a wet smack against a wall. Charles jerked his head to see the results of her unexpected violence and was instead yanked onto the bed. She sat astride him, wetting his chest, his neck, his face with licking kisses.

"Wait," he mumbled. "Wait. I've got… uh… protection."

"No need," she husked in his ear.

"Not to be rude but," he began, only to have her tongue lodged in his throat.

He pushed her back after a moment, and took a deep breath. "But even if you're on the pill, you know, um disease, and uh, stuff."

"Shhhhh." She slurped in his ear. "I'm clean."

She kept up her wet ministrations until Charles could hardly bear it. The walls seemed to pulse with sexual tension, the air filled with the musky stench of her need. And then she was fastening leather thongs about his wrists and scissoring his head with her thighs as she did the same to his ankles.

He made token complaint but she ignored him and he didn't really care anymore. Whatever it took to get her on top of him, that was fine. Because God did he *want* her...

She did sit on him then, her eyes bright with lust, the white skin of her chest flushing with excitement. And she began to grind, slowly, so slowly, and when the rhythm was set, she began to sing:

> *"I made it through the rain*
> *I kept him from protection*
> *I made it through the rain*
> *His cock it grew and grew*
> *I made it through the rain and chained him unsuspected*
> *like the others who*
> *got rained on too*
> *those cocks I blew..."*

Charles didn't know what she was singing about, or why; he only drove up and in to her, watching the perspiration bead on her forehead, the jet ringlets sticking to her head as the rest of her sultry twists bounced and bobbed on her shoulders. He was yelling out in orgasm as she finished one song and began another.

> *"Somewhere in the night*
> *I'll screw him deep and sweet as sin..."*

Her voice shrieked and she bucked on top of him as she reached her climax – still singing.

Charles collapsed limp in his restraints as she groaned and rocked herself slowly, bringing her hips back under control. Then she rolled off of him with a gasp, and licked his chest. Her fingers stroked his face. She poked his nose again.

"Beep."

He smiled.

"I just want you to know," she began, averting her eyes and trailing a long red-painted nail down his sternum, "whatever happens, you were good."

Her fingers played upon his nearly flaccid member, sliding across its stickiness.

"Whadaya mean?" he slurred drowsily. The liquor and sex had left him without a spasm of energy. He just wanted to sleep as he watched her hand raise from his crotch, thumb and forefinger rubbing together on a gob of white.

"Good, good good good," she repeated, a quirky edge to her voice. She rose from the bed and walked as if dazed to the far corner of the room. There was a circle painted on the floor, and some kind of triangular diagram within. She sat at its center, positioned her legs to cover two of the stripes within the circle, and pressed her soiled thumb and forefinger to the floor. Then she began whispering something. It was a chant of some kind, and while the words seemed like gibberish, the cadence felt familiar. Her voice rose and though he still couldn't make out the words, he felt the impulse to join in. Words rose from his mouth without conscious thought. He was singing the chorus to "Mandy."

Somehow the juxtaposition of Manilow and occult magic shredded the curtain of exhaustion and Charles felt afraid. He tested his bonds, quietly straining against them one by one, trying not to draw her attention. He was locked down tight. Naked and vulnerable. With a woman who didn't believe in any furniture but a bed. This, he suddenly decided, was not a good thing.

"Um, Ceiran," he croaked.

Her chanting didn't slow. "Could you, um, let me out of these? My arms are starting to hurt.

The chanting got louder, more intense. He felt an overpowering urge to sing along. To cry out for the love of some dog named Mandy.

"What did you mean about 'whatever happens'?"

There was a blinding flash, an explosion. Lightning seemed to strike in the room, though how it could get in, he didn't know. For a second he thought he heard voices, screechy wails answering Ceiran's incomprehensible syllables. Her chanting was abruptly silent.

He tensed with fear, straining to see through the smoke to where Ceiran had been a moment before. What if she had been struck by that flash, what if she was dead and couldn't let him out? Who would hear a man yelling from this house surrounded by muffling growth? In this room apparently hidden away in the middle of the building?

But then he saw her silhouette rise through the fog. She extended a hand as though offering him a fruit. But she still had to cross the room to give it to him.

"Are you OK?" he asked, totally confused. The smoke swirled around her in fragrant eddies tainted with pine and sulfur, moving with a life owing nothing to wind. She did cross the floor then, and the look in her eyes made him fear for his life. Worse. It made him fear the manner of his death.

She held a knife in her other hand, its tip smudged with red. A thin trickle of blood crossed below her bellybutton, dripping to disappear in the dark thicket below. He pulled now without subterfuge at his bindings, but they only constricted further. He was trapped by a naked woman with a knife and something in her hand that instinct told him was even more dangerous than steel.

She laid the knife on his throat and her teeth suddenly looked carnivorous, not carnal. "Now whatever you feel, don't move," she cautioned.

With the other hand she cupped his balls, which he feared she was about to excise. But the knife didn't leave his neck. Instead, a warming sensation seemed to wash over his skin from her cool, cupping palm. And then a shaft of needles ripped through his bowels, a mix of pain and pleasure that grew to a white-hot sword before receding again to a dull pressure. She retreated from the bed then, hands at her sides. The knife slipped from her hand to clatter uselessly on the floor.

"I really am sorry," she said, the little girl back in her voice. She sounded genuine. "I only need you for a couple days. There's even a chance you'll be OK afterward."

"After WHAT?!" he shouted. "What have you done to me?"

"I took the seed of our love, and called in two Direkits from the eighth plane. They need to incubate for a few hours before they'll be fit to grow outside the body. They've taken hold of your balls now, and should grow five or six inches by tomorrow. When they come out they'll be mine to command. And they can do some pretty cool stuff."

"You're crazy," Charles shouted, growing increasingly annoyed at her simplistic, silly speech.

"I'll come back later when you're in a better mood," she said sulkily.

The door shut behind her, a lock clicked into place. *Great*, Charles thought. *I'm now the prisoner of a bonkers dominatrix.* He didn't believe the Direkit B.S. But what had she done to his balls. They felt swollen, sore. Was he bleeding? He could barely lift his head enough to see them, but he strained against the cords and shook his penis to the side. His testicles looked inflamed, chafed red with pulsing purple veins raised angrily throughout the skin.

And then one of them moved.

The motion sent a wave of dizziness through him, but before his head fell back, he saw something that stretched the thin testicular skin. A leech, a snake, something dark squirmed within his sacs. "Holy shit," he breathed. He leaned back and started to cry.

Eventually, he drifted into sleep.

Ceiran woke him with a kiss.

"Morning stranger," she giggled. He opened his eyes and felt a momentary confusion. A pale girl with a rebellious tousle of curly black hair rampaging across her head and neck was locked to his lips. It felt so good, so comforting that he began to surrender to her tongue. Until the ache in his groin reminded him of the events of the night before. He twisted his face away from hers to stare at the pit of her belly button.

"Oh, you're angry at me still. Maybe you'll feel better after breakfast."

He stared up past heavy ivory breasts to glare at her. He hoped the anger in that look did something to her. What, he wasn't sure.

"I'd feel better if you'd let me out of here."

"Not yet," she smiled.

It was the smile of a nurse to a terminally ill patient, he thought.

"What did you put inside of me?"

She perched a perfectly formed thigh on the edge of the bed, and pulled a TV tray closer.

"You eat, and I'll explain it to you," she said.

She spooned a mouthful of Cheerios into his mouth from a bowl on the tray.

"I suppose you would call me a witch. And I don't mean a nasty woman. I mean honest-to-gosh, call-on-the-forces-of- darkness witch. But," she paused as she worked another spoonful into his mouth. "I don't believe that what I do has anything to do with magic. I use some of the trappings, true," she pointed to the circle on the floor across the room, "but I don't believe I am invoking demons here. Quite frankly, I don't believe in spirit stuff like God and devils."

Charles' eyebrows crossed in puzzlement.

"Then what do you call this speaking in tongues stuff you were doing last night, and flashes of lightning indoors, and whatever it is you jammed into my balls?"

She ruffled his hair between his fingers. "I said I didn't believe I was calling up spirits. I think what magic is – what people *call* magic – has to do with opening the doors to a different universe. Or perhaps a different plane. What I do is borrow some of the power in that place to use it here. It's not magic, but sort of like a UFO stopping here and abducting someone for a few hours for their own purposes – maybe humans are *magical* creatures to other races. Anyway, it takes a person with a weird talent for opening the door between, and it's very dangerous, because the same power that you want to bring through can as easily destroy you. I searched for years for the secrets of the calling, for the right frame of mind, for the right – you would say – spells."

He shook away a spoonful and she spilled the Cheerios on his chest. She bent down and tongued him clean.

"Mmmm," she grinned lasciviously.

"Cut it out," Charles complained. "You say you only borrow power. Then you're going to give back these things you put in me?"

"The Direkits? No. This is not a borrowing. I've worked for years to understand, to communicate with the Direkits. We have traded gifts. This pendant I wear," she fondled the necklace lovingly. "This is of a Direkit in its adolescent form. And you have Direkit babies inside you. They agreed to give me eggs to join with your seed to hatch here. They will grow in this house, they will be my consorts, my protectors. And they will get me whatever I want."

"What do you have to give in return?"

"Nothing," she laughed, and looked away. "Nothing at all."

He didn't believe her. Suddenly her elfin features seemed indefinably drawn and pinched, her childish charm only a facade covering a heart of black bile. He divined from her evasiveness that he, somehow, was the currency of exchange in this serpentine contract, and that he would not survive.

"Eat some more now," she coaxed another spoon into his mouth. "We've got to keep your strength up for the birth."

He glared at her, but accepted the food – his stomach growled even as he swallowed another mouthful.

"OK. Say I believe that you've inserted alien dragons into my balls because you have the unique ability to open some kind of interplanetary doorway."

She brushed her hand between his legs. He winced at the touch. "What's not to believe?"

"So what does the sex stuff have to do with it?' he asked, looking around the room.

"Nothing really," she answered, touching the tip of her tongue to the edge of her front teeth. "I just enjoy it. Helps me clear my mind."

She bent to work on his cock with her mouth then, and despite his repeated negations, his tool was quickly receptive to her advances. She threw a leg over his middle and sat on him. The ache in his balls flared to an unbearable mix of pain and ecstasy as she rocked. As he came, he screamed, and she joined her voice to his, a bizarre wailing of shared desperation. When he quieted, she moved forward a bit, resting provocatively astride his chest. She watched his face in silence for a moment, and then poked his nose.

"Beep."

She was almost to the door when Charles cried out.

"Why? Why me?"

"I thought you were cute, and you looked lonely," she answered. "I thought you deserved at least one good time."

The door slid closed.

\/\\/\\\/\\\/\\/\\/\\/\\/\\/\\

The day went by slowly, the churnings in Charles' lower anatomy growing more painful, more frequent. He looked down at one point and swore he could discern an eye staring back at him through the enraged veins of his distended scrotum. He might have been suffering from having his penis connected to a gas station air pump. Normally slightly smaller than golf balls, he thought his testicles now appeared the size of baseballs.

They hurt like hell.

He felt feverish too, probably the result of his body's immune system going haywire trying to fight this strange invasion. Dizziness passed over him in waves, and he fought the urge to puke several times – Ceiran hadn't been around for hours, and he didn't want to lay trapped in a pile of vomit until she returned. He had a plan if she would only untie his feet; but now he didn't even know if he could carry it out. He was drifting in a sea of red; all that mattered to him anymore was a release from the pain. Death would be fine.

\\/\\/\\\\\\/\\/\\\\\\/\\/\\\

"Wanna screw?"

The tinkly voice of Ceiran wrenched him from his haze.

"Sorry I was gone so long, but I had to work my shift, you know."

She was wearing some kind of sheer black leotard tonight, with neon blue lipstick. She began peeling off the outfit and Charles began begging.

"No, Ceiran. I can't. It hurts so bad. Please don't."

She began humming the theme to "American Bandstand." He didn't think he wanted to hear the words.

"Please, just undo my feet," he cried. "I can't go anywhere with my hands tied, and I've got to be able to move my thighs, the pain is killing me…"

"I'll tell you what." She stood naked beside the bed, hands on her hips. Reaching out a hand, she touched the bloated surface of his balls and watched him twitch and moan. "I'll release your feet after we fuck once more. It shouldn't be too much longer anyway and you'll be free of them."

She climbed on him again and seemed to be making an effort to be gentle, but his resultant cries and grunts of pain as she slid down his shaft didn't convince her to stop. The feel of his swollen testicles beneath her was an incredible turn-on. When she finished, she did undo his foot restraints, and kissed him once more.

"Thanks," she said, crushing his cheeks between her hands. "You're a nice guy. You make a girl feel real hot. G'night."

She laughed and left the room singing: *"I've been in heat forever…"*

Charles waited until the pounding, racking pain in his groin subsided, until the tears on his face had dried. And then slid his legs to the edge of the bed. Every motion was an agony; his calves dangled in space for minutes before he stopped biting his lip and committed himself to going over.

The shock of his feet hitting the floor sent a rip through his balls that almost made him scream. Instead he bit down on his tongue until it bled. He took several deep breaths. He willed away the nausea. And inched his feet along the floor near the bed, stretching and straining his back and arms to give his legs the farthest possible range. Sweat poured down his forehead into his eyes and ran in rivulets down his chest. He was going to collapse soon, he knew it. Rhythmic bites of pain shocked him from his unwanted babies, and he fought back tears.

Then a toe poked something cold.

He got his big toe on top and began dragging the object towards the bed. Maneuvering his lower back on the edge of the bed to act as the fulcrum, he pulled his upper body flat to the sheets, and grabbed the metal between his feet. He fumbled it the first time, opening a stinging gash on his right foot. He tried again, this time losing it as his blood greased it away.

The third time he got it up on the bed.

He lay still for a few minutes to catch his breath, and then, with a silent "now or never," he inched Ceiran's discarded ritual knife up the bed with his left leg bent backwards. Every inch was like pushing a hand into the fire – his entire mid-section burned with throbs of retribution. When it was high enough, he levered his body on top of the steel, and inch-wormed it up his back, nicking himself several times in the process. At last he gripped the knife in his hand, and used it to saw the leather straps restraining him. The angle was tight, and he dropped the knife with exhaustion twice, but he finally freed one hand, and then quickly slashed free the next.

The next step he'd considered for hours, and it was no more acceptable now than it had been upon first rejection. But he also didn't have a lot of choices here. Doing it, he might have a chance at coming out of this alive. Without? Dragon food.

His entire body felt swollen and hot now, and he hoped what he was about to try was worth the effort. He slid from the bed to the floor, sitting down with legs splayed as far apart as he could get them. Something moved in one of his veined grapefruits, and he stared at it closely, trying to separate the monster parts from himself. Then he placed the knife over the spot where a dark shadow twisted. Gritting his teeth, he pushed down.

A stream of milky liquid spurted from the wound. Charles lost his breath from the pain and stars swam across his eyes. His testicles deflated in an expulsion of white and yellow pus, a tide of dark crimson oozing behind it. He lifted the knife and saw that he had, indeed, spitted one of the monsters. A cold blue eye stared blankly at him from the head of what looked like an iridescent green toy crocodile. Only this croc had vestigial wings and eight fingers. Its tail whipped feebly a time or two before the entire creature went limp. Ivory ichor dripped from its breached midsection down the blade of his knife. Charles swung the knife in the air and the creature flew off to splat on the ground a few feet away.

And then he did scream, as a tearing sensation worse than the rip of the knife bit into him and he rolled back on the floor in anguish. The other Direkit had apparently witnessed the fate of its brother and wasn't having any. Charles screamed again and then pinching feet tread across his thigh, trailing a wreckage of wetness. Charles craned his head to stare at the creature which had moved across the room to investigate the Direkit corpse. A thin shaft of white hot flame met him in the forehead, shriveling his hair and causing him to roll over again.

These things really *were* mini-dragons.

The door slid open.

"I heard you yelling and I..." Ceiran stopped as she saw the empty bed, Charles' curled, bloody body on the floor, the knife in his hand. Then she saw the dead creature at her foot.

"Oh, Charles-with-a-C what have you done?"

She put a hand to her mouth.

"Where is the other one?" she asked quietly, her tone more serious than he'd ever heard it.

"I don't know," he answered weakly.

"Do you know what will happen if they realize we killed one of their babies? Do you know what will happen if the other one gets loose in this world without being impressed on me? Damn."

She quickly confiscated the knife he'd momentarily forgotten in his hand, and looked around the room sharply. She paused then, thought a moment, and returned to the singsong voice that had so bewitched him.

"Let me help you over here to the circle. There's some magic I can do to heal you up at least."

He didn't believe her. Didn't buy it at all. This was his exit cue. But he had no defense. She dragged him to the circle, which he now saw was inter cut with a pentagram. He left a trail of blood behind.

"I thought you didn't do magic," he coughed.

"I don't, silly," she answered quickly, then realized she'd negated her ruse. "Oh. I mean…" She didn't continue. They both knew what was happening here.

She knelt with him at the circle's center, began chanting the runic words to "Mandy," and then sliced her finger with the knife, pressing the damaged member to the center of the pentagram.

Charles threw himself at her with his last strength then, catching her by surprise. Grabbing her knife hand with both of his own, he shoved it into her belly.

She yelped in surprise and he rolled himself out of the circle. Ceiran was clutching her middle and screaming now, the runic language interlaced with "No, No."

He was sliding through the doorway when he heard the explosion crash. It lit the hall before him and Ceiran's cries grew frantic. Without looking back, he stumbled to his feet and lurched down the stairs and out the front door into the chilly night. He limped as fast as he could down the sidewalk and the world became a blur of shadow.

The ground rose up to meet him.

\/\\/\\\\/\\/\\\

He awoke in a hospital bed, a wealth of tubes and machines charting his life signs around him. The police were waiting. He'd been brought in, an officer explained, following a neighbor's call to 911 to report that a bloody, naked man was lying on the sidewalk in front of her house. The woman's call probably saved his life. A fresh-faced officer prodded him for a reason someone would cut his balls and leave him for dead. Charles gave the cop an annotated story of a bar pickup gone bad. The officer smiled oddly at him as he related the events of the past two days (minus any mention of ball-burrowing lizards, of course). The cop went away then, and he drifted back to a troubled sleep. When he woke again, he flipped the hospital TV on, thumbing through channels for the radio feed.

"Oh Mandy, well you came and you stopped me from shaking..." blared the speaker with unnerving synchronicity.

Charles punched the station switcher angrily. He settled on the news. A trench-coated reporter was standing in front of the violent orange glow of a house fire. Charles' car was behind the reporter.

"Firemen have been battling this blaze for many hours now, and are puzzled over its tenacity. Chief Dobrin expressed concern that some explosive material may be contributing to its stubborn hold on the house, which as you can see, barely has a timber of its original structure left. The building has sat empty for several years, according to neighbors, so there's no telling what caused, or is sustaining, the blaze. Back to you Chuck."

Charles clicked the TV off and lay back on the bed. No mention of Ceiran. Had she gone through to the world of the Direkits? Had the baby escaped – or was it the source of the unquenchable fire?

\/\/\/\\/\\\/\\

A taxi dropped him at the site to pick up his car a few days later. The police had left him alone after a couple more visits – no body had been found in the fire, so there was nothing to charge him with. Nothing remained of the house but a plain of black rubble. The yard's evergreens had burned to a few spiny skeletons. Charles walked over the ruined landscape, questions still burning in his head. He found that for all she'd done to him, he hoped that somehow, Ceiran had survived. *Why?* he thought. *So she can sing warped Manilow to other victims?* He didn't know. He just felt as though, sex aside, she had actually *liked* him.

His foot knocked a charred scrap of wood aside and the sun glinted off something amid the charcoal at his feet. He bent, pushed aside more debris, brushed away ash.

The sparkling eyes of the silver Direkit pendant stared back. He picked it up and wiped it off, considering the implications of Ceiran's abandonment of the medallion. Then he shrugged it over his head, adjusted it beneath his shirt and hobbled stiffly back to the car. His skin tingled oddly at the touch of the cold metal. *She'd want this, if she ever returns,* he thought. In the meantime, he figured he'd be scanning the supermarket tabloids. Looking for headlines like "Scientists Discover Dragon."

A shiver of anticipation shook him at the thought.

Pornography can give people the release they need without the dangers of reality. But fantasy holds the obsessive seeds for its own dangers. We all need a little fantasy in our lives, but like any other obsession, the single-minded pursuit of its enjoyment bears a high price. And if we need fantasy so, what does fantasy need from us?

Every Last Drop

His breathing grew ragged. In the shifting kaleidoscope of electric light, his gray eyes reflected obscene plays of color, did not shine out their own. The woman was tan, California style – no lines. Her lips were shiny pink, an erotic complement to the nipples of her bobbing brown breasts, currently matching – or more correctly, setting – the rhythm of his respiration. She flipped a strand of sand-blonde hair away from her face, ice-blue eyes flashing with lust, sweat collecting on her forehead, lips pursed and moaning...

The holovision abruptly went blank-blue, and Tony zipped up.

That was not your ordinary porno-blonde, he thought in admiration. Most of the blondes they used these days were like plastic dolls – the parts were all there, but the energy, the spirit – the spark that sometimes transfigured a 3-D bimbo into an orgasm-inducing fantasy – most just didn't have it. They looked bored. They looked... faceless. Tits and ass a dime a dozen – sex goddesses were hard to find.

On the cyberbooth door he paused a moment to read the obscene graffiti. He didn't know why, it was depraved and depressing and yet he always did.

"Looking for black cock to suck? Call 546-..."

"My wife screws you while I watch – ask for Leo (313)…"
"Homos go to hell…"
"The perfect blow job: no names, no faces, no price, all privacy, unspeakable pleasure. Cum to Redroom Hotel #112 after 9 p.m."

He read the last one again and shook his head. Nobody gave the perfect blow job for free. He couldn't *pay* Loni to give him one anymore at all. Tucking in his shirt he pushed open the door and walked quickly out of the back hall of the peep show. Men paced in the shadows, faces illuminated by the orange glow of silently smoking cigarettes, looking for the newcomer to proposition, waiting for the booth they wanted to free up. He grimaced in disgust and left the place, nodding at the wrinkled, bored cashier watching a "Dick Van Dyke Show" rerun.

Back when Loni had first gone out with him, she'd been eager to please, spreading everything for him just about anytime. She'd never been nuts about fellatio, but she serviced him dutifully. Their first couple years he'd nearly forgotten what the insides of these peep houses were like. Guys looking for anonymous sex with other guys, just for thrills or because they were too scared to admit they were gay and come out of the closet. Here it wasn't gay or straight, it was diversion. Businessmen on a lark, husbands on desperation runs. He wouldn't let these desperate men touch him, but he had no problem touching himself. If you couldn't get it at home, you had to go somewhere…

Tony gunned the car and screeched out into traffic. He hoped Loni was in a good mood tonight – the blonde with the ice-blue eyes and pure-copper bod had left him wanting more. The new cyberbooths at the adult video store he'd frequented for years were great – but even though the women surrounded you like real life, you still couldn't *feel* them. But thinking of that last scene made the crotch of his pants uncomfortable. He shifted in the seat and willed away an erection – which only served to increase its growth. Gripping his thighs together, he aimed the car onto the freeway and tried to relax. *That place was supposed to relieve the tension, not create more*, he grinned to himself.

\/\\//\\\\/\\\/\\

Loni was not in a good mood.

"You're an hour late and I've got to make that train," she fumed, shimmying out of her skirt in their bedroom. At 34, she looked good, he observed, better than when they'd met. Her chest, while not that of the goddess, was ample, if over-nippled. Her middle was potting out a bit but her hips always nailed his eye to their hidden valley, something which, at this particular moment, did not work in his favor.

"I'm changing Tony, you've seen it before. Go get something to eat."

He reached out to massage her exposed behind. She slapped his hand away. "Go. There'll be plenty of time for that next week. Right now I'm late and you're pissing me off."

Her dark eyes pierced the mental fog that arousal always drew around him. Loni grew easily irritated with his physical obsessions. Sometimes it was flattering; now it was in her way.

"Alright, alright," he grumbled. "Did you leave me anything?"

"There's Chinese in the fridge, some spaghetti from last night. You'll have to warm it up yourself. If I miss this train, there's not another one until 11 and Angie will be sitting at the station waiting for me all night."

She finished pulling on jeans and drew a sweater over the bra strap Tony had been admiring from behind. She turned and caught him still staring.

"It's only seven days. Go rent *Vampy Vixens* or something. I've gotta go. She slipped on a pair of black flats and grabbed her suitcase from the bed.

"I'll call ya tomorrow. Now goodbye."

She pecked him on the lips and was out the door.

The ache in his crotch flared again as he realized *that* was all he was going to get for quite awhile. Shrugging in defeat, he shambled into the kitchen.

He decided on the Chinese, but after aimlessly poking through pea pods and some mutant pygmy chicken, ended up re-Saran-ing most of it. He wasn't hungry, damnit, he was horny! He tried watching TV, but none of the canned laughs took his mind off the vision of pink lips wrapping around his erect member, a halo of beach-blown hair teasing his legs.

On a sudden impulse he pulled out the telephone directory and looked up the address of the Redroom Hotel. It turned out, as he'd expected, to be in a run-down section of the city, maybe a 20-30 minute's drive. He watched some more TV, knowing in some way that he was killing time. Waiting. Waiting...

...until the clock said 8:37. That would put him there around nine. Tony turned off the television and went to the garage.

Run-down is not the word for it, he thought as he pulled into the lot. The unlit sign (which was big enough that he still picked it out from a couple blocks away) didn't exactly promise the Hilton, and nobody seemed to be around. *Who knows how long that note had been markered onto the peep show door anyway*, he admonished himself. It was probably put there by someone in town for a night or two who was since long gone. He stopped in the hotel courtyard and shook his head. This was asinine. He could get mugged, get AIDS – maybe this was the site of ritual sacrifices. The newspaper'd just run an article about the rash of them downtown this year.

A clomping noise broke the pensive silence; made him whirl around, his heart kicking in double time. A sudden wind blew a drop of cold sweat from his forehead into his eye. There, on the brown brick wall at the end of the courtyard, a shadow grew, larger with each staccato slap. The clicking was footsteps, he realized, and they were coming his way. Go back – go forward – he didn't know which way to turn. And then, as the shadow reached gargantuan, grotesque proportions, its Dr. Frankenstein stepped into view – a short, Asian fellow carrying a briefcase and striding quickly towards the parking lot. He bent his head as he passed Tony, seeming intent on not making eye contact. Tony relaxed; abandoning his thoughts of turning back to the car, he decided to check and see if anyone was in room 112. He was here after all, and had a whole night to kill.

Night cloaked the courtyard sidewalk in shifting mystery. Bushes and weeds poked tendrils across the path, slowing his progress, their cold, tenuous gropings of his legs and belly made him shiver. The encroaching undergrowth made him wonder if this hotel was still in operation, but then, when he glanced around, he realized there were lights on in some of the rooms. The sign was out, the sidewalk beacons were unlit, but a blue glow poked through the curtains of the occasional occupied room. Upon reaching 112, his fears were confirmed.

No light at all.

He knocked anyway, and the door creaked open an inch at his attack.

"Hello," he called through the black sliver of an opening. It was somehow darker in the room than it was outside. "Anybody home?" he drawled with mock levity.

There was no answer, only a heavy stillness that seemed to press against him like a smothering blanket. He wanted to turn and go home, but a stubborn duality drew him to stay. He wanted to see *the* room, *why* he didn't know. It was not like there was going to be some tangible remnant of sex-gone-by to see. Still, he pushed the squealing door open some more and stepped inside, his hand trailing along the wall for the light switch. He found it, flicked it, and nothing happened. Except the door slammed shut. Tony backed against the wall, eyes straining to make out something through the inky black air.

"Who's there," he said, trying to keep a desperate quaver from his voice.

"Shhsssssssssssssssssss," something answered. It could have been a rattlesnake or a cat as easily as a human.

Something touched him, grabbed him at the waist. Tony froze, not knowing whether compliance was safest or if he should strike – and possibly risk getting stabbed or shot by his unseen assailant. Actually, he supposed the hands on his body couldn't be accused of assault. He was the intruder here, after all.

The pressure on his left side abated and he felt a tickle at his crotch. His zipper protested in the dark, and then his belt loosened. Still he couldn't move. He was so scared he wanted to scream, to run, but he could do neither, only stand flat against the wall in the groping night as his underwear dropped to his feet and something cold and smooth brushed against his cock – which completely ignored the paralyzed fear of the rest of him and responded with an instant erection.

His hard-on was first gripped and tugged by a cold hardness, *like the surgical probing of a doctor wearing rubber gloves for a prostate exam*, he thought. And then there was a wetness, an engulfing, and the two gripping appendages began working the rest of him, pinching his buttocks, sliding down his thighs, moving with icy grace across the hair of his chest. They were warming now, as was Tony, who had surrendered the fear, surrendered his questions. He pressed his hands to the wall as the caressing hands worked their erotic way across his skin, the unseen mouth working with unbelievable expertise up and down his hardened member. Teeth trailed lazily across just the right nerves, fingers pinched his nipples at just the right moment. As the tingling in his groin grew to a waterfall of breath-stealing sensation, Tony realized that this was, indeed, the perfect blow job and closed his eyes as the moment exploded.

When he opened them again, the hands had receded. He was sitting on the room's short, sandpaper-rough carpet and could see now, sort of, in the darkness. There was no one else in the room.

"No names, no faces, no price," the peep show graffiti had said. "Unspeakable pleasure."

It delivered what it advertised, he thought, just as something small and hairy darted across his leg. Tony jumped up, ending his reverie with a shiver. Pulling up his pants, he left the room still buckling his belt. Too weird, he thought, hurrying back to his car. He was weak as he slid in behind the wheel. The experience had been so intense, so draining…It was incredible, he thought, *but too weird for me.*

\/\\/\\/\\/\\/\\/\\/\\/

"Tony? Tony?"

The vision of the blonde goddess from the peep show burying her head between his legs in a shadowy derelict hotel room vanished, replaced by the less welcome sight of his balding overweight boss, leaning over the desk and staring at him with a perplexed expression."

"Tony, you've been drooling into space for the past 15 minutes. Are you alright?"

Tony shook his head to clear away the stubborn ache of his daydream.

"Yeah, Bob. Sorry. I just… didn't get much sleep last night."

"Why don't you go lay down in the lounge for a few minutes?" Bob Mackenzie smiled. "I'd tell you to go on home, but I do need to have that web report by the end of the week, you know."

"I know. You'll have it. I'm just having a little trouble concentrating today is all."

Bob chuckled, a dry, lifeless sound, and clapped Tony on the shoulder. "Well, wake up, man." He turned and lumbered back into his office. But Tony caught his watchful eye staring across the hall at him throughout the rest of the afternoon. And try as he might, the blonde kept nuzzling back into his consciousness. It was embarrassing. He couldn't leave his desk without first taking several minutes to meditate on bloody images of mutilated animals and abandoned babies to deflate the tent in his pants. First the incredible movie with the goddess and then the bizarre blow job last night – the two were merging together in his thoughts, a union so powerful his sex was reacting as if he were a male dog surrounded by females in heat. When five o'clock rolled around, he moved like a zombie towards the door, praying nobody was looking at the zipper of his pants. It was bulging, and as he fumbled in his pocket for car keys he suppressed the almost unstoppable urge to grab and go for it, right there in the middle of the office.

Bob watched his trance like gait from his desk and called across the office just before Tony reached the door.

"Get some sleep tonight, Ton."

"Uh-huh," he mumbled in reply. He knew what he was going to get tonight.

He threw the Chinese in the microwave when he got home, and this time managed to fork the mess down, though with little enjoyment. Loni called while he was rinsing off his dishes. He let her do most of the talking – she missed him, hoped he was fine. Did he eat the Chinese she left?

She got in OK, her sister Angie was waiting on the platform with her husband Dan. They were going to the zoo tomorrow. Tony answered automatically when necessary, while his attention focused on watching the blonde goddess who had somehow materialized in his kitchen. She spread her legs apart on the dinner table, her shockingly pink lips opening and closing with mesmeric rhythm while her mouth whispered: *"Come to me, Tony. Cum in me, Tony. Come to me, Tony. Cum in me, Tony."*

"Tony."

"Huh?"

"Have you heard a word that I just said?"

"Yeah, hon, I just got, um, distracted. There's some kids running through the backyard."

"Well, go shag them out. I'll talk to ya tomorrow. I love you."

"Love you too, hon. Bye."

He cradled the phone in its receiver. The table was empty but for some delinquent grains of rice. But he could still hear her soft, crystalline voice – pleading like a pony-tailed little girl, yet husky like a woman with a bad need for a man, any man.

Then it was nine o'clock and he was walking down the sidewalk towards room 112. He didn't really recall driving there, he realized, as he knocked on the door again. He didn't really remember what he'd done since hanging up the phone. But the door swung open with its raspy complaint and his cock was so hard he felt he might burst with anticipation.

The door closed behind him and this time there was no delay before the hands were taking down his pants. *It was strange, this silent sex*, he thought. There was no sound but his breathing, the beat of his heart, both increasing in tempo and timbre until he cried out in passion. "Yes. Yes. Suck me dry, baby. Take every last drop."

And with that command, somehow, she did. At the summit of orgasm he suddenly drew a breath of pain as her demand increased. He could feel her pulling him inside her, sucking him out through his penis. His head was spinning, a glittering fireworks display lit up before his eyes.

And then it was over, and he was collapsed on the floor, drained of the power to move. He had never experienced anything so powerful, so pleasurable.

"Who are you?" he whispered, as her hands pushed at his chest. He laid back on the floor as she directed and felt her hair trailing up his thighs to tease his belly. It was just like his daydream, he realized, and as he closed his eyes to imagine the glowing naked skin of the goddess, the woman between his legs began to work on him once more. This time when he reached his peak, he passed out.

It was after 3 a.m. when he crawled into bed, a painfully erect pole between his legs.

At 4 a.m. he was staring at the L.E.D. light on his clock radio, sweat streaming from his forehead, his hands, uncontrollably glued to his cock.

This was insane. He'd seen a porno with a hot babe, and then gotten sucked off a couple times by some nut who freaked about being seen. Why couldn't he let it go? He'd never been this horny in his life. What would Loni think? She wouldn't care much about the movie or the little fantasies, and getting an anonymous bj wasn't exactly cheating – she ought to be happy someone took care of it for her, he thought. No, she wouldn't be too angry about that stuff. But if she saw him here sweating with lust over another woman – actually two, one of which he'd never, in the strictest sense, seen – that, she wouldn't relish. In an attempt to snap himself sober, he fastened onto an image he'd seen in a documentary. Soldiers dead on the battle field, arms and legs streaked with red, entrails leaking out from between clenched hands, heads lying 10 feet from the crater where the rest of the body was mangled...

The erection in his hands didn't even flag. And then his

conscious mind lost control and the soldier with his guts hanging out suddenly stood up and pushed the bleeding mess back inside with one hand while unbuttoning his pants with his other. They fell to the ground and Tony saw the golden triangle of the blonde goddess below the ruptured belly. The soldier rubbed his face and her ice-blue eyes and pink lips were suddenly speaking to him.

"Come to me Tony, cum in me."

Tony rolled over and began to cry.

\/\/\/\/\\/\\/\\/\\/\\/\\

When 9 a.m. rolled around Tony was in his chair at the office, but Tony was not *in*. Black circles ringed his eyes and his right hand lay useless and twitching at his desk. His left hand was in his lap.

"Report coming along OK, Tony?" Bob asked from across the hall. He hadn't seen Tony move since he'd stumbled in a half hour before.

"Uh-huh," came the answer. But the man still didn't budge.

When afternoon arrived and Tony didn't seem any more aware, Bob sent him downstairs to the corporate doctor. There was a wet spot on the man's pants which left Bob praying silently that his key employee was not sicker than he looked.

"Well Tony, your blood pressure is low today," Dr. Regsic chirped at him. "Let's get up on the scale." The meter flashed 156 lbs and she looked down at her chart.

"You've lost almost 20 pounds over the past couple months, Tony. Have you been on a diet?"

He shook his head no.

"Exercising?"

No.

She shook her head.

"Get up here on the table and unbutton your shirt."

He did as she asked.

"How did you get those?" she frowned and bent towards him for a closer look. He hadn't noticed this morning, but there were 10 red trawls down his chest, starting with a weak red glow at his shoulders and turning dark purple as they narrowed to converge in a single thick corridor at his bellybutton.

He was silent for a minute, and then offered: "My wife gets, um, excited."

"Drop your pants, Tony."

She didn't sound like she'd take an argument, so he stood and undid his belt. His pants slid down immediately, revealing first, that he'd somehow forgotten underwear this morning, and second that the purple bruise led downwards from his belly to the tangle of hair beneath.

The doctor gasped at the sight. Tony thought she was impressed with his size – he was, of course, still erect. But her eyes did not look lustful, rather, they were disgusted. He focused on the object of her stare and saw that it, too, was red and purple – and swollen to twice its normal size.

"Look, Tony. I don't want to tell you what to do in your bed, but if your wife is responsible for this – I'd consider divorce. I don't even want to know how this happened, but you'd better rule out sex for the next week or two. I'm going to give you an antibiotic just in case you've got that infected."

She walked over to the white cabinets across the room and pulled out a tube.

Instead of a dumpy fortyish woman in an overly long lab coat, Tony saw the bronze muscular buttocks of the goddess crossing the room, the dark lure of the crack between her legs led his hand to his lap. Her stride was lolling, casual. Her hips swayed suggestively, the ripples in her back and across her waist invited his tongue. She looked across her shoulder at him, flipping a mane of bleached hair over her shoulder. Her eyes touched his with electricity and she winked.

"*COME TO ME, TONY.*"

She turned around to show him all.

"*CUM IN ME, TONY.*"

"God, what is wrong with you?"

Dr. Regsic stood in front of him, her jaw hanging open.

"I'm not going to say anything about this Tony, but I am going to recommend a counselor."

She reached over and pulled a paper towel from a roll on the wall.

"Here. Clean yourself up and go home. I'll leave a prescription of antibiotic for that – you better hope it doesn't scar – and some ointment as well. Come back tomorrow, I want to see how you're doing."

\/\/|\\/\\\/\|/\

She was there again at 9, just like before.

"Who *are* you?" he asked again, as his jeans bunched around his ankles. Still she would not answer, but her hands were hot tonight, full of rhythmic lust. He felt a sticky wetness on his leg. With the rest of himself, he felt only her power. Her fingers blazed trails of ice and fire across him, but it was her mouth that centered her magic. As she pulled him inside her, the pleasure radiated back into his body, a feedback of ecstasy. He knew now the purple trails across his chest were her conduits of pleasure, he could feel every pulling sensation electrify those paths with heat. It could have been the intoxication of the moment, but a dull cobalt illumination seemed to leak from the weave she worked upon him, growing brighter and dimmer with the waxing and waning of her pressure upon him. And as she reached up to carve another channel on his chest, he saw why she insisted on darkness.

Her left hand was maimed.

The thumb and pinky fingers were whole, their long, red-capped nails raked his flesh as any woman's. But the middle three fingers lacked nails – in fact, they seemed to lack flesh as well. It looked as if she'd dipped her hand into a radiation soup. That would explain the hard coldness he had felt the past three nights as she first cupped and cajoled his loins. *With cold bony fingers...*

But her skill made up for any deformities. Again and again she brought him to orgasm, he groaned and begged her to suck him dry once more. And every time she did. Again the night ended with his losing consciousness in the throes of release. Again he awoke to find her gone, and spent the remaining hours tossing in his bed. And the next two nights were the same.

On Friday, Bob put him on report and turned the web project over to another department. Tony went back to Dr. Regsic.

She tried to keep the alarm from reaching her voice, while noting that his blood pressure had dipped dangerously low and he'd somehow lost another 10 pounds since Tuesday. But when he removed his clothes, her breath hissed with disgust. The purple bruising covering his torso looked like a gridmap. And it all led to a penis the size of a cucumber. Not an overly healthy looking one at that. She handed him the name of "a good doctor" at the hospital scribbled on her business card.

"Go there. Now," was all she said. It was three in the afternoon, but he went.

Not to the hospital, though, to the hotel.

As he pulled into the parking lot – for the first time in daylight – he saw how truly decrepit the place was. Weeds sprouted everywhere through cracks in the asphalt. A "For Sale" sign was tacked on below the big Redroom Hotel placard above the main office door – which was boarded shut.

Apparently the Gentech Laboratories, whose fence butted up to the back of the hotel property, weren't bringing in enough business to support a hotel. Or maybe after the outcry a few years ago about GTL's genetic testing program, they had steered business away. The hotel windows that weren't covered in graffiti-ed plywood were broken, ragged glass massaged gently by shredding curtains in the low breeze.

Yes, this hotel had been closed for awhile, he supposed. *So how had there been lights on in some rooms the other nights? And how long had She been there?* This was probably a prostitution pit even when it was open for legitimate business, he guessed, wondering if his goddess had plied her strange trade here even then. *Were there others like her in the other rooms? Could the cold blue lights he had seen night after night have been the flares of others undergoing the same consuming pleasures as himself, not the glow of cathode ray tubes?* He found that he no longer cared, and strode unerringly towards 112. Closed or not, he knew of one room that had a vacancy.

The room was a lot creepier in the daylight than hidden in the moist shadows of night.

The paint, a dull, putrid green, was peeling away from the walls, especially in the corners where water damage had left brown stains on the cinder block the paint was separating from. The carpet was once charcoal gray, but now was pockmarked with circles of brown and black stains. Portions of it were frayed and pulled up. Spiderwebs crisscrossed the corners, and something scuttled under the unsheeted bed when he stepped towards it. The mattress looked too dirty to sit on, let alone sleep on. Now he knew another reason she said to come after 9. It would be hard to get off knowing that you were likely taking rats, spiders, or any number of vermin along for the ride.

"Hello. Anybody home?" he called into the silence that seemed to hang around him like a breath taken and held.

Something rustled nearby.

"I know I'm early, but I couldn't wait."

She came out of the bathroom, her skeleton legs joining neat as knickers with golden-skinned thighs and a blonde tuft of pubic hair. Her belly button was exquisite, a hollow darkness on a flat-planed bed of sensual muscle that promised both pleasure and mystery. Her breasts were as tan and supple as her belly, full, alert and capped by the lightest shade of pink areolae.

He saw now that both her hands were incomplete, but each by only two fingers – which was puzzling because he knew he'd seen three skeletal tips on one last night. But white-boned calves, feet, and fingers were not a turnoff to him now. And she could have hidden these odd deformities if she'd wanted to, he thought.

Her face was the real problem. A lipless mouth showed the white teeth within glittering savagely against a gash of wet crimson. He could see her cheekbone jutting through pink flesh on one side, while the other half of her face seemed nearly complete, and as coppery brown as the rest of her fleshed body. Her eyes were piercing sapphires, but on the visible cheekbone side the eye was lidless, and the white line of her skull seemed to poke through above it. The lightly kinked, wind-blown blonde hair that turned him on so much ringed her face and draped across her shoulders. She held her arms out in offering.

"Is this what you want?" she asked. Her voice was gentle as a girl's, yet somehow throaty, wanton. But despite the velvet of her tone, without the cushion of lips, her words revealed themselves like daggers plied from carving meat.

"Yes," he said without hesitation. "But, *what* are you?"

She smiled with her eyes. Her ivory teeth ground cruelly.

"I'm your dream lover. Come to me, Tony. They designed me to be filled up by men. And it's really been too long."

He started towards her. She moved past him to the bed and laid down. He could see dots of scarlet and curdled cream on the bones that were her legs, and on her feet, tiny red lines that looked like unsheathed capillaries. She wiggled her toes and they clinked together invitingly. She spread her legs and he saw the heaven he'd thirsted for all week long. She was his dream lover. She was the girl from the porno vid. He could see it in the eyes now, in the perfect breasts, in the pinkness that glistened so invitingly. His crotch throbbed painfully while his head ached with fear and longing.

"Cum in me, Tony. Let me suck you down to make me whole."

His pants were so loose now they slid to the floor with no unbuckling. He realized briefly that however he'd written off his previous indiscretions with this woman, this was, unalterably, adultery. He knew somewhere in his head that Loni would be back Tuesday, and he should put himself back together by then. And he knew he wouldn't.

Couldn't.

And he didn't care.

He straddled her unfinished body and bypassed foreplay. She was visibly ready, and her hands now raked at his back as they had all week on his chest. He felt as though he were being diced and licked at the same time. Her tongue snaked out of her lipless mouth and teased and moistened his eyes, nose and neck.

She bit him hard on the shoulder and then caressed his lips with her tongue. Her eyes sucked him into another world, her vagina was a utopian tunnel. He was making love like he never had before, bucking and pumping like a male hound on a bitch. Then she rolled atop him, the bones of her toes scratching at his calves, sounding like nails on hollow wood as they met the bones beneath his muscle. Yet he didn't howl; he could feel nothing but her force fed ecstasy. And she drove him on, harder and harder, the trails in his flesh burned and froze in alternate coursings. He could see them glow with power released. And when at last he answered her plea and came, he knew with fatalistic certainty that it would never stop.

She laughed as he came and came and the skin on her cheek grew thick and tan and her lips went from baby pink flesh to full pouting sex teases.

...*And he came* and felt her legs pressed upon his own growing, the red and white seeds of flesh drawing the essence of him to her, nursing, nourishing their growth.

...*And he came* and as her shinbones ceased clicking together he heard his own begin to clatter. He felt light, empty, but trapped in some sick, twisted compulsion as his hips smacked against hers of their own accord.

...*And he came* and she laughed and pressed her arms upon his chest. Her fingers were perfect and whole and she said in that husky girl voice, "take me again, stud," and laughed when he did and she bent to kiss him and his tongue was caught in a vacuum; his cheeks sagged, receded. She lifted his arm in passion and he saw the white bones protruding from the unraveled skin of his fingers.

...*And* still *he came* and the night came and the morning too before she pushed his trembling bones away from her flesh.

She stood then, and stretched, a lithe cat of a woman. Running her fingers across supple, muscular skin, she drank in herself inch by inch in a shard of mirror across the room. Her body was whole, tan, California style – no lines. Her lips were shiny pink, an erotic complement to the nipples of her perfectly brown breasts. She flipped a strand of sand-blonde hair away from her face, ice-blue eyes flashing with abating lust, sweat drying on her forehead, lips pursed in humorous consideration. Gazing back at the bed, she saw the eyeballs in Tony's meatless cranium staring back at her, still with a longing, and, she felt, appreciation of her new form. She'd best finish the job.

She sighed and bent over him, tongue lasciviously ready. When she rose the skull was sightless, the bones no longer vibrated on the floor. A long transparent tube of skin trailed between his femurs. She pulled it off with a rip and swallowed it. "Every last drop," she murmured and licked her lips.

She pulled on his jeans, cinching the belt to its furthest hole. It left her thighs baggy and ill-defined, but it would do for now. She fastened one button of the short-sleeved blue cotton shirt, and tied the rest across her belly, leaving her midriff and much of her chest exposed.

She pulled at the uncomfortable weight on her behind and came up with his wallet. Thumbing through $20s and $10s, her white canines flashed hungrily.

Good.

She didn't relish hanging around this dump any longer. As she went to flip the wallet closed, a snapshot of a woman caught her eye. She was raven-haired, dark-eyed, with high cheekbones and an intense look of vibrance in her mouth. The woman was hot. Just looking at the photo made her mouth dry, and even after its recent use, her groin ached with desire. *Probably his wife*, she speculated, checking his license to find an address. She *knew* where this house was, she realized, as Tony's cannibalized cells merged and shared their knowledge with her own. It had taken her too long to find a host after the Gentech engineer had abandoned her here to wither away. She laughed, thinking of his reward if she could track him down. Sex goddesses were hard to find – or make! And she intended to feed regularly to keep her full goddess form from now on.

Maybe he could be one of her snacks.

Kicking the sated bones under the moldering bed, she wondered, in the meantime, if Tony's wife liked blondes. Opening the door to step with anticipation into daylight, she resolved to find out.

What is justice and who does it serve? While it may yield a brief feeling of satisfaction for the wronged, it can't undo deeds already performed. It can't bring the dead back to life. Its taste is often fleeting and sours quickly. Yet, who hasn't wished for justice to be done?

When Barrettes Brought Justice to a Burning Heart

He staggered from the smoky heat of the bar into the chill autumn wind. The street outside was empty, the cloud-scummed sky a leeching black. Bill Frond's stomach sloshed as he weaved to the corner, but all the liquor his wallet could afford hadn't assuaged the burning in his chest. In fact, through the haze of inebriation, he actually felt more wounded now than before he had stomped into Ale's Head Tavern several hours ago. The fire in his heart had contracted to a pinpoint of heat, leaving behind a blackened void. He feared when the little acid flame that still burned was extinguished, he would stop dead in his tracks, a flesh appliance whose batteries had spurted their last current.

But another fire was lighting in his guts; it surged past the dying ember in his heart to race through his throat. Bill froze a moment, staring sickly at the dark alleyway just ahead. As his binge lit to purge, he dashed for the privacy of the narrow street.

Ten minutes later, exhausted, slumped on the ground near a pool of bitter vomit, Bill pulled a tissue from his jacket, wiped the tears from his eyes and blew the acid from his nose.

"Feel better?" a voice grated from the darkness. Bill's heart leapt at the unexpected sound. He squinted at the uneven bricks and shadows around him. The dim outline of a man began to take shape from the depths of the darkened street.

"Not really," Bill answered, wondering if, after all this, he was now going to be mugged. Or killed. Preferably the latter, a voice within him begged.

"Tell me," the voice asked, its owner settling just far enough away that Bill couldn't make out his face. A white flash as the man spoke, a glint from eyes turning down. That was all. A hint of a face.

"Tell you what?" Bill snapped. "That I feel sick inside? That I just wasted 30 bucks trying to drink away reality? Please leave me alone; I'm not in the mood for company."

"Don't worry, I'm not anybody's idea of company." The hint of a face blurred, shifted, moved closer. Bill caught the sour odor of alley trash and felt his belly kick in complaint.

"Tell me why you're here, while you still can," the voice demanded. The roughness of its tone sent a chill through Bill's neck. *If this guy was going to beat him up – or worse – what difference did it make why he was here?*

"You want to know? I'll tell you," Bill began, slipping easily into the words recounting events he had already relived a hundred times this night.

"Seven months ago, Lissa, my daughter, was walking home from school. We live just a few blocks away from Sanders High, and she always walked home. In the rain, in the snow, in the summertime. She liked to walk. And she always came straight home. But on that particular afternoon, she didn't come home on time. Cheryl – that's my wife – worried a little, but figured Lissa had stopped off to talk with someone. When it got to be dinnertime, Cheryl started calling the parents of Lissa's friends. No one had seen her. After I came home from work, and she still wasn't home, we checked the hospitals. Then we called the police."

The shadowed figured nodded slowly, as if hearing a familiar story.

"They found her the next day in the woods behind the school. She was naked, her body smeared with blood. Her own. Her eyes were open. I think that hurt me the most. She was aware of every touch, every violation, I know she was. Her skull was crushed – she'd been hit on the head with a rock. Then raped. But she felt every minute of it. Her eyes were screaming.

"They caught the boys who did it – a couple 17-year-olds who thought they could just knock her out with a rock, rape her and leave before she woke up." Bill's face wrinkled in silent agony, then he coughed out a sob and shook his head clear.

"But they hit her too hard," he finally continued, tears now wetting his cheeks. "And somehow, she didn't fall unconscious. I wanted them to die like my daughter died. I watched them smirking to each other in the courtroom during the trial, and I pictured myself smashing their heads together until their brains pulped through my fingers."

He paused, unclenched his hands and laughed sadly.

"The violence I planned for them! I wanted to castrate them, bash in their brains, stab holes in their hearts. Every night during the week of the trial, I cried myself to sleep. And when it was all over – the boys walked away free. Their lawyers managed to get every scrap of evidence the police had found thrown out of court on technicalities. They walked away free while my daughter rotted in the ground."

A flash of white, as the stranger's face nodded once again, inched closer.

"The day after the trial was over, I stepped out on my front porch to get the paper. And found these."

Bill pulled two triangular shapes from his coat pocket. They glittered in the faint light filtering into the alleyway from the street. "Lissa's barrettes. I know the boys left them for me to find. A joke. It was *all* a joke to them. And I hated myself, because instead of going after them, instead of giving them what they gave my daughter, I tucked these in my pocket, went back in the house, and cried some more."

The pale face again shifted closer, its outline now distinct, long in the heavy shadow of the alley. "Revenge is an expensive enterprise," it whispered, near enough that Bill could see the stranger's lips move. They seemed crooked, off-kilter. The alley stench had grown stronger, its character led by the nauseous aroma of rotting meat, but filled out with the bitter taste of old milk and neglect. Bill began to breathe through his mouth.

"Well, I wish I had paid the price now," Bill retorted. The fire in his chest had flared briefly with the retelling of his child's murder, but now flickered lower than before. He was beaten. It was over. He couldn't avenge his daughter and the remaining foundation of his life, which he'd spent years building upon, had, just today, been swept away in an instant.

"You're not here tonight because of your daughter," the voice breathed. Bill heard a pain in that tone that sounded not unlike his own. "Tell me," the stranger demanded softly.

Bill looked up in surprise at the stranger's appraisal, then nodded. It seemed right. He wanted to tell *someone* everything. And so he did.

"My wife looked into my eyes this morning. I thought she looked sad, and I asked her what was wrong. She just kept staring at me, and a tear rolled down her cheek. Then she kissed me. I knew something was bad. Real bad. She'd been so quiet since Lissa died. Actually, she'd been quiet before that, but I hadn't noticed – until I thought about it tonight.

" 'I don't love you anymore,' she said. Her eyes were blinking fast and her voice cracked.

" 'I've been trying to find it for a long time, but I'm sorry, I just don't. It's gone,' she said. I looked at her then, and maybe saw her for the first time in years. It's funny, after awhile, you start to see your wife as part of the furniture. She's there, you know? But in that instant I *saw* her, Cheryl, the girl I met at a beach party 20 years ago. And in her eyes I saw an unknown woman – still with all the mystery of a first date. I thought I knew her inside and out, but quite suddenly I realized that all I really knew about Cheryl was her skin. That I knew by heart. And her routines. But her? The woman staring at me with tears and pity in her eyes, I didn't know. And the man who cried, and begged, and finally fled here to the Ale's Head Tavern… I'm ashamed to know."

A hand patted him on the shoulder and Bill looked up into the startling eyes of the stranger. They were milky white, shot through with veins. They had no pupils. They rested in a face that seemed to move and shift in a manner no muscles could control. The rest of the man was cloaked in a long gray coat which didn't hide his gauntness. His bony fingers were also covered-in half-gloves, hobo-style.

"And what are you going to do about it?" the stranger asked, his breath crossing Bill's nose in a putrid wave which made him realize the alley stench was not of the alley, but of the bum.

"Nothing," Bill whispered. "I just want to die."

"That wish, I will grant," the stranger answered, and with a leap, pinned Bill to the ground. He didn't struggle.

"Go ahead," Bill said, all resistance leaving him. "I don't really care."

At close range, the stranger's oddly twitching face appeared mottled with sores, violent explosions of purple standing in grotesque relief against bone-white skin. The hands which pinned him to the gravelly asphalt were cold, sticky.

"I can give you the tool for revenge," the lips offered, mucousy spit dripping from them to moisten Bill's face. "Or I can simply kill you. I give you the choice because it wasn't offered to me. I would have chosen death. The cost of revenge is higher."

Deep in the burnt-out shell of Bill's heart, a tiny flame guttered higher. An insane thought crossed his mind. *This was not your ordinary alley bum.* Looking into the bloody whites which passed for the stranger's eyes, seeing the pus oozing from the cracks in his neck, smelling the decay which was not garbage, not bad breath, but this trench-coated bum's *rotting flesh*, Bill concluded that this was the devil himself. And suddenly that long unslaked thirst for revenge poured gasoline into his heart.

"I'll pay the price, whatever it is," he gasped through gritted teeth. "If it's my soul you want, take it, I don't care." Anger flooded his mind like the bile still lodged in his throat. "I just want to make them pay. All of them."

The being hesitated a moment, and a word of warning gurgled in his throat. His eyes lowered to stare into Bill's own. The stench was overpowering. Bill's stomach threatened to lose whatever acid remained trapped within when the eyes suddenly pulled away and then with a watery cry, the man buried his mouth in Bill's neck. He only got out one yelp of surprise and pain, and then the night sky blurred. His body went rigid and a stream of cool ice froze in his head. He could hear the stranger slurping, hear the beat of his own heart, *thud-thud, thud-thud, thud-thud…thud .. thud……. thud…. thud………….. thud.*

\\/\\/\\/\\/\\/\\/\\/\\/\\

The stench. God, it was bad! Bill lifted his head from the cushion of a plastic sack and stirred a hive of flies from somewhere below. They swarmed across his face and landed on his lips. He shook them away and realized in doing so that, amazingly, he had no hangover. But where was he?

Rolling off the bag, he felt the surface shift beneath him with a metallic heave as bags slid away and his feet scrambled to find purchase on solid ground. Reaching above him, his fingers met cool metal that lifted with a push. He rose to full height, his back and legs creaking at the unaccustomed stretch. A garbage dumpster. He was standing in a garbage dumpster! In a dark, stinking alley.

And then the events of the night returned to him. The drinking, the stranger, his story, and then – an attack? He reached up to feel his neck. Sure enough, two big sores where the bum had bit him. Bracing his hands on the side of the dumpster, he vaulted himself to the ground and brushed off his clothes. Something moved in the dark and he froze.

It was the expectation of hearing his heart pound wildly in his chest from fright that tipped him off.

His heart *wasn't* beating fast.

Odd.

He put his hand to his chest, felt around. *It wasn't beating at all.*

Odder still. But the worst part was, while intellectually he expected to break down into hysterics at any moment, the fact that his heart was not pumping blood to feed his fear didn't bother him. In fact, he *felt* very little. Rubbing an index finger along his neck and jaw, he realized he could feel the texture, but it was dulled. The equivalent of a black and white movie versus color.

The shadows stirred again. The stranger from last night emerged from a lean-to shelter behind the dumpster.

"Well, you asked for revenge," the bum said in a grating voice. "Now is your chance. Don't waste it. You don't have much time."

The blotches covered the stranger's face now; a tattooed blur of motion, its lips twitched out of sync with its speech, which was now slurred and indistinct – as if his mouth was slow to respond to the twitch of his muscles.

"Who are you?" Bill asked, his eyes drawn with abnormally detached interest to the shivers coursing across the man's exposed flesh.

"My name is Lawrence," the man said, milky orbs meeting Bill's own. "And, as you've probably guessed, I'm a vampire. You wanted revenge, so I gave you some of *my* blood last night." He pointed at the bruises covering his cheeks. "And this is the result of my thirst. This is *your* blood."

Bill thought that he should have known anger, should have smashed his fist into the prune face before him. But his head remained cool, empty of rancor. He'd been attacked and bitten by a man with a revolting skin disease, and here he was shooting the breeze with the same guy.

"I think you're just a sick bum with an S&M side," Bill laughed bravely, already trying to figure out if he should attempt to gain entrance to the couch at his house or head to a hotel for the rest of the night.

"You're dead," the voice before him gurgled. "And you don't have long to act if you want your revenge."

"Uh-huh," Bill said, starting to step away from the stinking, disease-ridden bum. But Lawrence shambled quickly to block the exit of the alley.

"Pull my finger," the bum begged, holding out his left palm. Bill laughed at the incongruous offer.

"Humor me," Lawrence demanded, ice in his tone.

Bill stared at the outstretched hand, its wrinkled whiteness a thoroughly unhealthy looking offering. Deciding that the faster he did what the transient wanted, the faster he could get to a bed, Bill grasped the extended finger and jerked.

And found himself holding the finger.

This appendage wasn't one of those trick pieces from the magic shop. This was real skin, real bone. And the red-black ooze at its disconnected end was, Bill suspected, his own blood.

"You're dead," Lawrence croaked. "Live with it."

Bill threw the digit away from him with a frown. He was now becoming somewhat disturbed at the situation. Things were looking, well, *unreal*.

"OK, let's say I'm dead. What happens now?" he asked.

"The same thing that happens to all dead people," Lawrence returned, stepping away from the alley mouth. "Decay. So get your revenge. Fast. And stay out of the sun. It won't stop you, but it will make you unpleasant to be around a lot faster."

Lawrence turned and disappeared behind the dumpster once more, leaving Bill alone. He felt again for his heartbeat. *Dead.* Stepping out onto the street, he decided to find out just what a man with no heartbeat could get away with. Remembering his impotent rage at the two boys who had stolen his daughter from him, he began walking towards the southeast end of town. There was a growing burning in him that sought release, a fire that consumed not only his heart, but his limbs, his head, his lips.

At last, he thought, *I will have some justice.*

\/\/|\\/\\/\\|/|

It wasn't hard to find them. There were only a couple of likely teen hangouts in this part of town, and the Angel's Park basketball court was one of them. Taking the bum's advice, he'd slept the day away in a cheap hotel, waking with the dusk to smooth his trash dumpster-scented clothes and step out onto the street once again. He briefly considered stopping at a McDonald's, and then realized that not only wasn't he hungry, but the idea of grilled beef made him somewhat nauseous. A drink wouldn't hurt though, he thought, and ducked into a Walgreen's to buy a pint of whiskey.

"Is something the matter?" he asked the aged woman behind the register inside the store. She wagged her head 'no' while staring at the stubble on his cheek. Her nose crinkled obstinately in complaint. Bill smiled as he accepted the paper bag. Her hand shied from touching his in the exchange. *"How quickly we devolve,"* he thought. *"Two days ago she wouldn't have looked at me twice."*

Outside the store he opened the bottle, tilted it back. The amber liquid slid easily down his throat – but lacked any kick. It might as well have been grape juice. He felt it travel his throat, detected a thin hint of flavor, and that was all.

By the time he'd reached the basketball court the bottle was empty, and he'd realized that, as liquor lacked any ability to warm his palate, so did it lack the power to make him drunk. *"Maybe it will preserve my insides longer,"* he thought. And then he noticed the dark stain spreading down the insides of his pant legs. Droplets fell to the sidewalk from his cuffs with each step. *No control*, he realized. If he drank, it simply ran through him. If he ate, it would probably putrefy inside him.

His attention was suddenly wrenched from his deteriorating condition to the fenced-in asphalt lot before him. The two punks he'd come looking for were here! They dashed from side to side wrestling for the basketball with a group of other teens. Bill settled unobtrusively on a bench just outside of the lot.

He could wait.

It wasn't a long one; it was already dark. The boys played under the blinding white glare of the park's lights for 15 or 20 minutes after Bill's arrival, and then began to fragment. Soon, only his quarry and two other boys were playing two on two. And then, they too split, two of the players passing him on the way out of the lot, while the two Bill was after hopped the back fence and headed through the alley towards their homes. As soon as the others had passed him, Bill jumped from the bench and sprinted to the back of the brightly lit court. He vaulted the fence easily, and saw the boys just a block down the alleyway. The tall one – Marcus, he remembered – was punching the shorter blonde kid's shoulder. Terry, that was his name. *As if I could forget*, Bill shuddered. In the courtroom they had appeared like negatives of each other – Marcus tall, black, beanpole-skinny; Terry short, squat and blonde. But both had maintained those smirking "you'll never nail me" expressions that were so maddening as it became more and more apparent that they were completely correct. *Well, maybe not completely*, Bill thought as he began running down the alley after them.

As he ran, that hot feeling in his heart and gut began to build once more – the thrill of the chase could at least still reach his deadened nerves. And then he was on them, slamming open palms into each of their backs just as they began to turn to see who was pounding the pavement behind them.

Terry was caught off balance by the blow, and fell to the ground with a startled exclamation. Marcus stumbled, but with the grace of a true athlete, absorbed the imbalance, and turned to meet his attacker. His eyes looked like searchlights in the dark street as he saw Bill's maddened face.

"It's Lissa's dad," he yelled to Terry, who clutched a knee on the ground. "Lay off asshole, or we'll have you in jail," the taller boy boasted, dodging a punch.

But Bill wasn't listening now. His body was on fire, his blood boiling, his head…hungry. He realized that even if he wanted to stop this, it had already gone too far. He *had* to have these kids.

Now.

He leapt at Marcus, ignoring the knife the boy pulled. He absently noted that the weapon lodged in his back as he and the boy fell to the ground. His voice seemed to slur as he pummeled the surprised teen's face with his fists and at last vented his anger: "You killed my daughter, you bastards!"

Reaching into his pocket with one hand, he brought out a shiny barrette. "Thought it was real cute to leave these on my doorstep, didn't you?" Bill raged.

Marcus let out one "holy shit" as Bill's mouth opened to expose a set of elongated fangs. In the same instant, Bill brought the barrette down, lodging it in Marcus' left eye. The boy shrieked an ungodly noise, and Bill felt rage electrify his body. He hated the snivelling creature beneath him. The boy had stolen his life.

Something crashed into his back, knocking him off balance. Then hands were around his neck, trying to wrest him away from the boy on the ground. He looked up to see the frantic face of Terry, trying to use his weight to drag Bill down. He only laughed and clubbed the fat slacker in the side of the head, and Terry went down like a rifled deer.

Then he turned back to Marcus, still writhing beneath him, hands covering his punctured eye. Bill felt a meanness he'd never known in life course through him like liquid fire and with his fist he beat at the boy's hands, pounding the barrette deeper into the boy's skull, until only a glint of metal remained visible amid the punctured white and red Campbell's soup of the boy's eye socket. Marcus' screams turned to metronomic near-silent hissing squeals. His arms dropped to the ground and his hands clenched and unclenched, his entire body spasming. Bill pulled the knife from his back without even a wince and began to stab his daughter's killer in the heart, over and over and over again. With each thrust he hissed "you… killed… my… Lissa."

Marcus didn't answer.

Finally Bill stopped slicing and stared at the wreckage he'd made. Blood was smeared like an explosion of thick barbeque sauce across the boy's face and his t-shirt lay in dark stained tatters across a torso wet with crimson ruin. The scent of sweet iron filled the air and Bill realized he was salivating. Drooling over the carcass of a murdering rapist. His face inched lower to the boy's chest and he tried to pull back. But the pull of the scent was like a leash. The world faded out and all he could see was the slick red skin beneath him. He lapped at the chest wounds like a dog, and seconds later, Bill's newly grown incisors were buried in the soft, unmarked flesh of the boy's neck. He sucked like a newborn babe on his mother's teat, drawing the essence of Marcus within himself, mouthful by mouthful, suckling breath by breath.

It was good, so good! As the liquor should have felt, that was how this blood was. He was floating in a garish maroon cloud of lust and drunkenness. Every touch, taste and emotion he'd lost upon his death combined in this hot elixir. Bill felt as if he was cumming, drinking an exquisite wine and laughing all at once.
This was heaven.

He was blinded to everything for a moment as the dying teen shuddered once more beneath him. With a fist he pounded the boy's chest to still him and found that with each punch, the rush of heaven increased. So, long after the boy's life had finally slipped away, Bill continued beating Marcus' middle, cracking his ribs, and eventually, forcing some of those splintered bones through the skin.

As the blood began to taste different, cooler, Bill pulled away from his drunken orgy and looked around. The night was still around them; amazingly, no one seemed to have been alerted from the boy's screams earlier.

Then, all at once, he saw that Terry had disappeared. He was loath to lift his mouth fully from his feast, but some last vestige of sanity forced him. He couldn't let the other boy live. Rising from the carcass, he saw for a moment the slashed neck, the white tips of ribs hung with shreds of skin and blood, the white, rolled back eyes – one with a shiny barrette skewer. He pulled the knife from its soggy chest holster and then he was running down the alley.

Terry would go home, he thought dimly, and home for the boy was only a few more blocks, he knew. There were many times after the court trial that he had driven past Terry's house, wishing fervently that he could stop and go inside and beat the living shit out of the little rapist who lived there. But he never could.

He forced his feet faster; the neighborhood garages backing onto the alleyway became light blurs as he ran. And then he saw the blond head of the hobbling, injured boy, and the look of utter terror as Terry saw the bloody face charging towards him. Bill threw his body at the boy. Something cracked loudly as they hit the ground. But that wasn't enough. He wanted the boy to feel the way that his daughter had.

"How do you like your own medicine?" Bill whispered. Picking up a loose hunk of asphalt, he brought it down on the boy's forehead, ruining that golden blond hair purity with spatters of blood. Terry moaned and Bill stood up, dragging the boy's limp body with him.

"Thought you'd get away with it, didn't you?"

He threw the boy against the steel pole of a fence and didn't wait until the body had slumped back to the ground to yank it up again. Bill had never felt this strong in life. With one motion he slammed the body on the ground like a rag doll and when one feeble hand reached out to stop him, he stood on the boy's chest, grabbed the hand and yanked until with a loud pop it separated from the shoulder joint.

"You were never good enough for my daughter," he mumbled, and then retrieved the knife from the ground. Slicing through the boy's shirt, belt and jeans, he stripped Terry and stared at the white folds of unconscious flesh beneath him.

"And I'll make sure you'll never do it to anyone else."

With that he brought the knife down at the base of the boy's shriveled penis, and pushed down. And sawed. And with a spew of blood and other fluids, he yanked and flipped the loosed sac of skin away.

"Aaaawwwwhh," the boy screamed, coming to just as Bill finished his castration. Again the knife went down, this time through the boy's open mouth to bang with a jarring crack against the rocky asphalt beneath them.

The scream trailed off to a choke, and Bill finally gave in to the lure that had been growing with every touch of his hand on Terry's flesh. He could feel the life pulsing slower in the dying teen, and knew that he had to have what was left for his own. Pushing the knife handle out of his way, Bill bit down hard into the soft, warm flesh of Terry's neck. Again the rush of heat, the ecstasy of orgasm, taste, life. He sucked the boy's last life, and when the flood lessened to a trickle, he began pounding the boy's torso, squeezing out the last drops into his own bloated belly.

After a time, it was done.

Bill sat back from the body as the fever receded in his brain. His stomach hung heavy and his whole body seemed suddenly weary. He wanted to lie down here, next to the battered corpse, and rest.

But no.

He shook his head, tried to clear his mind. The bodies would draw flies. And police. And he wanted neither near him. Pulling the remaining barrette from his body, he tossed it on the body, heaved himself to his feet, and shuffled back the way he had come, reaching his hotel room in the early hours of morning. He felt an odd discomfort as he collapsed on the bed, and reached to scratch the sticky hole in his back. In moments he slipped into a coma-like sleep.

Bill woke the following night with flies buzzing around his face. *How had they gotten in this room?* he wondered, lifting a hand to swat them away. The hand struck his face accidentally, and flopped back to the bed. He was getting stiff, he realized, and losing control of his muscles.

"I'm dead," he reminded himself aloud, but the words meant nothing. If he was dead, how could he be staring at the ceiling? How could he be swatting flies? How could he have killed two boys...

He broke the thought but it came back anyway. He'd *killed* last night. Murdered! Lifting his hand again, he could see the dark stains of the boys' blood. He had had his revenge.

But if it had been heavenly at the moment of action, it didn't taste sweet anymore. It didn't taste at all. His mind cried with the enormity of his act. He had *killed* them both. Sucked the life from their bodies with his mouth. Whether they deserved it or not, their lives had not been his to take!

But the memory of the blood – and its effect on him – made his body shiver. He realized with a twinge of fear that he only wanted one thing – to kill again.

Rising slowly from the bed, he saw that he had stained the sheets with blood. It had pooled near his head and beneath his crotch. A thin smear of it seemed to cover the sheets, as if he'd sweated it out through every pore.

The mirror said he had. The single bathroom bulb reflected off a purpling face and dusky reddish chest. His entire body seemed drenched in blood. Its sight didn't leave him nauseous, as it would have but three days before. He did feel weak. And hungry. Or more accurately – thirsty.

Stepping into the shower, he saw that his feet and calves had purpled. His penis lay half erect atop truly blue balls. *Dead*, he reminded himself. Three days dead. He must stink. As he rinsed the blood sweat from his bruised body, he gulped water from the shower head. It was an unconscious ritual, but as soon as he had, he knew it was a bad move. He could feel it slosh into his belly, gurgle through his intestines. And moments later, a pinkish stream dribbled from his dick. At the same time, a brown-black sludge began dripping from his backside. He could vaguely smell the foul stench of shit and rotting meat as his bowels released to the drain. This frightened him. What if these excretions continued? He would be forced to rot away in this room. He couldn't go out leaking sewage as he walked!

But the drainage soon stopped. Bill shut off the tap and dried himself. Then he dropped his clothes into the tub and began to scrub the bloodstains out. When at last he stopped wringing them, the stains were dulled. Though not completely obliterated, people would notice that he was wearing wet clothes before they'd see the stains on them. Luckily he'd been wearing jeans and a dark t-shirt on the night of his death. When wet, they hardly showed stains at all.

\/\/\/\/\/\/\/\/\/\/\/

The night was cool and quiet when Bill at last stepped onto the street from the dimly lit warrens of the cheap hotel. He should have been shivering in his wet clothes, but he wasn't. He could feel the cold, but it didn't affect him.

He walked, at first without direction. Images of the dead boys appeared unbidden in his mind. He angrily replaced them with the memory of his violated daughter, open-eyed and still on the morgue table. If he'd been alive, the battling emotions of the two visions would have led to tears. But he only blinked dryly.

He thought of the events that led to this: his own inaction, his wife's dismissal. *How could she cast him out after all they'd been through?* How could he have let it get to the point where she wanted him to go? He thought of the last time she had made love to him. As he'd settled into bed she had left one light on, and unbuttoned her blouse. Piece by piece, she'd dropped her clothing on the floor, not saying a word. He'd watched with growing interest, as the pink tips of her breasts grew taut and she stripped off her panties, as the kinky brown hair below her belly shifted, as she strode purposefully toward him across the room. Neither had spoken as she lowered herself upon him without foreplay. She had taken him hard, moved atop him brutally, and removed herself slowly when he had at last released a telltale groan.

And now she no longer wanted him in her house, let alone her bed.

He was angered, excited, lustful, thirsty. And he realized that he stood outside of his home. The lights were off; she was probably already asleep. Was she glad he did not snore beside her? Or had she regretted her words after the first night alone?

Quietly he eased open the screen door and tried his key. It still worked. The house was still, heavy. He moved through it slowly, not needing a light. How many times had he walked these halls, oblivious to life's fatal chasms yawning all around? Somehow, in the past few months, he'd fallen into all of them. His daughter murdered, his marriage in ruins, his life taken, and he himself had turned killer. As he passed the living room, he saw the dark square of the family portrait on the piano. *Those people don't exist anymore*, he thought, and stepped past.

Cheryl was asleep. He stood at the foot of the bed watching her chest move, hearing the soft hiss of her breathing. He touched his own chest, and felt the stillness there. He moved closer, could see the soft chestnut hair trailing across her cheek, could see the white of her teeth, as they touched, just barely, the warm blush of her lip. Could smell the heat of her blood pumping steadily through every artery, sending a reek of heady life through her pores. *This*, he could sense. With a trembling hand he touched her hair; she stirred.

The fire in his heart was growing again, feeding his anger at losing this, at losing her. This time he felt his fangs protruding, felt his erection at the nearness of bloody orgasm.

She turned on her back in her sleep, one nipple peeking seductively from the edge of the sheet. He leaned in to bite her, to steal her lifeblood. Yes. She should be even better to take than the boys. He would take her in lust and in love. As his teeth brushed her flesh, she murmured, "Bill?" in her sleep. Her voice was slurred, but seemed surprised and… *happy?*

No!

From somewhere beyond the vampiric haze, Bill found the strength to throw his body to the floor beside the bed. He had killed the boys for revenge, and what pleasure did he have for it now? Guilt. They were rotten kids, but killing them had solved nothing. They had no chance to atone for their crime. And Lissa was still dead. *He* was still dead – in fact, probably rotting faster for their infusion.

If he stole Cheryl's life now... Could she perhaps still find happiness, without him, without Lissa? Could he steal the chance from her, for a selfish moment of necrotic passion?

No! He rolled back and forth on the white carpet, inches from Cheryl, fighting back his instinct, struggling with his thirst. He could smell her, almost taste her. The nearness, the memories, the anticipation of her hot kisses, her hot blood! It was too much. His chest spasmed, his nose sucked air, just a breath. And from behind his drooping eyelids, a tear fell to stain the carpet red. In the morning, Cheryl would see it and wonder.

He took some fresh clothes from his closet, lingered a moment at her bed. "Goodbye," he whispered. "Be happy again." He went quickly then, to the only place he could think of to go. The alley by Ale's Head Tavern.

"Lawrence?" he called into the dark narrow street. "Lawrence, are you here?"

There was no answer. Bill leaned against the brick back of an old store, slowly slid to the ground. Even the companionship of his killer was denied. He thought of the power of the blood lust, felt it still, and forgave the bum for killing him. If it had been anyone but Cheryl, if he'd had an ounce less control, he would have killed tonight. He still might. But not her.

There was a shift, something sliding. The hollow metallic ring of the dumpster. From the shadow of the ancient alley, a lurching shape appeared. Even Bill's dead senses could smell the stench. The bloated man sunk to the street beside him. Bill could see the black and green slime that was once a face shivering, rippling. The figure reached a skeletal finger to its head, pried open its mouth. As the hand dropped, it scraped the shivering ooze of its cheek, releasing a stream of white, wriggling maggots. Bill cringed.

"Pretty, heh?" the bum gargled, almost unintelligibly. "Not long, not long now. Had your revenge?"

"Yeah," Bill whispered. "And yes, the price is too high."

"Going to…" Lawrence choked, spat a stringy stream to the ground. "Going to give someone else the chance?"

"No," Bill replied firmly.

They sat silent for awhile, occasionally kicking at rats which tried to steal the meat of their decaying, yet still animated flesh.

"Tell me," Bill said suddenly. "How did you… get taken? How many did you kill?"

Lawrence's sagging, rippling face turned toward Bill. One eye glinted whitely in the streetlight. The other socket appeared empty. "Tell me first; will you drink again?"

"How can I not?"

Lawrence's head shook stiffly, sadly.

"The more you take, the faster you'll go."

\\\\/\\\\\\\\\\\

The echo of an Ale's Head Tavern barkeep bellowing "last call" lingered over the alley as two rotting vampires quietly fought their thirsts and began to share the night with stories of when they were alive.

The taste was as bittersweet as blood.

In the ever-more-dangerous obsession with kink and extreme sensation, the most important aspect of human sexuality – the piece that can give the resulting orgasms a deeper resonance – is often lost. When emotion enters the equation however, the most perverse action can become a transcendent sacrifice.

The Mouth

Thrust.
Pull back.
Buck, fist, pound.
Thrust.
Pull back.

The heart speeds up, briefly, adrenaline pumping in crazed waves. The mouth opens and shuts, gasps for air. Moans fill the air like rain, musk melds with the stench of sweat. And then it's over, and the attack diminishes, the cries taper, the galloping heart slows.

The defining evidence that separates sex and murder is really only the amount of blood left behind on the bed. The amount of heartache afterward separates lust from love.

\|/\|/\\|/\\|/\\|\

I've been a slave to these passions for so long, the gaping mouths and gasping wounds have all blurred together in my head. There are memories of thrusting – hands, knives, cock – inside the mouths, mammaries and musk of blondes and brunettes, fat girls and thin, ugly trash and haute delicate-skinned models. In the end they're all sloppily the same and yet beautifully different. The tenor of their cries, the strange tics and angular movements that separate one girl from the next are delicious to watch, to feel. Some bleed heavy and thrash like mad. Others go wide-eyed in shock and disbelief. But in the end, sex or murder, fat or thin, it all comes down to moans and thrusting, hard nipples and harder cocks.

And the challenge of distancing yourself after. Both in heart and body. I've never had much of a problem managing either, and I didn't expect to today.

Kyla, a D.C. hooker who's played with me in my sex-death revolving roulette often over the years, told me the story that set me packing instantly. She knew I'd never resist the temptation. Her acne-pocked cheeks crinkled in a lop-sided grin as she measured my interest and excitement.

"They call her 'The Mouth,'" she whispered, and then ran a thin tongue tip across her lower lip. She knew I could rarely tear my eyes (or cock) away from an eager oral slave. That's why so often I had her videotape our little explorations with our chosen slaves. Or, as the case may be, victims. Later I could pick up the other details missed during my initial fixation. And rerun them, again and again.

"She's all fucked up," Kyla explained, leaning in to nip my ear. A light chocolate breast slid out of the silk entrapment of her slip, and my hand didn't hold back from trapping its eager nipple. She hissed and pulled away as I squeezed hard.

"Tell me," I demanded.

Her fist pounded at my shoulder, but I didn't ease my grip. Kyla would try to make me fuck her for the information, but I wasn't trading.

"Later," she moaned, nails now in action across my chest and back.

"Now."

The Mouth

And so, a few hours and a diseased fuck from Kyla later (sometimes I'm generous), and I'm in backwoods Virginia. "The Mouth" is apparently an Appalachian throwaway. A backwoods freak. Genetic disaster.

And the thought of it has me harder than nails. Kyla has her ways and her contacts and she owes me more than I owe her. Her fascination with dismemberment in the midst of orgies has been a logistical nightmare for me on many an occasion. And there's something highly unarousing about hosing the splatter of another man's sperm and bile off the dead girl beneath you so that you can finish your own fuck.

I hate it when Kyla cums before me.

The houses had thinned to one per mile, and for most, the only evidence that there was a dwelling behind the tangle of lush forest and vine was the rutted track that broke the barrier of heavy hedge along the gravel road. I couldn't go above 30 mph without fearing a hernia. This was not well-traveled country.

But every time I felt lost, I'd spot one of Kyla's landmarks passing by. A rusting John Deere overturned in a ditch. A wooden sign declaring "Keep Out. Property of O'Clannahan. Trespassers Shot First, Questioned Later."

I stuck to the road, such as it was, and watched for the only clue I had remaining on my list of landmarks. An outhouse.

Why anyone would put an outhouse at the edge of the road out here was beyond my guessing, and why anyone would be brave enough to step inside such a structure in the midst of snake and spider and hornet country was a better question. An outhouse on an unused road would likely harbor more critters than shit, and I wouldn't dare consider contributing to the latter given the threat of the former. Then again, many of the property warning signs might leave one a bit shy of pissing on a local bush. You might end up without privates.

The outhouse jolted out of the brambles like a bell tower, and the car jerked and slid as I slammed on the brakes. A lurch, a shuddering slide, and I was skating down the rocky hillside drive that the outhouse had marked. A canopy of fern and leaf left me with the impression of driving through a poorly lit tunnel. Just as my eyes accustomed to the shade however, the forest roof broke to a clearing and in the white shine of a sweaty noon, I caught my first glimpse of The Mouth's house.

Correction: *shack*.

It looked to be four or five rooms, a rotting testament to lazy carpentry. A series of mismatched gray planks jutted from the roof eaves and only a door cut through the warped boards of the front wall. I could see one window on the side of the structure, a four-paned bit of relief that threatened to disappear inside a nest of leaves. The hum of bees filled the air and as I stared at the decaying structure I saw why. A stream of fat, slow flying insects traded flight paths from the nearby woods to a dark fissure in the roof above the window. *Precisely why I avoided outhouses in the woods*, I thought.

Shrugging to myself, I trampled through the knee-high scrub grass and tentatively knocked on the peeling white paint of the front door. Could anybody really still be living here?

From inside I heard the squeak of old floorboards and the murmur of voices. And then the door opened a crack. No more than four inches. I could see the glint of a dark eye and the spray of gray curls.

"Yeh?" came a suspicious, guttural question.

"Kyla said you'd expect me."

The door opened wider and a wrinkled short woman inspected me, hands on hips, not moving aside to let me pass 'til her consideration was finished.

"You been fixed?"

"Not broken," I said.

She shook a heavy head.

"Fixed. You had a va-sex-tommy?" Her accent was heavy with the hills, and I stifled a smile.

Once her meaning sank in, I shook my head. "No."

"Then no oral for you."

I looked at her and thought that I didn't want oral, anal or anything else from her. She was a potato sack of a woman, and long beyond childbearing years. I started to back away but she grabbed my arm and dragged me inside the dark house.

"She likes the oral, but no fixed, no oral. Deal?"

I said okay and she slapped my face, lightly.

"Promise. You like her, you get it fixed. Then you kin fuck her mouth. Only then."

Again I agreed, and she led me past a brown couch, stuffing leaking from its belly and into a brighter kitchen. She pointed to an old white wooden chair and I sat, noting the drone of bees was louder here. I thought the window over the sink must have been the one I'd seen from the drive.

What the hell had Kyla sent me into? Was this a punishment for something?

The inside of the house was no more kept up than the out. And in the heat of summer, with no air conditioning and no open windows, the air was stifling. And sour. Flies bumped heads against a grease-blurred window, and on the table a handful of mugs and glasses remained full of recent leavings. A glass of tomato juice, another of some light golden juice, maybe apple. A mug of coffee was in front of me, and I pushed away its curdled contents in disgust. Something with a lot of legs ran across the broken tile at my feet.

The old woman came back then, this time with a younger woman. At first glance, she was a beaut. Long, raven-black hair flowed over her shoulders, and a thin, ratty tank clung tightly to her and did nothing to hide the fullness of her breasts. The dark point of her left nipple pressed tightly through the fabric. A wide trail of sweat ran from the hollow of her neck to the point just above the deep pock of her bellybutton. The shirt ended there, and so did her clothing.

I didn't disguise my stare.

Her hips were wide and full, her flesh cooly pale as winter. The V of her groin was hairless, and the distended, pink lips of a human face parted there. A cunt that truly smiled. It looked utterly bizarre, unreal. The twisted product of a demented artist who tortured his sexy models by distorting them on-canvas. And as I expected, it turned me on instantly.

My gaze returned to her face, and then I saw the sleek aquiline nose and intensely blue eyes rested above what some men crudely call a "gash." Even when I'm going to kill a girl I generally have more respect for her than to call it that. I stared forever at her face, taking her in pore by pore. The lips of her mouth were thin petals of pale pink flesh. Not firm at all, but rippled and wavy.

The lips of a pussy.

"Take off your clothes," the old woman directed, and before I could start myself she was reaching up and unbuttoning my shirt.

I brushed her away and finished the job myself. For a moment, I worried that she'd kill my fledgling hard-on; maybe this freakishness wouldn't turn me on as much as I'd thought. But before I'd even slid down my jockeys I felt a stirring again; it flopped out awkwardly and in seconds was pointing across the room at her.

The old woman was reaching into a cabinet as I kicked off the pants and the buzz in the kitchen grew louder. I looked up and almost screamed. Her hand was buried in the thick waxy comb of a bee's nest! We were only separated from being stung to death by the uneasy kiss of a cabinet door!

She pulled her hand back dripping with golden sugar and shut the cabinet door again, somehow not letting a single bee into the room. Then without a word she coated my cock and lips with the warm, sticky sweet liquid and nodded towards the back room.

"Go on then. Her pussy likes the taste."

I followed the silent girl to the back of the house. She reached out, almost shyly, and took my hand as we walked. The older woman, thankfully, stayed behind.

\/\/\\/\\\/\\/\

Her bedroom was unlike the rest of the house. It was tiny, but neat. The walls gleamed a fresh coat of lilac, and the mattress on the floor was covered in a light linen to match. There was one dresser in the room, a man's highboy, but aside from the dents and scars of probably 50 or more years, it was clean and uncluttered. She turned to me and made a grunting noise.

"What?" I asked.

Her eyes looked pained for a moment, and then her hands touched my chest.

Lightly. A feather's exploration.

The sweat was rolling down my back and forehead but her fingers felt cool as they traced the line of my sternum and then followed the faint hollows between my ribs. She grunted deep in her throat again, and then nodded.

I guessed I'd "do."

I reached out to lift her shirt but she shrunk back.

What the hell? She had her pants off already, and then I thought about it again. Of course she had her pants off. Her fucking mouth was in her crotch. She probably never wore pants. And if her pussy was in her head... shit. When the older woman said no oral sex, which hole did she mean? An abortion through your face would be a bitch! But maybe her ovaries remained where they belonged, in which case, no fucking with her "mouth."

I suddenly didn't know what to do. Did I go back and ask the old woman? My cock started flagging at that, and I laughed at myself. If this freak couldn't tell me which way or the other it was her own problem. I reached out and pulled her towards me, and kissed her on the mouth.

On the pussy, rather. Whatever. I kissed the lips in her head. What a messed up feeling. My tongue was buried in her cunt, but my eyes looked straight into hers. And she looked scared.

Of what??

She tasted salty, heavy. Not the sort of taste you expect from a first kiss. More like the taste of a woman after she's screwed your two best friends and then wrapped her legs around your face.

But usually it wasn't her nose that was in your face for that one.

I frenched her quickly, and the flower of her mouth seemed to expand around my lips. She grew wet; her eyes opening and then rolling back in pleasure. My tongue is legendary in some circles.

My hands caressed the rolling mounds of her buttocks, and slid upwards, dragging the dirty cotton rag she wore with them. She broke our kiss and shook her head no again, but I didn't listen. With a yank I pulled it up and over her head, and then she was naked in front of me, her breasts drooping with a heavy fullness, slicked with sweat, and covered with scars. I saw now why she was reticent. Why her eyes looked scared. Someone had used her poorly.

Circles of scarred buttmarks littered her chest, and one of those abused mounds had lost its nipple. Bitten off? Cut off? She wasn't telling. She crossed her arms quickly across her middle and lowered her gaze. But I would have none of it. Gently I massaged her shoulders, and then tipped her chin up to look at me. Her eyes were pools of tortured darkness, and I bent to kiss them, each eyelid. Then I tasted her forehead, her neck, and the bloom of her lips. Soon her arms slid around my back and we collapsed to her bed. The 69 position took a whole new meaning with her. In minutes we were slick with sweat, and her pussy lips were hungrily sucking my cock into her throat. Meanwhile, her thighs held my head like a vise as her tongue matched the timing of my thrusts. She stabbed me in the head with her tongue and I stabbed her in the head with my cock.

How fucked up is that?

It was heaven, and I wanted more. By the time I stopped slipping around on her bed, I had decided I might actually get a vasectomy so that I could get between her legs and do her mouth. I wasn't looking for kids in this lifetime anyway.

\\/\\/\\\\/\\/\\\\/\\/\\\\/\\/\\\\/\\/\\\\/\\/\\\\/\\/\\\\/\\/\\\\/\\

When I pulled myself together and got dressed, I went back to the kitchen in search of the old woman. She was washing dishes in a faded manila plastic washbasin.

"She everything you dreamed of?" she said and then cackled as she rinsed a mug with water from a tall pitcher.

"She was wonderful," I admitted.

"You like fucking freaks, then?"

"Never have before, but seeing as I've fucked just about everything else..."

"Well, that pays my debt to Kyla," she announced. "So next time, it'll cost ya."

"You her pimp or her mom?"

"Both."

"Nice."

"What do you expect me to do with a freak like that? She's good for screwin', and not much else. And then only by perverts like you."

"Sweet attitude."

"You paying for sugar?"

"Naw."
"Then fuck off."
Classy.
"You got a bathroom here?"
"Nah. That's what we use The Mouth for."
"You're a sick old bitch, aren't you?"

She looked me over silently for a moment. Then she reached up and put one large ham of a hand on my shoulder. I hate to admit it, but I flinched.

"Listen. We live out here in nowhere. The Mouth's a retarded freak. She got no teeth up top so she cain't eat nothing but sauce and syrups. I got no money. Given where her taste buds are, she likes the taste of piss and shit. Hell, she tastes her own every day. So I saves up what I can."

She nodded over at the glass of pale liquid on the table that I'd taken for apple juice earlier.

"You wanna drink, or donate?"

She laughed long and loud as I left.

Fast.

But I couldn't stop thinking of her. Every night, I dreamed of eyes staring back at me as I kissed the rippled flower of a pussy. And scat fantasies. I'd never been into it before, but suddenly I imagined myself pissing between her open lips, that mouth hungrily slurping up my waste.

She was suddenly all I could think of. Mostly though, I imagined plunging my cock into the pussy of her head. Fucking that mouth 'til she was choking. It was very disconcerting, this obsession. I'd had women live with me, naked on their knees for me whenever I called, and had them dispatched and forgotten quicker than most men can cum. Why did I keep going back to this freak in my head?

The Mouth

I was making a pickup near the Areland Costume shop when I hatched the idea.

I bought a scar kit. Hell if I was going to pay for a vasectomy. But I was going to fuck that girl's pussy mouth.

The bees were buzzing warm and loud as I pulled up the decrepit backwoods drive to The Mouth's house. I had a roll of $20s in my pocket for the old bitch pimp. The lust rolled off me in waves on the drive down. I could smell it. My cock got hard and long thinking of those pocked breasts in my mouth, that warped mouth going up and down on my pole. And afterward, I'd stand up and piss right down her pussy mouth.

I was ready.

\/\/\/\N\/\/\/\/\/\/\

The old bitch answered the door, slate gray hair matted to her forehead, a stain of sweat revealing the fat floppiness of her breasts. What a turnoff.

"You!" she snapped. "Lotta nerve, you!"

"The Mouth at home, today?" I asked sweetly.

She didn't answer, only glared at me. Then with a shrug of her head she motioned me inside.

"I take that as a yes," I answered myself. Still she didn't reply, only walked through the stink and hum of the kitchen and back towards the room of The Mouth. I followed.

"You gonna take care of this?" the old woman asked as we entered The Mouth's room.

She was lying on the bed, sweat from the heat of the summer day rolling off her forehead in lazy beads. Her eyes were large as cows', that same deep brown look of open innocence that a bovine faced with a shotgun to the ear has. Her fingers toyed gently with the pussy lips of her face, teasing and stroking it in a masturbatory fugue.

"This is all your fault," her mother announced. "What are we gonna do?"

That, was a very good question.

Apparently, I'd chosen the wrong mouth. The Mouth's neck was swollen to the size of a small melon, that delicate white skin stretched and almost translucent. Spider veins snaked around and up from her bare chest to meet in a web of blood pulsing right where her Adam's Apple would have been, had The Mouth been a man.

I'd chosen wrong. If her pussy was in her head, and she pissed from those same lips, then naturally her uterus was in the wrong spot as well.

Or unnaturally.

Which would make her about two months pregnant. And she was gasping for breath already. Three months would kill her.

Abortion through the head? Could they *do* that?

I went to her. Put my hands on her face and kissed her forehead. There was a sick pain in my heart that I thought had grown impervious to stabs of guilt. Not so.

Those brown cow eyes looked up at me in trust. In fear.

And the hands of an old bitch began pounding on my back.

"You did this. You did THIS!" she shrieked. "You gotta fix it. You got money. Take her. Fix her."

I stepped back, took the old woman by the shoulders and shook.

"I'll take care of it," I whispered. Sharply. "Go. Leave us alone for a bit."

She squinted at me then, as if not trusting my motives. But what else could I do to her freak of a daughter at this point? I'd already fatally knocked her up.

When the door closed behind her, I dropped my pants to the floor and pulled the shirt over my head. Naked, I joined The Mouth in bed and kissed her swollen neck, her musky lips. Her eyes rolled back with each thrust as I lay my cock between her teeth, between her legs, and fucked her the way I should have the first time. I wondered as she swallowed my cum in the mouth between her thighs if she could taste it there.

Afterward, when the sweat had dried on her chest and my hard-on had diminished, I asked her if she was thirsty. She nodded vigorously and I let her drink from me. I coated my finger with some honey from a discarded comb lying half eaten on the floor by her bed, and tenderly fed her glistening lips the sweetness. They slurped together like an infant's, hungrily sucking at the teat. Then I stroked her hair softly, until her lids closed and a steamy slumber overtook her.

She didn't stir when I put the cold steel next to her ear. But I kissed her lips before it went further. Once more for dreams. Her eyes opened then; confused but happy, they stared into mine.

And then with a small but thunderous pop, her brains were against the wall and The Mouth kissed no more.

I was crying when the door slammed open and the old bitch screamed. But I had another bullet and wasn't nearly as careful about where I placed it. The result was that I had to pull the trigger twice more to still the woman's wailing, choking cries. Those didn't phase me. All I could see were the deep brown eyes and trembling, half opened pussy lips of The Mouth as I gave her the abortion she – and our baby – both deserved.

Fuck.

When you're a kid there are monsters under every bed, killers in every closet and witches in every neighborhood. But sometimes the most frightening parts of growing up are the discoveries of our own nature.

Creaks

The noise broke through my dream as sharply as if somebody had tossed ice on my bare back. I woke up tense, heart beating so loud and fast, I worried it might pop. "And what a mess that would make," I thought.

Shaking and quivering under the downy comforter grandma had given me just last month, I listened hard at the night. I strained to hear and willed my heart and the blood pumping madly through my veins to silence itself. My body was drenched in sweat, but I wasn't hot. And then I heard it again: a faint shriek, as if a small animal – or maybe a girl – were being throttled somewhere in the house. For a moment, I pulled the covers over my head and hid from the sound, but a moment in the dead black tent of my bed convinced me I was better off if I could at least *see* what was going to kill me. I pushed the covers back.

I don't know where the courage came from. I was really quite a shy boy – not ever standing around where a fight might find me, never laughing rudely at jokes about the teachers or girls' private parts – the stuff the bully boys made their reputations on. But still, somewhere in my 10-year-old frame I found a spark. A monster was loose and I would vanquish it. Save the girl it was trying to eat. I crept from my bed and grabbed the only weapon I could find: my little league baseball.

I stepped into the hallway – and almost wet my pants. Ahead of me a sharp staccato sound reverberated.

Creak. Creak. Creak.

I knew houses settle and my dad had often told me the hows and whys of those midnight noises that used to send me quaking to my parent's bed. But this was different. This was… unnatural.

In my mind: a ghoul as it raised a blackened face, lips missing from around its fangs, eyes glowing with hellfire. It wore a black cape, but I could see the white bones beneath and smell the stench of decaying meat. It must be coming down the stairs, I thought, not being able to come up with any other explanation. The creaks were the pads of its hairy clawed feet coming down from the attic. One, two, three. How many stairs were there? I panicked, frozen to the spot halfway down the hall – completely exposed to its claws. Why hadn't I stayed in bed? Maybe it wouldn't have seen me. Maybe it would have eaten mom or dad – or better yet, my sister – and left me alone. Tears were filling my eyes and my bladder threatened to burst and still my feet were rooted. *Creak. Creak.* I'd dashed up those stairs a million times and I couldn't remember their count. Ten? Twelve? Thirteen? Then the creaking stopped and the house was still for a second.

It was going to leave me alive! I rolled the league ball in my hand and tried to listen over the angry noise of my heart. A freeway rushed in my head, despite the leaden silence of the dark hallway.

No. Everything was not still. Somewhere something moaned, or cried. The monster was here and it had somebody! *Maybe my sister?* I hoped. *Maybe my mom*, my heart leapt at the thought. I steeled my will one final herculean time and forced my feet forward. One step. Two. Three.

And I was in the living room of our house and the creature was not as it had appeared in my mind. Oh, it was there, but across the room it appeared bone-white and sickly. An amorphous blob of pulsating flesh that rose and fell on the couch. And as I quaked with fear, I heard what made the noise and I saw my mother's face hanging back in apparent agony over the edge of the cushions and I knew that I alone could save her. Taking aim through the murky darkness at the widest swath of flesh that lay atop devouring her, I let loose my beaten, rough, grass-stained little league ball with all the force of a future pony league pitcher just as my mother hissed through the pregnant silence, "Oh God, yes!"

The ball hit the monster with a resounding slap and it was only at that moment, as I heard the voice of my father groan "Yeah. Slap me baby," that I knew the severity of my error. The monster was my *dad*, and he was doing something horribly disgusting to my mother. And she was enjoying it! The couch was creaking and my stomach was turning inside out and the sight of his heaving white buttocks was the end of my childhood, I think. It was certainly far more frightening than any red-eyed monster I could envision.

For the rest of that night, and on many more to come, when the creaking took over our house, I lay awake, fighting back the nausea in my bed. I no longer feared monsters. I could only wish. Because now the smiling faces of my parents appeared to me as false masks. Beneath those gentle eyes and easy grins lurked the real monsters, the monsters that did unspeakable acts in the night.

The monsters that made my house creak.

I grew up a couple miles from Bachelor's Grove – an original "settlers" cemetery that now exists near a perpetually green-scummed pond behind broken down fencing in the middle of a forest preserve. As a Cub Scout, I learned (no doubt with wide, trusting eyes) that deep in the dark forest near our otherwise treeless suburban town, there was a haunted place where a dead woman walked and a strange house appeared to lure unwary travelers. As an adult newspaper reporter, I found that the hauntings of Bachelor's Grove were widely reported in the literature of ghost watchers, and as with so many "forgotten" places, it had become a hangout for vagrants, drug dealers and even, reportedly, Satan worshipers. I visited the place for the first time while researching a Halloween feature story on "area haunts" for my newspaper. The vandalized tombstones and forgotten air left me with a sad, spooky feeling that I had to try to capture.

Remember Me, My Husband

I'm married to two incredible women – one dead and one alive. Is this bigamy? Or since one of those wives was not married to me beneath the myopic eyes of a preacher, are my romantic dalliances in the graveyard merely adultery?

\/\/\/∧\/\/\\/\/\\/\\/\\/\\|

They came for my car first. Banks are funny that way. They'll send a couple of monkey men out to break into and drive away your auto over a couple grand, but when you owe them 50 times that on a house payment, they'll let it ride and ride. But even then, sooner or later, the man shows up at your door and makes the demand: "pay up or get out." It's funny, the guys who come for your car look like goons, but the guy who comes for your house wears a suit and tie, round glinting wire glasses and a nervous laugh. It was after the nervous laugh dissipated – slowly, as a cloud of sewer gas fades on a still-as-death summer day – that my living wife, Joanne, announced that as long as I was losing everything else in my life, she'd be taking a powder as well.

"I can't watch anymore," she cried, the words gurgling up in her fleshy throat from some deep underwater cavern. Her makeup ran like wax, her brown eyes shiny and ringed in mascara. *I love you baby*, I thought, but said nothing. What more was there to say? I couldn't blame her. I'd lost my job, lost my backbone, lost me. And with that despair, piece by piece my life was slipping away faster than the laugh of the nervous eviction man had stopped echoing in the empty foyer. It only takes a few months to erase the work of years.

"I love you but it doesn't matter," Joanne was still sobbing. "You won't *DO* anything and I can't help you anymore."

She stood in the middle of our dingy living room, suitcase at her feet, shoulders slumped. The 20 or 30 pounds that years of casseroles had congratulated her with were not attractive when she abandoned the strictures of good posture. My own untucked oversize t-shirt couldn't hide the blessings of overeating and under-activity, either. But as my mind shot Polaroids of Joanne's pathetic whimpering and my own listless carcass stretched lazily across our old brown sofa, I found I didn't care. Fat, skinny, tearful, laughing – the extremes of life affected me not in the least.

Eventually, Joanne's snuffling sobs and the ultimatum represented by the suitcase both drifted away. The shifting orange of sunset slid across the walls and still I lay motionless. I can't tell you myself how I came to be there – in this room in my head permitting no caring, no interest in living.

There were hard blows, sure, but why they affected me as they did…

The worst was watching my parents slip into the grave without being able to say goodbye. There wasn't much left to say goodbye to of dad, and mom never woke from the coma. It was a familiar story – drunk driver hits old couple head-on, he lives, they die. But it's never real until it's your own family that chalks up another scratch on the statistic boards. Joanne worked hard to pull me through, and then just as things seemed to be getting better, the factory closed. Mother GM couldn't afford to lose the millions of dollars a year our plant was flushing down the drain anymore. Those two events – and the thousand tiny fires on the soul that they engendered – burned out my will.

And on that, the night of my necrotic marriage, as the shadows died and the streetlight winked into life across the street, I knew where I had to go. Maybe I'd known it since I watched the green jagged line flatten on the tiny TV screen next to my father's bed. Or maybe it was my mother's silent passing, mere hours after his own – did she know somehow? Did she feel him slip away into the darkness? Did he call to her as his heart ceased to hammer?

I slid from the couch.

\/\/\/\\/\\\/\\/\\/\\/\\/\\/\\\/\\/\\/\\\/\\/\\/\\\/\\/\\

The forest whispered at its violation as my flash bobbed along the trail, sometimes reflecting, just for a second, off a pair of luminescent eyes. In all my years of coming here to bury my troubles, I had never run into another person stalking these trails. The animals lurking just beyond the bounds of my flash were not used to being routed from their hunting schedules by wayward humans after dusk. The stories were responsible for that. The same tales that drew the curious during the day – witness their discarded pop and beer cans littering the brush – kept them locked up safe and sound after dark.

I think almost every town has a place like Bachelor's Grove – a place of creepy stories to scare children, a place of midnight magic. Named for the status of the German men who pioneered a settlement here in the 1800s to rough out homesteads before sending back to the continent for their beloveds, little remains to mark their labor now. The forest betrays few secrets. The foundations they struggled to lay down are hidden beneath dirt and vine, the wood of their rustic homes long burnt or carted away. All that remains is a fenced in clearing, tucked inside the whispering forest, a short walk from the turnpike. From that road all that's visible is a green-scum covered pond. But beyond that rancid water is the subject of many a Boy Scout campfire tale: Bachelor's Grove Cemetery.

As a boy, I'd heard numerous ghost stories about the fabled cemetery – the woman who cried in the night as she paced the earth in a hopeless search for her stillborn child, the house of blue fire that beckoned foolish mortals inside to their death – but as numerous as the stories, were the descriptions of where the graveyard lay, and for many years I'd believed that even the cemetery itself was a fable.

It is not. On a boozing run with some guys in high school, we discovered the grave site during a search for a place to drink and not be seen by cops or parents. Under the harsh glare of a nearly full white moon we walked down a gravel trail and straight into the eerie stand of decaying stones. Being brash and brave as all 17-year-olds, we laughed loudly and scoffed at the stories of Ella Marie Steuben, the woman who reputedly drifted wispily and weepily out of her hallowed earth searching in vain for her baby every now and again. But the laughter fell falsely on the rocky ground and the night ended early. And somehow or other, our group never looked in that particular forest for a drinking spot again.

But I returned. Call it morbidity or stupidity, the stories of Ella and the blue house and of numerous other ghosts – including that of a manic stagecoach that supposedly appeared and rushed through the trees at breakneck speed to vanish with an audible splash into the green pond – these were the touchstones of my childhood, the cherished adrenaline pumpers that made me both pray that there was a ghostly life after death and at the same time beg that I never encountered it – in this life, anyway.

An older, more skeptical me returned with some regularity to sit at these stones when life became too thick to move through, but over the years, the thrill of flirting with the supernatural turned to heavy sadness. The latest burial date in Bachelor's Grove reached back to the 1960s, the earliest readable ones to the late 1880s. No longer, in my adulthood, did these crumbling stones speak of mystery or provoke a frantic heartbeat after dark. They stood only as sentinels to the void of death. Bachelor's Grove Cemetery cried out to me in loneliness, and in it I found a kindred emptiness of spirit. And on the night of my second marriage, this is where I came to die.

What better place? I thought, as I sat down heavily before the towering gray stone marking the final resting place of Ella Marie Steuben's bones. Next to the large pillar was a much smaller one, a nameless marker. It read with simplistic and chilling factuality: "baby girl." This, no doubt, was the source of the ghost stories about Ella's night walks in bereavement of her child. I uncorked the bottle of Wild Turkey and took a deep swig. "Bottoms up," I coughed and held the fifth of amber bourbon up in the direction of the tombstone. "I'll be with you soon, Ella," I whispered, and took another burning swallow.

The moon was not obliging this night. The sky writhed in thick roils of cloud, and as the temperature dipped, the ground too was clothed in cloud. It was as if I sat in a limbo between an earth and sky of gray, chillingly damp fog. But the liquor warmed a trail to my belly, and my flashlight lay beside me on the ground, its beam reflecting off the headstone with a sickly glow. 1854-1883 was carved beneath her name. A faded epitaph was still readable in the shadowy light: "She always took care of her own."

"Will you take care of me, Ella?" I asked aloud. "I've sat with you many nights, you know." The trees around me shivered in response and a shadow of dread seemed all at once to encircle my heart. Suddenly my witty repartee with the cold earth and stone seemed not altogether wise. I kept quiet then, concentrating on nothing but getting a good drunk going.

When I'd downed half the bottle, I decided it was time. I needed the steadiness and will of what remained of my sobriety to finish this. Withdrawing a razor from my coat pocket, I rested its edge on my wrist. If I owned a gun, I would have used it instead. I've never been a believer in the long drawn-out methods of snuffing oneself. Poison can be long, painful, and ultimately, uncertain. Hanging, if it doesn't break your neck, can also be a somewhat lengthy process. But without a gun, I thought a steady bleed of life under the anesthetic of bourbon should be relatively painless.

Holding my wrist out over the barren earth, I stared at the sky and drew the blade up my arm. The pain was more than I'd expected, and my razor hand was trembling in cold and fear before I finished. With hot red blood leaking out over my other arm, I used my injured hand to inflict a similar wound on my other wrist. I made the mistake of looking at them then, these warm wet crimson hands whose lifeblood darkened the black earth deeper. The blood steamed thick amid the fog. My stomach churned and with a rush of nausea, the liquor and acid of my gullet were abruptly dripping through my nose and mouth to the ground beside me.

When it was finished, I wiped my face with a bloody sleeve and slumped back to the stone. Taking a deep swallow of the bottle, I shakily spoke to Ella again. "I'll be with you soon, now," I said, as a tear worked its way through the vile smears on my cheek.

I leaned back and closed my eyes. The forest seemed insubstantial suddenly, as far away as the troubles that drove me here. Leaves rustled nearby, a coon or a possum no doubt spying on the source of the light. It wouldn't take long, I thought. Already I could feel my strength draining into the earth, my life rushing away from me like a river after the spring thaws. I didn't think I had the strength now to move, but I could hear every beat of my heart louder than the last. It pounded in my ears so strong that I almost didn't look up when my light suddenly rolled away and something grasped my leg.

But I did find the last ounce of strength to look. And that strength then led to a hopeless scream. Rising out of the bloodstained soil was an arm, or rather, an arm bone, its yellowed, worm-ridden hand wrenched my leg with increasing pressure.

Ella Marie Steuben was trying to pull me into her grave!

With a ripple of shifting, slurping mud, another arm appeared. Loose slimy earth dripped over my body as the second skeletal arm reached across and wrapped around my waist. I screamed again, this time in pain as Ella used my body – not trying to pull me in, I realized, but used me as leverage to rise. A skull broke earth, shaking the dirt from her eye sockets and gifting my face with the wet splat of decay. Inside my head, a sane voice screamed: "escape!"

It was like moving underwater, but I willed myself to roll away from the clutching bones and stumbled erect. She stepped fully out of the earth then, and came for me.

I wet my pants and gagged on my own saliva as my feet stayed glued to the earth. She stood nearly as tall as myself, a bony skeleton draped in tangles of thin dark roots and pink worms and the tatters of something I told myself was once a dress and not flesh. Something thick and glittery hung from her neck and dangled through her ribs. Her eye sockets were menacingly blank, and she stretched out hands lacking several crucial bones in my direction.

I tried to run, but in my drunken, dying weakness, I stumbled to one knee, and then those bones, ripe with the smell of deep ancient earth, encircled my neck and dragged me backwards. My head hit the ground and whatever will I had retained was lost in pinpoints of angry light. I lay still then, unprotesting, as those bones in incomprehensible animation crawled around my body, coming to rest atop me. I stared into the empty skull an inch from my eyes to see the cloud rumpled sky through her unhinged jaw. She was missing several teeth.

The rank perfume of worms assailed my nose and I felt the urge to vomit again. But instead, the skull leaned closer, touching its icy wet teeth to my lips. I slipped out of consciousness then, but in that instant between, I saw Ella not in death but in life: long, flowing golden hair tickled my face as her thick, blood-red lips disengaged from my own. Her eyes glinted blue in the dim illumination still available from the displaced flash, and freckles dotted her nose and cheeks. I think I said "I love you."

She smiled and her teeth were flawlessly white.

\/\\/\\/\\/\\/\\/\\/\\

The birds were chirping loud around me when I woke, cold and confused. When I finally forced my eyes open, the sunlight was blinding. Everything hurt. I sat up, reaching out a throbbing, cold hand to rub my pounding head. The wrist was bound with bloody cloth – a shredded piece of my shirt, I realized, and saw that my other arm was likewise bandaged. So even bleeding to death is taken away from me, I thought at that moment, and then noticed the ground beside me.

Etched in the ground damp with my blood were four words:

> *Remember me,*
> *my husband.*

Husband? I thought, and absently looked at the fourth finger of my left hand, the finger that for eight years had held my gold wedding band in a disengagable grasp.

It was bare.

A sickly white ring of flesh marked where it had once been. On the pinky finger beside it was a new ring. It didn't fit past the knuckle, but it glinted with the prism of a diamond in the morning light. It was a woman's wedding band, and I found that my neck was also cuffed by the muddy jewelry of my dead wife: a heavy diamond necklace.

I stared in disbelief at the words on the ground, the words on her headstone, and thought of the words represented by my new jewelry. I knew that somewhere below my trembling knees, the skeleton of a long-dead, freckled blonde now wore my wedding ring. Would she require a consummation? Had she already taken it?

Staggering out of the graveyard, I ran for home.

I probably could have used stitches and a transfusion, but instead I cleaned and disinfected myself, bound my wrists with clean gauze, and slept through the next haze of days. And then one morning, I pulled on my best clothes, got on a bus, and went to a jeweler. They apparently don't make many diamond necklaces like Ella's anymore, and I felt awful pawning it, but the money got me a used car for a couple hundred bucks and paid my mortgage back up for awhile. Maybe that's why she left it with me.

But nothing could make me part with the ring.

Joanne came back to me after I proved that things were turning around. She didn't even ask "how" when I said my wedding ring was lost, she just nodded quietly and took me downtown to buy a new one. I had one of the diamonds from Ella's set in the new band. I didn't tell Joanne. How could I tell her anything about Ella?

The new job stinks, but it pays the mortgage – and buys flowers. It's funny really. It took the love of a dead woman to bring me back to life. And I try to make her happy, I do.

In this gray, forgotten cemetery haunted by the ghosts of lonely souls, I hear the bones of one freckled blonde rustle with the pleasure of attention each time I lay a bouquet upon that discolored ground where the rain has yet to wash away her bone-etched plea: "Remember me, my husband."

Each night, as I gift her grave with roses the color of my blood, I read those words aloud and answer, "I do."

Love and lust can lead to trust... and trust to games of who can go further. But in the twisted mix of domination and submission, sometimes the line of play and prey can blur. Should you ever trust a lover with your life?

Wooden

The grass has stopped waving. I miss the motion. But she'll be back soon. And I miss her more. Waiting is hard. Waiting for the sole sweet drop of honey in a life of poison. Every time she touches my face I shiver, like a cat striving and shaking for just one... more... caress.

\/\/\/\/\/\/\/\/\/\/

Looking at her eyes, I'm struck mute.

Not just sometimes, always. I wonder, how did I deserve her? Those beautiful deep brown eyes suck me deep. Sliding down a slope of lust and love and self destruction. I go gladly.

When I kiss her lips, I feel like a trespasser. Waiting for the shots to ring out behind me, striking me with bullet bliss in the back, I thrust my tongue inside her, and she capitulates.

For the moment.

The laughter in those brown eyes says she's content with my descent. But laughter turns to curdled scream. Swallow and she's gone.

Naturally I've grown careful around her. Why would I

want to go from kiss to kicks? She tells me to cook her dinner and I do. I follow her when she takes walks in the forest behind her house.

"On all fours," she says.

"Naked."

It makes her happy.

The first time she told me to strip off my suit and crawl, I made the mistake of giggling.

The tip of her high heels caught me in the ear. I couldn't hear on my right side for two days. But I took off the suit.

Now I do what she says without question. She is still the only person who has ever made me happy. And, truth be told, maybe I like licking the dirt she plays in.

Maybe I like it too much.

Now I'm paying.

"You're a piece of wood," she screamed at me this morning. I had kissed her before leaving for work. She promptly stuck out her jaw and smiled. I know that smile well. It says, "I'm gonna fuck with you. And if you resist, you'll like it less."

"Lick my toes," she commanded.

That was easy. I started to get down on the floor to comply, but she shook her head.

"Not here. I want to come to the office with you. When we get into the lobby, I want to you get down on your hands and knees and lick my feet. In front of your secretary and your boss."

I have been well-trained. I got to my feet and opened the door for her.

By the time we got to my office, she'd turned dangerous. Apparently compliance was not what she was after.

"You're a wooden soldier," she spit. "Where are your balls?"

I think the moment that I crawled across the light gray carpet of my office, in front of the gaping mouth of Lorene, our receptionist, was the breaking point. As I ran my tongue in between the crevices of her feet, she kicked me in the nose, turned and walked out.

I followed her. My heart was a bubble above a pin cushion. I had done everything she asked.

Everything.

How could anything be wrong?

\\/\\/\\\\/\\/\\\\/\\/\\\

I think it's really wrong now.

I think I'm dying.

Have you ever seen those steel combs that end in a spike of a handle?

I'm staring at one now.

It's sticking out of me. And not because it's stuck in my hair.

\\/\\/\\\\/\\/\\\\/\\/\\\

She ignored me at first when I followed her from the office, but finally, she turned and kissed me. Hard and angry. Strands of her long spidery hair covered my eyes as she twisted me beneath her and we fell to the parking lot pavement.

"I'm yours," I gasped, out of breath from her sudden attack.

"I know. But you must do one more thing for me. If you can do this…"

"If you can do this…" had been her mantra since the day we met. I understood the motive behind Hercules' labors. But I had prevailed so far. And she still slept with me every night. Not some other, better looking, better hung guy. It was enough for me.

Oh, the steel comb? It's between my legs. A salad fork is beside it.

\\\\/\\/\\\\\\\\\\\\\\\\

"Since you've been acting wooden lately, I'm going to teach you what wood is," she pronounced suddenly.

I didn't like the sound of it.

She led me behind the house, into the forest. I had never before had to strip and crawl through the pine needles and rough branches, which made me nervous. She carried a bag with her, and wouldn't speak.

"Here," she said.

We stood in a small clearing. Near the center was a dead oak trunk. It looked as if it had been struck by lightning. About 15 feet up, it had snapped off and fallen to the ground. The bare trunk pointed jaggedly at the sky still, but it had been years since the tree had sprouted a leaf of life.

"Now you can strip," she said. I unbuttoned my shirt, and dropped my slacks without thinking. She had long ago flogged away whatever fears I had about showing my nakedness. When I had piled all my clothes to the side of the tree, she slapped me, hard, on the ass.

I grinned, secretly enjoying any kind of touch from her.
"Against the tree," she barked.
And then she opened her bag and I became afraid.
She took out a hammer first. And then a knitting needle. And a steel comb. And fork. And steak knife. She took out bobby pins and a spiked hair curler.
And she laughed.
It wasn't a good sound. I felt my penis get perversely, uncomfortably hard.
She used the hair curler first.
"Bend over," she said.
It burned like fire at first, then sent sparks of broken glass pain up my bowel. But I took it. I wanted to make her happy.
"Back against the tree."
I was crying, but I held my tongue. She plugged the curling iron into an extension cord, and proceeded to tie my waist to the tree with it. If I moved a muscle the teeth of the curling iron shifted inside me, drawing new gashes of pain. I remained very still.
"Wooden as a tree," she growled, and then slapped my obstinately erect cock with derision.
That's when she got the hammer.
"If wood is what you are, wood is what you'll be," she mumbled, and began to stretch the skin of my balls to touch the rough bark of the dead tree behind me. Before I could even try to move, she picked up the steel comb and pierced the skin she held taut, burying the point in the tree. With three strokes of the hammer she drove it solid, and then repeated the action on the other testicle with a fork.
I screamed then. I started to thrash, to kick her away from me, but the motion only drew the pain faster.
"Ah, some reaction," she nodded. "Good. Let's try for some more."

I'm looking at the comb sticking out from my testicles, and wondering if I can ever go home again.

There's blood on the ground at the base of the tree.

An alarming amount.

There's a knife buried in my left shoulder, a knitting needle in my right. She pierced the cartilage of my ear with a bobby pin, and then hammered it to the tree. She missed once, hitting the ridge above my eye. I can still see out of the other one. I can see the nails that pin my hands to the tree trunk, one at each side. I can see the dried blood that smears my body, and the razor graffiti that she wrote on my chest.

"Wood," it says, by my left nipple.

"Burns" it says, by my belly button. It's a little smeared where the blood ran, but still legible.

The sun set awhile ago, and the night has quieted. I watched the grass swaying in the breeze for a few hours, but now it's still.

The pain has dulled to background, and I'm almost floating above it all now. If she thought to make me more responsive to her little murders, I think the plan has backfired. I'm above the pain, above the blood, above the sadistic impulse in her that makes her burn and kick and spit on me.

And still, she makes me happy.

"Tonight," she promised. "I'll be back. I'll bring some matches. We'll have a bonfire, you and I. Dead wood burns best."

It looks like this time, I won't fail her.

One night at an Italian restaurant, I found myself trying to unobtrusively cut a pill in half with a dull bread knife for my wife, whose throat constricts on all but the smallest of pills. This seemed both absurd and yet, absolutely necessary (she had a splitting headache which threatened to ruin our getaway weekend trip). "It's all psychological," I've often said – not that this has any effect. Psychological constraints are just as constricting as a real-life straitjacket. Of course, there are a lot more things in life beside pills that turn out to be difficult to swallow...

Swallowing the Pill

In mid-sip Gerard coughed into his beer, sending a puff of froth over the edge. He turned his face away so the foam would drip from his chin to the floor, instead of wetting his lap.

"Jeez man, you need some codeine. And an antibiotic. You sound terrible."

Gerard nodded mutely, willing the spasms to still in his tickling, wheezing throat. "Got some," he gasped finally. Can't swallow the damn antibiotic pills though. They're effin' horse pills."

Andy laughed and shook his head. "Whaddya mean you can't swallow them?"

Gerard knew that behind the question was an accusation, the same disbelieving put-down that he'd heard from pharmacists all his life. *What are you, a baby or something? Be a man and take your medicine.*

"Believe me, I've tried, I just can't get them down."

"It's not a matter of can't, Ger," Andy clapped him on the shoulder. "It's a matter of won't. Your throat is big enough to accommodate the pill, but your mind says no. It's all in your head, my friend. If you really wanted to, you *could* swallow those pills."

Gerard coughed again, a prolonged hacking that left his chest prickling with deep-burning fire. He shook his head again, sniffed wetly and then shrugged.

"No, I'm serious here," Andy pushed, refusing to let the subject drop. "I don't believe your body is physically capable of floor vaulting from one end of this bar to the other – that's just not in your genes. But swallowing a pill…"

Gerard refused to argue anymore, and quenched the fire in his lungs with another draught of beer.

Andy leaned closer, whispering so nobody else at the bar could hear. "You can do whatever you want. Don't you realize that?"

Gerard squinted sidelong at his friend. "Whaddya talking about?"

"OK, take your boss. You're always complaining that the bitch takes shit out on you. Well, give it back to her. And don't say you can't. OK, maybe you shouldn't knock her out physically because you'd get fired – and that would hurt you. But there are ways to get even. Ways that only you will know about. Piss in her coffee cup. Hack into her documents directory and delete all the records she worked on the day before. Shit like that. You'll feel better."

Gerard shook his head. Andy was drunk again.

"Listen to me. Haven't you ever wondered what you're really capable of?"

Again Gerard shook his head. He was really wishing he'd stayed home tonight. In his bed.

"Man, you take everything lying down. You don't try. Push the envelope a little. I mean, shit, when you found out about Jenine and her boss, what did you do?"

Gerard slumped a little and mumbled something.

"What?"

"I said I forgave her."

"You forgave her. You didn't scream at her, wail on her

or give her anything that she deserved."

"No. I couldn't hurt her, she's my wife. I loved her. I still do."

"Ah, and there's where you're wrong, champ. You could've hurt her. She deserved some hurt for what she did to you. Hell, she might have even appreciated it. And you would have felt more like a man if you had."

Gerard looked away and Andy grabbed his shoulder.

"The very least you could've done is had a little of your own on the side. You've told me about that admin girl at work. What's her name, Trish? She comes on to you, so take her up on it."

"No. I can't."

"Make you a deal. You think about this. Every time you say to yourself 'I can't do that' this week, I want you to force yourself to do it anyway."

"Forget it," Gerard whispered.

"No, c'mon. You worried about going to hell? You don't do church, so if there is one, you're going there anyway."

Gerard sighed. "There's no hell, I know that."

"Well then. Time for you to break some boundaries, my man. C'mon, promise – every day this week you're going to do something that you say 'I can't' about. By this time next week, I guarantee you, that pill will be going down your throat without a second thought."

"Yeah right," Gerard laughed. "If I boff Trish I'll be able to swallow a pill all of a sudden? Get real."

"It's not *about* doing Trish or not doing Trish," Andy hissed. "It's about pushing yourself. It's about getting beyond all those little walls you've put up that don't do you or anyone else a bit of good. You can do whatever you want, man. For once quit staring at the ground and try to see what you're really capable of. I guarantee you, the world will be a much different place for you."

Gerard slept badly and dreamed worse. His nightmares were peopled with choking pills and knives and beautiful women who grabbed him by his silk tie and dragged him beneath a sea of black water.

Jenine was already in the shower when he staggered to the bathroom feeling worse than he had the day before. When was he going to shake this cold?

"How ya feeling, honey?" came a silky voice from behind the curtain. Splashes of water slapped at the walls of the shower as she soaped her head and underarms.

"Worse," he croaked, and uncapped the horse pill bottle. Andy was right. He didn't try hard enough. He filled the bathroom cup with cold water and stared at the long, daisy-yellow pill in his hand. Then, closing his eyes, he tilted his head back and brought a hand up to his mouth. His other hand brought up the cup and with a gulp of cool liquid, he sent the pill to the back of his throat.

Where it lodged.

His eyes popped open and he shook his head in panic and the remaining water gurgled from between his lips into the sink. Leaning over the basin he coughed violently, freeing the pill to shoot from his throat to lie on the silver ring at the bottom of the sink. Tears wet the corners of his eyes as Jenine peered out from the curtain, black hair white with the foam of shampoo.

"OK?" she asked. He nodded quickly, not daring to talk. Replacing the cup in the holder by his toothbrush, he left the bathroom to her once again.

As Andy had so often reminded him, Gerard was a bit of a doormat. In college, with his boyish face and weight-bench augmented biceps, he'd never lacked for dates. But he'd also never been the one to call the relationships off. He was dumped and dumped on. Things hadn't really ever changed. Now at work, he carried the yoke of blame for every department misstep, and at home his wife had, at least temporarily, dumped him over for another man.

Gerard accepted it all and called himself lucky.

Well, sometimes.

It was easier to just take it and not cause a scene. Not that he didn't fume inside. He amused himself, placated himself, really, by imagining scenes where he took his petty revenges and emerged victorious from his complacency. But every fantasy held a bitter undercurrent of self-loathing. Because he could never act any of them out.

Now, as he sat in front of Angela Harper's well-polished mahogany desk, he thought again of Andy's taunts of the night before. The spill of shrill rhetoric spun past his ears like white powder from the spout of a snow blower. It was Angela who had fucked up this time. It was her paperwork that was amiss. But as usual, she was playing pin the tail on Gerard with a tirade of self-righteous vinegar. Idly he stared at her coffee cup and grinned at Andy's suggestion. No... he could go one better. He could serve the bitch coffee and cream, he could. And she'd suck it up and like it.

"Yeah right," his inner self laughed at him. "Like you could ever have the balls to do that. You can't. You CAN'T."

But what if he could? What stopped him, really? Maybe it was the codeine, but he warmed at the thought. Hell, he got hard at the thought.

A spat of coughing made him bring his own cup to his lips, all the while nodding and pretending to humbly accept Angela's abuse. It was empty. And from somewhere, he found himself saying:

"I'm sorry, Angela. I need a bathroom break. And some more coffee. Do you want me to get you some?"

Her thin lips stopped in mid-sentence, both amazed that he would interrupt her and thirsty for some more hot coffee.

"Yes," she said, slowly. "But be quick about it. We need to straighten this thing out this morning."

His hand was cold as he gripped himself in the stall, but the vision of Angela's lips sucking down what he intended to give her warmed him. He thought of his wife, taking the cock of another man down her throat (how could she…?) and then of Trish, kneeling right here in front of him, blouse undone to her navel…

The black liquid swirled into the mug, its heat dissolving Gerard's revenge like sugar. He topped it off with a splash of half and half and took the two cups back to Angela's office, groin lax and warmly sending out signals of satiation, heart meanwhile pounding with a mix of disgust, fear and excitement. What was he doing?

Oh, it felt good watching her drink his revenge down, licking her lips as if he tasted sweet as sugar. And maybe he did. He certainly felt a rush that was sweeter than any candy in his heart. For once Gerard Ambrose had the last laugh. Andy was right. Revenge, silent or not, brought a whole new view of the world. When the last of the coffee had disappeared between Angela's pale, frosty lips, Gerard nearly split a gut.

"I'd say suck my dick, but you kinda already have!" his inner child chuckled.

And then, high on the moment, he did something else untoward.

You can't.
I can do anything I want.
You can't.

"You know Angela, if you'd filed the right paperwork for this with the home office, we wouldn't be having this conversation," he said out loud, shocking himself nearly as much as her. "It's not my problem. You figure it out."

And rising suddenly, he snatched his coffee cup in one hand and turned his back on her. He did not have to suffer this. His exit was marred by a spate of deep, croupy coughs, but behind him, Angela sat speechless, lips coated in the spunk of her coffee.

That was the beginning.

But it was a corner turned. Almost every hour afterward, Gerard began testing himself in other ways. His imagination had never lacked for ideas. As he walked down the hallway next to the enticingly bouncing tush of Trish, he brought his hand back...

You can't.

...and connected with a solid slap on that spongy rear.

She turned to him, wide blue eyes bugged, jaw dropped, red glossed lips hanging open in a wide 'O' like the open-mouthed Trish he'd imagined kneeling before him earlier in the bathroom.

"Wha..."

"Hey Trish," he said simply and winked.

She looked confused for a moment, then laughed. Haltingly.

\/\\/\\/\\/\\/\\/\\/\\/\\/\\

Those were the big things. But the little things he challenged himself on, too. His feet were hot, sweating. They kept the office building too warm in his hallway. No windows to suck out the overflow of heat. With the toe of his right foot, he touched his left heel...

You can't...

and kicked off first the left shoe, then...

what are you doing? This is an office...

...his right.

Instead of going outside in the cold to have a smoke...

You can't!

...he lit up in his office with the door closed.

And then, high on the nicotine and codeine and just plain insanity of it, he slipped his slacks down to the floor, pulled out his penis, and lovingly enjoyed a vision of Trish, breasts pressed to his thighs, mouth pressed to his…

It felt good.

In his heart, he knew it was too good to be true. You couldn't just jack off on everyone and expect to be OK. The ax would fall. Angela would fire him somehow. Then Jenine would leave him, probably go back to sleeping with her boss.

His mind was awash with conflicting emotions; self-loathing arm-in-arm with a rare appearance from self-love as he walked through the garage entryway into his kitchen. The TV was blaring in the background and Jenine came rushing in from the living room, her kinked black hair frizzed up as if she'd been sleeping on it.

"Hon, would you go back out and pick up some dinner," she begged, planting a dry, chaste kiss on his lips. "I didn't have time…"

Automatically, Gerard did an about-face, then broke into another fit of coughing that left him bent over, wheezing for air.

You can't…

"No," he said quietly. Without another word he went up the stairs to change, absently noting that the bedsheets were a mess, something Jenine never put up with. So.

He stripped naked, walked to the bathroom and swallowed half the bottle of codeine cough syrup. As the hot trickle warmed his throat and spread its flame to his belly, he climbed into those sheets, still musty with the scent of his wife's sex, and cried himself to sleep.

She did not join him.

When he awoke, Jenine's perfume still hung in the air of the bedroom, but the house was silent. She'd left for work already, without a word. She knew that he knew. And what could she possibly say?

He coughed himself awake and went through his morning routine. Lather, rinse, gargle, comb. The wheels were now turning faster than ever before. And yet he was so calm. Emotionless, almost.

At work, Trish paged him to help her with a software glitch, and as he leaned over her shoulder, smelling the flowery musk of her hair, he reached out a...

You ca...

...hand and cupped her right breast. It was full, deliciously heavy in his hand. She looked up at him, surprised, but didn't pull away.

"I thought..." She didn't finish her sentence.

"Wanna do something tonight?" he asked.

Her eyes dimmed a moment, then met his. She looked afraid. Then nodded.

\/\\//\\\/\\/\\/\\/\\

Trish's apartment was purple. Lavender carpet, violet drapes. Her bedroom walls were pink with a bed topped by Princely royal purple sheets and comforter. Her body felt as silky as the sheets, and Gerard entered her without...

You c...

...a condom. Her mouth sucked his own inside of her, and for a moment, he remembered the flash of searing ecstasy he'd once felt with his wife as she took him within her. When she was his and only his...

He bit wildly at her neck and bosom and she raked her hands down his back, first in passion, then with insistence.

Gerard swam back from the brink of... something... to see her widened eyes and hear her cries of "Gerard, no, no, no!"

She pushed him from her, red welts already swelling on her skin, tears streaming from her eyes.

He didn't say anything, just pulled his pants and shirt on. In a second he was out the door, coat in hand. Trish wasn't the woman he felt this way about. His problems were at home.

Maybe.

The house was dark when he got in, but her car was in the garage. He hardly even thought now about what he...

You...

...was going to do.

The rope slipped around her sleeping wrists and ankles with ease. She didn't even stir until he was lifting her up from the bed.

"Where..." she asked sleepily.

"I could say the same," he said.

He laid her in the bathtub. Stopper down.

"I can't take any more," he said, as if that explained it all. Her eyes widened as she tested the tightness of her bindings and he leaned over her to tie the gag. Her head shook wildly and he sighed, loudly.

"Once I could forgive, but twice..." She started arching her back, trying to flop herself out of the tub, and with hardly a...

You...

...thought, brought his hand down on her face. With five sharp raps on the tile, she was still.

Then he went to the garage.

The chlorine barrels for the pool were heavy to get up the stairs, but he had managed to get them from the store to the trunk before. And so he managed to cart them through the kitchen, up the stairs and into the bathroom.

Slipping a razor from his Bic, he sliced through the thin cotton of her night shirt, and then her panties, leaving her naked and unconscious on the bottom of the tub. He looked at her then, slack lips parted, hair curled in ringlets up the sides of the tub, where soap and a trickle of blood had pasted it. Soft, full breasts ripe for kissing and a belly that even now brought a throb to his pants.

Enough. You can do anything. You've proven it already. You've punished her. You can't....

Methodically, he emptied the jugs of chlorine into the

tub, watching with a scientific indifference as the yellow fluid crept up between her thighs, soaked her hair and then covered the closely cropped tuft of secret hair below her belly.

How long would it take for her skin to burn away? he wondered.

She stirred then, and her eyes opened. They looked foggy, confused. And then, in pain.

"I'm not buying dinner tonight," he said coughing. The fumes were stifling now, and Gerard started coughing again. Grabbing his medicine, he left her alone in the bath, closed the door and went down the stairs to the kitchen. His eyes were watering as he poured a tall glass of milk from the fridge. There was a dull pounding sound echoing from upstairs, but he couldn't think about that, he couldn't seem to stop coughing; his chest was an agony of phlegmy irritation. Uncapping the bottle of antibiotics, Gerard popped one in his mouth and took a gulp of milk.

Y...

The pill went down easy.

I've learned two things about romance. Every heart holds secrets best left unseen. And the tease of the veils of mystery provoke more desire than the most perfect form unmasked. Oh… and one more thing – be careful what you wish for.

Broken Window

"You're a mystery to me," I complained. "Sure, I can *interpret* the spark in your eye. I can *theorize* over the meaning of the mischief in your smile. But I can never really slip past your guard. I can never stare directly into your heart. It's always veiled. A kernel of you is always hidden."

She smirked.

Not smiled. Katrina never simply smiled. There was always a twist attached. Which, in fact, was the point of this conversation.

So she smirked.

"What would you say if I told you that I am *never* really guarded with you," she cooed. "If I told you even though I joke and play with you, that I am always naked to your whims."

"I'd say you were deceptively poetic and I wouldn't believe it," I snapped.

I even crossed my arms to underscore my point.

How masculine.

How above reproach.

How foppish.

She brushed my caged chest with her lips. The shadowed almond shape of her eyes seemed rounder than usual. More doe-like. Another affectation to twist my feelings around her tongue.

"How could I believe it?" I railed further. "When you want me to buy you something or take you somewhere, don't you put on a slinky top and your tightest stretch pants – the purple ones with the flowers that I like so much – and tease me? Isn't that a deception? And when you talk on the phone, don't you close the door so I can't hear? And don't you go shopping with your sister and conveniently never show me what you bought? You *get* what you want by winks and kisses and hurt looks and you *do* what you want in secret. How can I know *what* goes on inside you without a window to your soul?"

"Is that all you want?" she asked, strangely calm after my accusations.

"What?" I said, confused now.

"A window to my soul? If you want it, I'll get one. It can be done tomorrow."

I didn't really know what to say. I'd been blustering my way through to win the argument up to this point. In truth, I liked her to coax me into doing things her way with a kiss and a jiggle. It was an unspoken, admittedly sexist but effective agreement we had. And I certainly had had my share of private conversations and excursions which I never spoke of. But I couldn't back down now.

"Yes," I said at last. "Have one put in."

She neither smirked nor smiled now. But she nodded her agreement.

Our bedroom was strangely silent that night.

\\/\\/\\\/\\\\/\\/\\/

When I came home the following day, Katrina was not there to greet me as was her usual routine. I called out her name, but she didn't reply.

Dropping an armload of papers on the kitchen table, I

walked through the house looking for her.

"Katrina?" I called. The dusk shadows were still.

"Katrina?"

The house remained silent. Yet, I could feel her presence somewhere.

"Here," she answered at last. Her voice sounded weary.

She stood in front of the bathroom mirror with her shirt off. She was staring at her chest. I joined her.

She'd had the window installed.

"That was fast," I said.

"I didn't want to lose my nerve."

Gently, I turned her to face me. I kissed her mouth, but she was unresponsive.

I bent to stare into her newly transparent chest. Her once magnificent breasts were gelatinously see-though. Her sternum was crystal clear. You wouldn't think it, knowing how powerful the erotica of glass sculpture can be, but I found Katrina's transformed chest suddenly a dead zone. An erotic zero.

The view itself?

Strange.

What else can I say? Can I tell you I saw almost nothing? Or shall I describe the flashes: a wisp of pale blue smoke, a hint of crystalline lattices that wound amid a garden of silken rose, a toothy multi-eyed creature of purest ebony that sweat crimson stains. All these strange visions and more I stared at. I saw a flash of Katrina the child, and even a glimpse of my own face staring back at me for an instant – a far more porkish visage than the one that appeared to me every morn in the mirror.

Mostly though, I saw emptiness. But at each image that flew fleetly past the window to her soul, I felt what she felt. And as I stared with a completely new and different interest than I'd ever had before at her chest, I can tell you better what I felt than what I saw.

I felt robbed.

Violated.

Empty.

When at last I looked up from her glass bosom, Katrina and I were both crying.

In giving me absolute entrance to her soul, Katrina had given up too much, had kept nothing for herself. I tried to hold her tightly, to soothe her pain, but she pushed me back.

"I'll break now," she warned.

"C'mon," I said, mustering a grin. "You're stronger than that. Give me a good smirk."

One of those multi-eyed black creatures bit bloodily into my own soul as the expression on Katrina's face changed.

She smiled.

When I was in grade school, I inherited a treasure trove of 1950s science fiction books from a neighbor. I read many of those novels – by Simak and Asimov and Clarke and Heinlein – two or three times. But perhaps my favorite of the bunch was an anthology collection of "Golden Age" short SF fiction called Children of Wonders. Richard Matheson's classic "Born of Man and Woman" was there, a perfect marriage of horror and SF, as was Theodore Sturgeon's "Baby is Three," probably the best "wild talent" story penned about children with "psi power." When I took creative writing in college, these were the type of stories I wanted to create. "Tomorrow" and "The Last Plague" are among the first stories I ever completed and certainly yearn to capture the same malignant, futuristic cautionary sense of those great 1950s authors.

Tomorrow

I went to the tree today. I thought very much, about me and Mum, and Dad. The tree helps me think – everything gets cloudy sometimes. Like tears and smoke. The tree stretches branches around me; it protects me. I told this to Mum when I first began going to the tree, and she got mad. That night to Dad she said "Charles, what are we going to do with him? We can't shield him from the world forever. What will he do when he has to interact with other people? What will he do to us?"

Dad told her not to worry, I just needed love, that was all. Then she started crying like always and asked how she could love a freak. Dad told her I was her child, not a freak, and that made her cry louder. She wanted to send me away, but Dad wouldn't let her. He said I was just...*different*. But he was afraid. I was learning fast.

VVIANMVIAI

I think at first they were proud of me. "Prodigy," they said. "Talked when he was two. Crawled at three." The doctors said no operation could make me walk, so I got extra brains. I heard them tell Dad not to have more children. Chromosomes. Radiation. Even then, I think Mum had trouble loving me. She cringed sometimes when I hugged her; she always turned me over to Dad when he got home. Sometimes she'd lock me in my room, and let me scream for hours. She smelled bitter – like the tree when you rip the bark away. She tried to look the other way as she fed me, but I stared straight at her. When her eyes glanced at mine, her lower lip trembled. Her teeth clenched together. Her hand shook, but the spoon forced its way into my mouth. Sometimes I spit it back in her face and laughed. It was a little revenge. My mother hated me, and I knew it.

That was when I started *doing* things. Little things. Like spilling grape juice on her favorite blouse, or hiding her keys in the toilet, or crying in the middle of the night and then stopping just when she entered my room. Harmless, but effective.

I would lie awake at night, and listen to them talk. Mum would cry a lot and call me a monster. She told Dad my little pranks, and he told her she was exaggerating. "In fact," he would say, "it shows he is developing like every other boy. A little mischief is good. He's been withdrawing too much lately. This fall he's going to have to go to school."

"But Charles, these… these *things* he does… They're malignant. It's just not normal. The way he looks at me…"

I had to try hard not to laugh out loud and give myself away.

Then came the Day. It was mid-summer, nothing to do. I was really bored. We had a cat named Spider, because she tiptoed around everything. I got some yarn, a coat hanger, and a steel brush and built my very own custom Spider trap. When it sprung, there was a howl like you wouldn't believe. I was laughing and rolling on the floor.

Mum went running into the utility room and found the cat shrieking in its litter box. Every time Spider tried to get out of the yarn strands holding her in the box, the steel brush swatted her like a fly. There was kitty litter everywhere. Mum lost her temper, and came after me with the brush. She hit me over and over, and screamed when she saw the blood on my shriveled legs. I was red inside, and I turned over to see her raising her arm again. I hated. I felt fire in my head and I wished it at her. And she stopped. She froze in mid-motion and the brush fell from her hand. A sound came from deep in her throat. An ugly sound. Like a grating door. Or that sound you make just before the vomit comes up. I looked away, because her face wasn't pretty anymore, and I hurt. I heard a dull thud behind me as she fell to the floor. Later, when she began breathing slower, she got up quietly, slipped out the back door, and ran from the house.

When she came home again, Dad was with her. His face was all wrinkly. He was scared. Not scared like they show people scared in horror movies, but I could tell. I was watching TV and I smiled as they came into the room. "Hi, Daddy," I said. "Mummy spanked me today. See what she did." I rolled over to show my scabbing backside.

His wrinkles dropped to a frown. I knew I'd won, and they went in the bedroom to fight. "Don't be ridiculous," and "He's just a kid," I heard. And from Mum: "He's a devil. He tried to kill me!"

We moved after that, and nobody talked about me going to school anymore. Our new house was in the country. Dad thought it would soothe everyone's nerves and bring us closer. He started teaching me himself. That was when he started to understand. By the time I was nine, I was mastering physics. I had discovered the tree in the back of our yard and often took my books and struggled through chemistry and mathematics there. When a problem got too hard I pulled myself close to the tree and felt the cool bark against my skin. The tree supported me, and I felt its strength. Then the problems were easy, and the smoky webs in my head went away. I just wanted love, and the tree loved me. I could feel it.

I tried to make Mum do what I wanted, like on the Day, but it didn't work. Sometimes when I tried, a funny look crossed her face, but she kept on with what she was doing. One night I laid awake listening, and heard Dad telling Mum that I would be going through puberty soon, and that it might open new doors for me. "His mind is so incredibly developed, who knows what extra hormones will do for it," he said. Mum murmured something unpleasant, and I smiled. Dad had books on everything and one was on ESP. I read it and realized that what I had done to Mum was like the powers the book talked about. Maybe I could learn to do it whenever I wanted.

So I practiced by the tree. I'd look at an ant, and follow him a while with my eyes. Then, when he ran in a straight line, I made him stop and turn around. I did it over and over. At first it didn't work, and I just got a headache, but gradually, the ants did my will. I played with them for hours, making them build grass towers and have mini-skirmishes.

I started getting tiny black hairs popping out on my body. I felt strong, and I couldn't play with the ants anymore. When I tried to make them do something, they curled up and died, like when you touch them with a lit punk. I realized that playing with the birds and squirrels was more fun anyway. Once a sparrow was sitting on the line making noise while I was sleeping, so I stared at it. It flapped its wings for a second like it was trying to keep its balance, and then rose from the phone wire and flew in a straight line through the kitchen window and onto the table where Mum was making dinner. She screamed and screamed. When Dad got home she cried again and called it an omen.

Tomorrow

On my 13th birthday, Dad brought me home a lot of electronic equipment from work. He works for the government with experimental nuclear stuff, and I had gone through all the texts he had brought home. I said I wanted to try some of my own experiments, and he made me a workshop in the garage. I built a laser and teased the cat with moving strobes of heat. Spider soon avoided the garage. I worked alone now, and went to the tree often.

One night, I asked Dad about the neutron bomb, and he wouldn't tell me how it worked. "You are not old enough to fool around with that kind of science yet, kiddo," he said.

He smelled acrid, like Mum when she wouldn't look at me.

"You stick with building the better mousetrap for a few more years."

"C'mon Dad, I need to know," I begged, but he merely shook his head. His shoulders were slumped.

I got mad. I hadn't made a person do anything since the Day, but now I looked at him. His eyes widened, and gasping, he began reciting. When he was through, I thanked him and went to the tree.

The night was clear, and the branches pointed to the stars. A jet left a wispy trail to the south, and the west was lit by the dull glow of the closest town. The wind blew hair in my face, mixing it with the tears streaming from my aching eyes.

"I hurt my Dad!" I yelled at the tree. My tears ran down the white bark to wet the empty anthill below. I had killed all the ants. There were no birds or squirrels for miles. My fists beat bloody against the tree, and after a while I lay still panting. The stars shone steady and strong. I longed to go to them. But they were so far. I knew that I would find a way to them, but not yet. Dad had more to teach me. He had brought stacks of technical books home for me, but I yearned for his touch. His voice. His love.

I slept.

And woke in the dark. I sat up and knew I was imprisoned. The floor was cold cement in place of warm soil. The air was damp, and water splashed somewhere. I was blind and helpless. I knew all at once that I was trapped in our crawlspace. My mind woke, as my anger built. I strained to see and hear, and suddenly I could feel my parents just meters away. I pulled, and Mum screamed. A trapdoor opened, and Dad's face was silhouetted in the opening. "I'm sorry," he said, "But until you learn never to…" His voice cut off as his whole body went rigid and fell through the opening to the cement floor. I crawled over him and dragged myself up the short ladder.

Mum and Dad learned to behave quickly. I didn't feel bad, because they locked me up, so I just did it to them. I showed Dad what I was building in the garage, and a tear ran down his unshaven face. I noticed how large his bald spot was growing. He tried to tell me that I should use my talents to help humanity, not to destroy it, and I smiled.

"Would they help me?" I asked.

He turned away and wouldn't talk anymore.

I decided I wanted to see if other humans were like Mum and Dad. They would make fun toys. Then maybe I would visit the stars.

\/\\/\|\\/\\\/\|\/\|

This morning I woke up and they were gone. I guess I didn't put them to sleep enough last night. It's OK, though. They weren't a challenge any more. If I need them, they'll come back. Going to the tree helped ease my mind. If I go to the stars I have to take the tree.

Somehow.

Tomorrow I think I will go into the world. I rewired Dad's car so I can work the gas and brakes from the steering column. I will see what people are like. My memories are fuzzy. All I remember is a doctor leaning over me with yellow, smelly teeth, and some ugly old ladies. Aunts, Mum called them. I could have fun making them stand on each other in pyramids like with the tree ants. "It's a big world though," Dad always said. It should at least prove more interesting than squirrels and birds.

And if I don't like it?

I'll go see the stars. And maybe use what I built in the garage when I leave. It would be fun. I could just push a button, and the earth would crack up like an egg, the slimy, yellow yolk oozing out of the middle.

I've always liked eggs.

Especially crunching them in my hand.

Tomorrow should be a very good day.

Voyeurism is an increasingly accepted pastime in our society of confining cubicles and don't-need-to-leave-home satellites and Internet sex photo swapping. In our splendid isolation, the kink of anonymous others provides affirmation of our own "normality" and gives us, at the same time, a way to release the fantasies of our own darker natures. Despite our increasing amount of time locked in our own heads and space, sometimes the hardest thing to do is to look away from the perversities of others and stare hard at the black core within ourselves.

Mirror Image

My reflection is not a nice guy. I've known him all my life, but I first met him – really got to know him – last week. I was straightening my tie in the antique mirror in our bedroom when he frowned at me. "Just your imagination," I told myself, but when I turned away, I could feel him watching; laughing, silently.

The next morning, I kissed my wife Janine goodbye and then turned once again to the tall oval mirror in our bedroom. As the necktie looped, my reflection mimicked every move but one. While my face remained sleepily still, his began making moues – sarcastically imitating my recent kiss.

My heart raced; this reflection had a mind of his own! The half-knotted tie dropped forgotten to the floor and I lifted a hand to touch the surface of the mirror. His palm rose in answer. When our fingers made contact with the glass, the surface of the mirror shimmered as if the touch was a droplet hitting a pool of mercury.

Something icy wrenched my hand and I stumbled into the mirror. Instead of tumbling in a crash of splintering wood and glass to the floor, my senses suddenly cut off and I was pinned *inside* the glass. My perspective flipped; my reflection now stood outside the glass, and he was again laughing at me. This time out loud. I opened my mouth to scream, but there was only silence. And the cackles of my reflection, who whispered one thing as he turned to leave the room:

"You've always told your bimbo wife you liked to watch. Well, I'm sick of watching. Now you'll see how a life should be led."

As his steps echoed on the hardwood floor, I felt myself fade.

\/\\//\\/\\\/\\/

Then he was back – and so was I. Hours had passed; the streetlamps shone sulphurous on my reflection, who was hungrily kissing Janine! My arms mimed his caresses, stroked nonexistent hair. Alarmed and enraged, I struggled to still my limbs and step through the mirror to reclaim my wife. But I couldn't even slow my fingers from following the intricate map of his lovemaking. The worst part of it was hearing Janine call out my name to him.

"Oh, Terry," she moaned, when they were finished. "That was the best! What's gotten into you?"

My double turned his head to stare back at me in the mirror.

He winked.

The next night he moved me closer to the bed.

"I want to see you everywhere I look," he told Janine as he scraped the mirror along the floor. She blushed and squealed. "Ohhh, kinky!"

I couldn't look away as two feet in front of me my reflection took my wife with savage glee.

\/\\//\\/\\\/\\/

In the morning, he kissed her passionately in front of me. When she was gone, he peered into the glass as if I were far away. "Are you enjoying this?" he asked. "Your wife sure is. What a twit. Now watch closely tonight." He grinned so wide I could see the silver in my back teeth. "I have a special surprise for you."

It was night again. I heard Janine's moans before I could see her. And then she landed heavily on the bed before me, her eyes wide with a mix of lust and fear. Her wrists were bound together, but rather than trying to work her way free, she arched and stretched for him on the bed.

As my double walked around the bed, he paused to stare directly into my eyes: "You always said you liked to watch, so you must be observant. Look around the room. What's wrong with this picture?"

My throat clenched at his tone. Something bad was going to happen tonight. I squinted hard at the room, trying to see beyond the limits his motions placed on me.

They were well on their way to orgasm when I saw it. On my dresser. An open curio drawer.

Empty.

My reflection straddled Janine on the bed and I struggled to see what he held in his hand. I prayed to God it wasn't what I feared – the gift my grandfather gave me when I first began to shave, a token from the days when his shop was the center of gossip in town, not the local bar.

His barber shop.

"I have a surprise for you," my reflection crooned to my wife wriggling beneath him. His hand – my hand – glittered in the pale light from the street as he held the ivory-handled razor for a moment over his head before bringing it down.

I opened my mouth to scream, to warn her.

But all I could do was watch.

Believe it or not, most of my stories have little to do with my home life (and given the nature of the women in many of the stories in this book, I should probably take this opportunity to point out that my wife is a sweet-natured girl who never turns up in our bed at night anointed with demonic sigils or brandishing sharp objects. Not often, anyway). The following story does have a real root, however. When I was in college, I brought home a handful of my roommate's Elric books by Michael Moorcock during a vacation. My mother read the bit on the back covers about Elric being a "dark lord" and promptly shredded the books to keep their evil from her house and my head (never mind that they were not hers – or my – property to dispose of). If books and magazines represent the exploration of all aspects of the human mind and spirit – which by nature ranges from the bloody abominations of hell to the saintly missions of heaven – then whether books are filled with sacrilege, science, porn or prayer, they should all be sacrosanct.

Murdering the Language

Gretta's breath hung heavy in the air as she huffed and gasped her way up the steps. The final load – at last. Her brown paper shopping bag (she never accepted plastic at the supermarket) was filled, not with carrots and Campbell's soup, but with books. Library books. Gretta Dowler was the new President of the Parkville Library Board. She loved that title. Every time she thought of the election last week, a smile stole across her face. At last the good citizens of Parkville had come to their senses and unseated that liberal homosexual, Gary Worth. He lived with another man, for goodness sake! What kind of example was that for the children of Parkville?

But now she could start undoing the harm. Mrs. Fellier, the fat busybody librarian hadn't liked it, but she, Gretta Dowler, was personally going to review all of the fiction.

The trash would be put where it belonged. Never again would an innocent child – or adult for that matter – leave the library with a novel to read, only to be led into sin and ill thought by stinky, perverted smut hidden inside. Gretta's heart warmed with the thought. And the best place to start was the horror/science fiction section. It was unconscionable that publishers allowed some of these cretins to print such immoral evil. But if they wouldn't be responsible...

Carefully holding the storm door from slapping shut with her back end, Gretta stepped inside, dropped the bag on the kitchen table and shut the heavy wooden inside door. It was cold tonight, even for November. She unknotted the scarf from around her head, noting with dismay the pure white hair that clung to it. Her handsome silver curls were steadily losing even that vestige of color. Old and gray. It had happened so quickly. Her once thin and supple hands now looked gnarled, spotted with brown and lined with blue. Old and gray. She shook her head. The colors of age were not at all festive.

Ice sparkled on the panes of her living room windows, she noticed while hanging her coat in the hall closet. Shivering slightly, she decided this would be a good night for a fire. Yes, a bright, happy orange, and red fire. And a pot of tea. That would set the mood just right for reading.

Twenty minutes later, Gretta sat down on the couch near the fireplace, a book bag beside her, a steaming mug of tea on the lamp stand. She took a sip and closed her eyes momentarily, savoring the moment. The tea was sharp, the fire hot. Every few seconds it popped, like a cap going off, as it reached a pocket of moisture in the wood. Reaching into the bag, she pulled out a book at random. Clive Barker *Imajica*, it read. The cover showed two people of ambiguous sex curled about each other. One of them was purple. What sort of picture was that? Turning to the title page, she began to skim. He seemed a learned author, Gretta thought, noting his use of words like "vociferous" and "blandishments," right off. But the tone... somewhat sinister.

She went to chapter two and right away found him writing of "hard-ons" and "unloading his balls." Simply disgusting. She turned the pages faster, noting references to sex on almost every one. "Deathbed fucks," a ruthless murder, "conjuring," and then, a three-*page* description of a man – contrarily named Gentle – sharing the sex act with a strange woman who turned out to be male. Gretta slammed the book shut. She felt soiled, dirty. How could someone so obviously educated contrive such filth?

She tossed the book to the floor and grabbed another. *Queen Of The Damned* by Anne Rice. Now this woman she'd heard of. She wrote smut under another name. Dreading it, she flipped open the book anyway. It was about a vampire rock star. Ridiculous. Skimming the chapters, she saw that this, at least, did not use such foul language to accomplish its aim. But perhaps that only made it more insidious. For, as near as she could tell, it glorified these devils, these vampires. They sucked their victims dry, chatted over the quality of their evil, and slunk off to kill another day. In one chapter, one of the despicable characters turned to the hero – another murdering vampire – and proclaimed "Now you shall be a god with me." Sacrilegious! And at the end of the book that same "hero" laughed "I'm a perfect devil. Tell me how bad I am. It makes me feel so good!"

Gretta tossed *Queen* to the floor. Glorification of murder and sex. Glorification of murder and evil. How could she let people be exposed to this trash?

The pile grew through the night. Peter Straub, Robert Silverberg, Harlan Ellison... Gretta couldn't believe the trash these people concocted. The pile grew further. Isaac Asimov *The End Of Eternity* – men making themselves gods. Robert Heinlein *The Number Of The Beast* – she didn't even have to read that one, the title itself was enough. Dan Simmons *Hyperion Cantos* – immoral pilgrims going to worship some murderous monster on another planet. Michael

Moorcock *The Revenge Of The Rose*. Gretta got so mad reading that one – which cast a horrible vengeful dark being named Elric as the hero who sacrificed souls to a devil named Arioch – that she ripped out the pages.

"Trash, trash, trash," she pronounced, tossing the remains of *Revenge* into the fire. It caught with a whoosh of yellow flame. Satisfied, she went into the kitchen to refill her tea. It was almost midnight, and she hadn't found a keeper yet. Mrs. Fellier was *not* going to be happy, but this was for the best. Couldn't have people getting these warped ideas. Why do you s'pose there were homosexuals like Gary? She liked pronouncing that word to herself. Ho-Mo-Sex-U-Als. It sounded appropriately dirty. People like that Clive Barker made simple folk think making love to a man who looked like a woman might be a good thing. He perverted innocence. And why were there serial killers? Reading about vampires ripping people's throats out and worshiping the blood, and some devil named Elric riding around lopping good people's heads off with a soul-sucking sword. No wonder the world was in such sad shape.

With fresh determination, and another steaming mug of tea – this time with some lemon in it – Gretta returned to the couch. From now on, the bad ones were going directly to the fire, she decided. No point in holding back. And if Mrs. Fellier didn't like it – well tough. That's what she was elected for. And she was sure some of those romance novels that chatty librarian was always carrying on about were going to be hitting the fire too.

Lord Foul's Bane by Stephen R. Donaldson caught Gretta's eye next. The title certainly wasn't promising, and she saw right away its main character was a leper called The Unbeliever.

It crackled well in the fire. As the fire tackled the binding, it gave off a high pitched wail.

The evil little book is screaming, Gretta thought with a smile.

Just reward.

Another Donaldson title was in the bag. *The Real Story.* It seemed to be about some outer space pirate who captured a nice girl, put this thing in her head, and forced her to have sex with him. Perversion! It quickly joined the other Donaldson titles.

EEEEEEEAAAAAAAAHHHHH, the book keened as its pages quickly blackened, curled and died.

Gretta shivered despite the warmth of the room. It really *did* sound like screaming. Angry screaming. The fire was getting smoky now, and Gretta realized if she didn't want black spots on the ceiling and ashes drifting through the house, she was going to have to stop feeding it the books.

But what could she do to destroy these evil things?

Revenge, someone whispered.

Gretta shook her head. She was starting to hear things.

Revenge.

There it was again!

"Who's there?" she called.

Foul, someone else said. This voice was louder, crueler.

Gretta got up and tiptoed to the hall closet. She kept a hatchet there, for when the bushes out front started blocking the walk. If someone was here, it ought to take care of them too. As she hefted the weapon a voice yelled shrilly:

FOUL FUCKING. Fucking. Fuckingfuckingfucking...

The voice seemed to be all around her. Then a whole clamor of voices began taunting:

FOUL REVENGE! FUCKING! FUCKINGFUCKING-FUCK-INGFOUL! REVENGE!

But no one was there. The kitchen was empty, the bedroom empty, the frontroom – just the books on the floor. And a chorus of wicked reedy voices.

TRASH! Trash. Trashtrashtrashtrash.

"Shut Up!" she screamed, brandishing the ax at the empty room. "I'll show you trash."

She brought the weapon down on the pile of novels

she'd left on the floor earlier. Yes! This was what she needed to destroy these wicked books.

Bitchhhhhhhhhhhhhh!!! The voices screamed as the axe bit through the Clive Barker book and into Anne Rice.

You're a perfect devil, one screeched.

There was no one here, Gretta realized. These books. They were possessed! They were so evil, devils lived in them!

She went to work in earnest, hacking at the pile. Lifting the ax, bringing it down. Something splashed on her hand and she realized the Rice book, cleaved in half by her third stroke, was bleeding. Wiping wet black ink from her fingers, she noticed that all the books she'd chopped were bleeding. As she watched, the ink ran from the pages, trickling and coagulating into dark, evil pools on the floor.

You think you're a god, Gretta?

This voice was cold, steely. Not like the teasing, angry voices before.

And this one knew her name.

You want a little lesson in literature, Gretta?

"Who are you?" she yelled, turning slowly about the room in a circle.

Something snapped behind her. She twisted around, ax at the ready. One of the books on the kitchen table had flipped open. Its pages were riffling as if caught in a strong wind. And then, as suddenly as it had opened, it slammed shut. She recognized the book now. It was by that horror writer everyone talked about. She'd read some of his stuff before – disgusting filth filled with "fucks" and gore and sex talk.

"You're murdering the language," she yelled at the now-still book. Turning towards the living room again she raised the ax once more. "You're all murdering the language!"

You want a little lesson in literature, Gretta?

The voice was everywhere.

The good guys always win.

The ax lifted from her hands and Gretta was falling. Falling through an inferno of debauchery. Her body recoiled: her stomach heaved, her bowels opened, her head was exploding.

Hands touched her beneath her skirts, men sucking on other men leered at her; women flogging themselves held out their vile instruments for her to take; blood streaked the sky in violent trails; arms, legs, heads rolled between her legs where crimson smeared faces grinned back; adultery, sodomy, disembowelments were performed on her, under her – she was immersed in filth, filth, filth.

A little lesson in literature, Gretta.

Gretta clawed the floor around her in desperation for the ax. If she could only find it again and still the voice.

\/\/\/\\/\/\\/\/\

Sgt. Gates stomped through the little old fashioned kitchen nook, letting the storm door crash shut behind him. He wasn't too worried about letting in the dawn chill.

"Marty? You in here?" he called.

Lieutenant Marty Weis straightened up from his appraising crouch over the body.

"In here, Jack."

Gates' feet echoed heavily on the hardwood floor as he entered the room. He whistled slowly, taking in the view. Blood spattered the walls and floor, where the torso of a wrinkled older woman lay amid a pile of shredded, bloodstained books. One of her arms was near the fireplace. A leg poked out nauseatingly from beneath the couch.

"What the hell happened here?" he asked.

"We got a call from a neighbor around 3:20 this morning saying he was woken up by screams," Marty explained. "I got here at 3:26. There was no sign of forced entry – no evidence that anyone else had been here. And she's holding the ax that took off her limbs so tight, I can't pry it out of her hand. She chopped up these books Jack, and then she chopped up herself."

Jack Gates whistled again. He'd been on homicide investigations plenty – but this one might well go down as the creepiest. Certainly the bloodiest. There were pages from those books stuck to the ceiling and walls – obviously stuck with the woman's blood.

"What's that black stuff on the floor?" he asked, pointing to a deep black stain.

"This?" Marty ran a fingertip through the puddle and held it up for Jack to see. "It's ink! The fire must have melted it right off some of these books – look."

He held up a piece of one of the lesser wounded volumes and leafed through the pages. Some were pure white, others had dark smears where there might once have been text lines. "I ain't never seen the like though," he admitted ruefully.

Jack shook his head. "Archie and Jim are on their way over to help you finish up. I'm going back to the station. Make sure you guys document everything – I don't want anyone crying foul on this one."

He noticed a book on the kitchen table.

"Hey, is that the only novel in the place she didn't hack up?"

"Looks like it," Marty replied.

Jack picked up the hardcover copy of Stephen King's *The Shining*.

"My kid likes this guy," Jack mused aloud. "Think I'll take it home for him."

He shoved the book into one of the wide pockets in his coat and thumbed back at the body of Gretta Dowler.

"I don't think she'll mind," he grinned, trying to dispel some of the horror from the scene. Marty didn't laugh.

Jack let the storm door smash shut behind him once more.

This story originally appeared in the last issue of one of my favorite magazines in the mid-'90s, Dead of Night ("Pumpkin Head" was slated to appear in its next issue, which, sadly, never materialized.) For me, this story was an exercise in trying to take an old horror trope and look at it in a new way. And about those special days that all relationships celebrate. Some of us celebrate things a little differently than others, of course…

Anniversary

Margaret looked at the calendar rune and tickled her lips with her tongue. Full moon tonight. She'd been pressing her thighs together in anticipation of this day all month long. Charles only came on the night of the moon, and though her body ached for his visits, she knew that once a month, realistically, was all she could handle. There was so much to prepare for – and so much to recover from, afterward.

She made the bed, called in sick to work – did anyone notice her sick days always coincided with the phase of the moon? – and went to the closet to find what Charles called her "ice cream" outfit.

"Those guys all think you're a cone waiting to be licked and caressed," he'd grin, evilly. "But I know better. You're a tigress. And I screeeeeem for you!" He'd howl as he said it and she'd strip out of the skin tight catsuit before letting him lay a hand on her.

"You don't want to be licking the napkin around your cone, do you?" she'd tease.

Staring at herself in the mirror, she could feel her body starting to sweat and moisten, just thinking about Charles. Her average 34 A-cup breasts looked like 36 Cs in the immodest display of the sheer, deep blue suit, and she knew her butt jiggled tantalizingly as she walked, every dip and tuck bouncing. She was not a well-endowed woman, but she made the best possible use of her assets. Of which, she realized staring at her reflection, her hair was currently not. Charles forbade her a shower on the day of the full moon, and her hair hung in flat, lazy twists across her shoulders. She'd dyed it auburn this month for a change and prayed he'd like it. Running her hands through it in a useless attempt at styling, she decided she'd have to rely on her other allure tricks. Charles wouldn't allow hairspray, either. Made him sneeze.

At the vanity in the corner of the bedroom she applied a heavy coat of electric red lipstick to match her nails, and lined her eyes in sooty black. She was ready.

First stop was the K-Mart. More than a few graying heads turned her way in shock as she paraded through the white-tiled aisles. To any close stare she was stark naked in a coat of blue spray paint. An old woman stood fingering a fuzzy pink nighty in the underwear department and happened to look up as she passed. The nighty dropped to the floor. "Young lady," a scratchy high-pitched voice chased her. There was a strong element of chastisement couched in those two simple words. Margaret glanced over her shoulder and flashed a crinkle-eyed look. "You keep your man your way and I'll keep mine my own way," she smiled sweetly.

God, she hated people, she thought, picking up a white cotton tank. Confront them with the truth – a human body, un- or thinly veiled – and they went to pieces. Religions had been built on hiding the truth of the human form. Laws had been passed on how it should be shielded and where it could be kissed. Human beings lived in denial of what they were, and she hated them for it. She knew what she was, and she was unashamed.

Shaking her head, she took the cotton tee and matching bottoms, grabbed a box of popcorn, and went to the register. A high school-aged girl with braces and plastic framed glasses rang her up, pausing every few seconds to stare at her chest when she thought Margaret wasn't paying attention. "Yeah, you'll have them soon," she thought wickedly. "And you'll bind them and hide them and offer them in trade for a chain noosed around your lover's neck. Happy hookering, hon."

Striding purposefully from the store, she drove to a park nearby. The sun shone golden bright through the trees as she tossed handfuls of popcorn to the pigeons. They crowded her feet, scrambling over each other in their haste to eat. Others swooped down from the trees periodically, disturbing the complex pecking order of feeding. "Whoever pecks the most ruthlessly rules the dinner table," she thought, and wondered if she and Charles stood at the top of the food chain.

A pickup pulled into the parking lot a few yards away, and a middle-aged man stepped out. He was maybe 5'6, white, looked like a going-to-seed blue collar. Handleable. With a deliberate stretch, Margaret put her hands on the back of the bench, thrust out her chest, and spread her feet far apart on the ground. Within seconds the man answered the call.

"Mind if I sit down?" a tremulous voice asked. She did her best Madonna. "Sit or spit, I don't care," she answered, calculatedly bored. It was best not to act too forward – only look that way. She felt his weight settle onto the end of the bench, but didn't look at him.

There were only the noises of the scuffling birds for a few moments, and then he tried again.

"Um, my name's Bill," he said. She turned to meet his gaze. "Hi Bill."

"You, uh, come out here and feed the birds a lot?" he pressed on.

"Now and then."

"Married?" he braved.

"No."

Quiet again. Probably time to help him a little.

"You want to toss some," she offered, holding out the bag of popcorn.

His face lit and he slid closer to her.

"Sure."

It barely took an hour. Bill was an electrician, supposed to be at a job site. But sometimes, he admitted, he came here during lunchtime, looking for "company." She got the impression he didn't care what kind, as long as he got off. He let it slip that he was married, while his eyes massaged her chest and crotch guiltily.

"Sometimes," she said, "I like a little company, too."

She stretched, put her arm around his shoulder and trailed a nail down his biceps. He stiffened, and then looked at her face in unveiled lust. She leaned over, kissed him, and then stood.

"Want to come back to my place?"

It wasn't always this easy, but it was never that hard.

She led him by the hand down the stairs through the basement and into a nearly bare room. The walls were black painted cinder block, the floor black tile. A white vinyl couch stood out in violent contrast in the room's center.

"I like to pretend it's night when it's day," she explained when he looked in dawning fear at the oddly decorated room. His suspicions evaporated when the blood rushed from his head to his cock as she knelt at his feet. She stripped them both, moving her supple body sinuously around his thickening waist and wrinkled rear. Laying him to the couch, she twisted and turned atop him, rubbing every inch of herself on his skin. No baths, and the scent of the man she'd brought him, that was what Charles asked. Smells drove him wild. But she would not let the "other man" enter her. When he began to grow anxious for the act, she slid from the couch and worked him with mouth and hands as his own beefy palms grabbed and kneaded her flesh.

This was always the hardest part for her. Having to touch some disgusting strange man in the unclean places. She was not turned on by this – rarely did she pick up a man to whom she was sexually attracted. But she did this for Charles. She thought of the first time they'd met, when in her forward passion she'd reached inside his jogging pants in the very same park she'd picked Bill up in. Charles had kissed her lightly, and with a firm hand, had pulled her probing fingers from his crotch.

"I can only cum beneath the light of a full moon," he said softly. She was not convinced – other women just hadn't been as skilled as her, she thought somewhere deep in her lust-clouded brain. His eyes looked sad as he watched her ego-deflating, vain attempts to prove him wrong. But filled with stubborn pride – and a telling, nagging wetness between her legs – she stuck out her chin and challenged, "Then visit me on the night of the full moon."

His strong features both grinned and frowned at that invitation. "I will," he promised.

She laughed inside now at her foolish naivety in extending that offer. She knew he had struggled not to accept – he'd liked her, and knew what would come of such a tryst. But ultimately, he had lost his internal battle. At her doorstep, 8 p.m. on the night of the moon he had appeared, a thin wiry man in a black t-shirt and jeans. He'd brought her roses and asked if she'd reconsidered her invitation. In answer, she'd leaned into his body, inhaling his musky, woodsy, animal scent and inserted her tongue between his lips. In moments, they'd been naked and rutting on the couch in the living room.

Beneath her absent ministrations she felt the warm stream that signaled an end to her duty. As Bill groaned in ecstasy, she reached a hand beneath the vinyl cushions searching for the chain. She needed a new couch, she thought. The cushions were cracked with age and scored with scratches. Her hand grasped what she was looking for. With a fast pull and snap, she efficiently cuffed Bill's right arm to the couch.

"Huh?" he exclaimed and grabbed for her with his free hand. She skipped easily out of his reach, watching in sad amusement as his cock deflated instantly. "What are you doing? Let Me Go!" he ordered in false bravado.

There was fear in his voice, but nothing like the tremors that would shake it as the day wore into night.

"Sorry Bill, but I need you tonight. Get some rest, why don't you."

Ignoring his angered yells and curses, she picked up the clothes that littered the floor and left the room. The door clicked shut to leave Bill in blackest darkness. His bellows diminished to murmurs as she climbed the stairs to wait for the night.

\|\\|/|\\\\/\\\\|/|\

When the doorbell rang at eight, Margaret was ready. Dinner was in the fridge, a crisp medley of carrots, spinach, lettuce, onions and other vegetables. The house was spotless – her only means of passing the time between locking up her guests and meeting her lover in the evening was to clean. You could eat off her floors. And maybe they would tonight, she thought entertaining erotic designs. Maybe he would spill the salad across the tile and feed each chopped vegetable to her with his lips.

Her body pulsed with anticipation as she crossed the room to let him in. She wanted this night to be perfect – it was their first anniversary. A carafe of deep ruby wine rested on the coffee table – his favorite vintage. She wore only the thin cotton underwear she'd bought this afternoon.

"Margaret," he whispered, admiring her near naked figure from the stoop. He held out a bouquet of red roses. She took them and pulled him inside. "Your hair is beautiful," he complimented, warming her to the bone.

"I need you so bad," she said, staring up into his face. He had those eyes that shifted, looked green one moment, brown the next. His face was smooth, but sharply drawn. She leaned to kiss him, and in her hurry, caught the roses between their bodies. "Ouch," she jumped and stepped back. A thorn had pricked her thigh. A thin line of red ran from the puncture to a crimson tear.

"Let me," he breathed, and knelt to lick her leg. His tongue was hot, but felt sandpaper-y, like a cat's. She shivered at his attentions, tousled his hair with her free hand. "Come have a drink, baby," she said, stepping back to break their contact. A few more minutes of this and they'd be fucking right there on the floor, and she wanted this night to be slow, thick – a steady building to perfect passion.

He stood, and flashing a row of gleaming white teeth, fingered her nipples, which poked like nails through the thin material.

"Whatever you say, lover."

She trembled at his voice. So much power there. A quick look at him would not give this impression. A thin nose, deep set eyes, smooth white face on a fit but not obviously muscled body. He was Joe Average, but she could sense the strangeness, the exotic reeking from his pores. Maybe that's what had attracted her to him in the first place.

They clinked glasses of heavy Bordeaux together, and

Margaret felt the sweat begin seeping from her body as he rumbled in his sexiest deep tone: "to us."

She drank deeply, closing her eyes to feel the fuel of the wine mixing with the fire of her lust. God, it was so hard to wait. The days between grew longer and longer and once he was here, she struggled every moment to stop herself from ripping his clothes off and mounting him without a word. But at the same time, she wanted these moments before, when they could talk and just be together as the musk of their mutual lusts rose around them like a fog.

When she poured the last drops of the bottle into his open mouth, Margaret could wait no longer. His features were wild with the pull of the moon, his movements jerky as a palsied man. He licked his lips and husked the word as she pounced.

"Now."

His hands wrapped around her body in a bear hug, drawing her close. "You smell divine," he growled and proceeded to lick her arms and legs, his nose chasing cool trails across her skin. Leaping from his lap, she dragged him to his feet and in fumbling haste undid his belt and pants as he unbuttoned and shed his shirt. He stood before her then, naked, yet covered with a manly down. His pubic thatch was thick and long, almost braid-able. But its wildness couldn't hide the scope of the tool that hung hungry there. With a rough finger he traced a red line up her thigh.

"So, have you missed me this month?" he said from between gritted teeth.

She smiled at the ritual, and nodded affirmatively.

Tucking his finger inside the cotton panties," his voice dipped even lower. "So I feel." His hand cupped her, made her tingle, his head dipped to inhale her smell. "So I smell."

She scratched the thickening hair on his chest, her hand resting on his engorged cock. "You're the only meat for me, Charles. Let me eat you."

Acceding to her request, he dropped to the floor. Her

tongue lashed him then, her teeth threatening to chew him to a bleeding pulp. But he only scraped his nails deeply into her back, shredding the cotton shirt and staining it in spots with drawn blood.

He was panting then in the thick of the moon's pull, and she knew the change would soon be complete. Moving from his crotch, she posed on hands and knees beside him. He was quick to rise. With an excited tear of cotton he freed her breasts from the remains of the t-shirt, and at the same time shredded her panties, leaving a waistband dangling around her middle and swollen trails of blood on her behind. Her sex only ached more at his rough violations, and then, at last, he was mounting her doggy style there on the floor. She could feel him changing faster now, as he pounded his cock between her thighs. The nails gouging her shoulders grew sharper, the flesh meeting her butt grew prickly, as if she were being slapped by a bristled broom. And within her too, his cock altered, grew, until she screamed in spasms of ecstasy and collapsed on the floor as his frenzied motions peaked in a warm, wet rush.

"God," she huffed, "God, God, God."

A strangled "No," answered her, before turning into a howl. She felt his teeth gripping her leg, breaking the skin, sinking into the soft flesh of her calf. She had to get up, she thought, or he'd devour her. In this state, his desire overruled his mind and it didn't matter who she was.

Kicking out with her free foot, she slammed his head from her leg and launched herself down the stairs, a trail of blood marking her passage. He followed, raking claws at her thighs, tearing skin from her back as he tried to bring her down. She knew some part of him was fighting for restraint – or else she would not make it down the stairs.

With a twist she turned the knob of the door as his teeth sank into her arm. She felt a rush of wetness between her legs in answer to the pain and laughed out loud. If she let him, she'd cum again as he ripped the flesh from her bones. One day, she thought, that's exactly what would happen.

But... not... now, she grimaced, and pushed the door open.

"So you came back, finally," Bill's voice trembled from within the pitch black room.

Margaret felt Charles' weight shift as he heard the voice. She could see his ears pricking up, feel his paw leave her back as, for a second, he pointed, and then sprang.

Bill screamed his loudest then, because Charles generally went for the throat when he was really hungry.

She remembered hers' and Charles' first time, when, as she watched the hair growing from his limbs like cheese from a grater, she'd realized how it had to end. And as his wolfen cock had spurted its seed within her, she'd called out to her roommate.

"Cathy," she'd bellowed, in the midst of an orgasm herself, "I want you to come down and meet somebody."

Charles had flipped her over with a huge hairy paw and was going for her jugular when Cathy had cautiously peeked into the room, mere seconds later. "Bitch was probably listening to us," Margaret had thought, and with all her strength she'd pushed Charles' muzzle in Cathy's direction.

"Get HER," she'd screeched, and somehow, even that early in their relationship, Charles had been trying to hold back the beast he was. He'd sprang and ripped out Cathy's throat in seconds. And so, their monthly routine had been born.

Behind her, Charles' growls and Bill's wails were fading.

"Shoulda stuck with the noose you knew, Bill," Margaret thought as she limped up the stairs to the kitchen. The gurgled "helps," "stops" and "oh Gooooods," quit before she'd even pulled her salad from the fridge.

She went back down to eat with him, flicking on the light and sitting naked on the floor. Feral eyes looked up at her from the disemboweled carcass on the couch. She didn't share his meal. She trapped his food out of necessity, but she herself was a vegetarian.

Across the room, he slurped and chewed, wolfen head disappearing in and out of the gory chest cavity. She wished she didn't have to handle his food so much beforehand, but Charles said the scent of the other man on her was what ultimately, kept him from killing her. It got in his nose as he made love to her, and when that wolfen olfactory sense picked out the origin of the smell, his instincts took over and he was after it instead of her.

Crunching a carrot between her teeth, Margaret melted inside at the sight of her werewolf. Five feet of iron bone and sinewy strength, his paws shredded and picked apart the man on the couch as if he were butter. Her body warmed again in anticipation as she thought of him returning to her at the end of his meal. Before she uncovered the drain beneath the vinyl couch and hosed down the slaughter room (and herself), Charles would pad across the tiles to her, green eyes filled with lust. Then he'd hold her down with a vaguely human paw, and lick her clean with that rough and tumble tongue. He'd mount her again, fast and hard, before disappearing up the stairs and into the night.

She didn't have to cuff him to the couch and he didn't wear a collar, but she knew he'd be back. Real men didn't fight their chains. Sated and relaxed, she propped herself up off the cold floor with one arm, and watched protectively as Charles enjoyed his meal.

She lived for the nights of the full moon.

A dozen years ago my college literature professor wrote on the top of this story that my writing showed promise, but that I should expand my literary horizons and stop writing stories like Stephen King. I've never had better praise.

The Last Plague

"Why?"

Silence greeted his vocalized query, but he expected little else. Silence and he were brothers – Siamese twins joined at the lips, he thought, twisting his own into a grin. He felt terribly alone tonight, more so than usual, but the clammy wind and the sterile world around him could not hold back his witticisms. He thought perhaps that was why he still lived. He laughed while everyone else went comatose.

"And Gram cries," he thought.

His name was Dave Rogers, but for all practical purposes this identification was unimportant – no one called him any name at all.

"Names don't amount to much when there's no one around to call them," he sometimes thought.

The road he traveled groped its way down a rugged slope, chasing the twilight. His bare, dusty feet plodded slowly, carefully, avoiding the shards of broken windshield and bottle glass, thistles, rusted metal, and rotting garbage heaps which overran what had been the rural town's main thoroughfare. Flies buzzed their healthy appreciation of the unburied, unmolested decay. The air teemed with insects unscourged by lethal sprays and blue electric arcs couched in cozy backyards. Lately, backyards had taken on the appearance of untamed jungle. The pavement was crisscrossed in cracks and reflected a dull, peeling, crumbling gray, rather than a healthy, sticky black. The roadside vegetation had not missed entropy's siege signal, and encroached with increasing vigor upon the concrete surface with the abandonment of ice salting and roadside tractor mowers. Grass has always been nature's first and best re-possessors.

"A funeral song," Dave murmured in response to the call of a wild dog. "But what a quiet funeral when the dogs have to sing in the chorus! Hardly a sob from the three or four relatives attending. Fitting, since the deceased went down without a fight. Kind of like Oedipus doing his mother," Dave laughed again. "Took the pleasure without investigating its source. Afterward it was too late; too final."

A brown and cream mottled Labrador suddenly darted between his legs and performed a quick 180-degree turn. The tail writhed like a wounded serpent as Dave wrestled the playful dog to the ground, rolled him over, and scratched his ears and chest. Then in a fluid motion the puppy-like exterior was gone, replaced by a fanged carnivore which disappeared into the tall grass, chasing a scent.

Reagan had been Jack Crepin's dog; now he came with Dave on his nightly walks. When Dave and Jack had been kids, Reagan went on family picnics with them, exploring creek beds and bramble-infested forests searching for hidden treasure and forgotten graveyards. Jack's mother always brought a stupid-looking red checkered tablecloth, but Dave's low opinion of the design never held him away from the plates of food she pulled out of the cooler and placed on it. But sunny family picnics were part of an almost forgotten past now. Dave couldn't even remember when he had last seen Jack.

Since the last plague, Dave had befriended a wide assortment of animal friends. They were former pets, forced to fend for themselves when they found their owners staring fixedly ahead on couches, chairs or beds, ignoring every and all screeches for food. Most perished, after the generations-long shelter was ripped away, but some succeeded in returning to the instinctual world of their ancestors. A dog pack now holed up somewhere to the north, and occasionally came to the town on foraging missions. Dave knew later in the evening they would probably hurl their frustrations at the moon – as countless canines over the centuries had seen fit to do. "This generation sure has a lot more to complain about though," he thought.

Reagan returned the dismal howl coming from the town while romping through the weeds. He had adjusted well to the change. Dave didn't mind the company on his nightly walks, and Reagan showed up at his doorstep every evening at sunset.

"That mutt's here again to take you for a walk," Gram'd grumble sarcastically. "Better hurry or he won't take you out."

Gram hated the idea of him being out in "that savage world" on these walks. But he had to go. It was an exercise of freedom which gave him time to reflect and relax, and sometimes, for a little while, to forget.

If he sat at home every night he'd lose his grip on sanity listening to the old wind-up mantel clock tick away an endless benediction. He couldn't understand how Gram could just sit there, night after night, feeling the cold gray shadows creep in around her until all that remained of the once warm and glowing sitting room was the icy arms of the leaching moon. Dave imagined the moon sometimes as an entity to itself: "A heavenly carnivore, sucking the energy and life from every sphere its chilling light could reach." He imagined lifeless Mercury and Mars its past victims, and wondered where the moon would go when Earth too was just another lifeless empty orb. He shook his head. "No, the only predator to man is man himself. And time. Gram and I just observe it in different ways. I walk the nights searching, and she stays at home waiting. It's all the same in the end, though. I wonder if anyone will be able to find this road at all in another hundred years."

He walked on, tossing the shoulder length curls behind his ears. Gram still held the old maternal worries. Once she had attempted to dissuade him from his jaunts, filling him with horror stories of unarmed travelers accosted by thugs, rapists and murderers. He had absorbed all of these reasons and after some thought calmly answered her.

"But Gram, we don't have those anymore to worry about."

He hadn't understood then why she had slumped at his words, and retreated to her room sobbing.

On impulse, in the middle of the weed-wrecked road, he threw his arms up and settled into a pitching stance.

"All right buddy, ya want the old screwball, do ya? Well, try and find this baby when she crosses the strike zone."

The invisible ball left his hand and he shouted, "Ha, strike three! Yer outta there!"

The silence was only more palpable.

"Looking pretty stupid aren't I," he asked the street. "Well I've seen worse – I'm not nuts yet. Maybe next week. For now I'm the best philosopher, pitcher, lawyer – you name it, I'm it."

He glanced at his watch. Really a useless object at this point, but he was slowly becoming obsessed with time. It was always slipping away, bit by bit, until nothing outside of its flow remained. Especially life. He inhaled a deep breath, trying to clear the cobwebs of pessimism from his brain.

"It's better this way," he told himself without conviction. He'd been over this subject countless times before. "No more wars, murders, noise – and God, the clamor there used to be. Freeways packed with screeching cars, blaring stereos, and bellowing drivers. Everywhere, masses of irritable people yelled and cursed, laughed and gossiped, always talking, talking, talking…"

Now the cacophony of man was still; the jets, and radios,

and shrill voices, gone. And the smells," he thought. "The stale choking odors of cigarettes and sweat, and auto exhaust, and smog, and air fresheners, and public bathrooms. . ." His nose wrinkled in remembered disgust.

"Justice works cruelly," he mused. "Yet what better, more effective punishment, than to unseat man from his despotism over nature – his creator – and place him at the mercy of that which he created. The irony is devastating. And if I keep up this line of thought much longer, I'll go nuts... or become a philosopher. Same difference, Gram would say... I hope she's OK."

Tonight he had tried not to leave her, but she had insisted.

"Look," she said. "Your faithful mutt from hell is out there waiting for you. Don't disappoint him. You can't do anything around here – unless you've discovered a new way of pressuring the crops to grow overnight." She smiled that weary smile which meant don't fight with me about this, or I'll have to use the rest of my strength to win, and you don't want to live with the consequences of that. "I'll be alright. I'd like some time alone right now anyway."

That afternoon Gram's old school friend Becky McClinger hadn't shown up for their game of penny ante poker.

"Stupid old coot probably forgot to wind her clock up again," Gram had said as she stormed out of the house to find her. Becky was at home when Gram stomped into the house, pausing in her flow of caustic rhetoric only on seeing her friend, sitting on the couch, eyes glazed, lower lip drooling, a disorienting rainbow in the background. Gram tried to break the trance, but it was too late, impossible. Dave found Gram crying in the den that afternoon when he returned from his scavenger run. He pushed the door open and approached her slowly, not sure what to do. She was a proud woman, and didn't admit tears often.

Bent and gray, and her head barely reached his shoulder. "What is it Gram?" he whispered.

"We used to joke about being matriarchs," she said, her voice rising in an unnatural cadence. Dave knew at once something had happened to Becky.

"We were so proud. The town, the world, everything was ours. We played cards and bought Tupperware and gossiped, and compared our men and our," she shuddered, "our children. And then it was all gone: our kids, our husbands, the town, our entire world. But still we had each other. And our card games. Those damn, endless card games..." She stared in bitter longing at the deck on the table in front of her.

"We were... lifelines to each other. Like a tightrope connection to another world, a ruined, past reality. And now," her voice quavered, "now she's not real anymore. That damn thing has robbed me of everything I ever loved." She slammed the deck of cards into a drawer and collapsed into her grandson's embrace, her tears soaking into his shirt. He felt awkward, unsure of how to comfort her.

"I'm here for you Gram, I won't leave," he told her. But she only cried louder.

Dave wiped a tear from his own face as he remembered Becky and reached down to pick up a chunk of asphalt, weighing it in his palm. She had been his only friend other than Gram for over three years now. She had given him his first book of Shakespeare, and satisfied the corresponding thirst for literature which that volume awakened in him. Becky had once been an English professor, and her tutelage gave him the education which the state never again would provide. It was she who had coined the phrase "the last plague" and now she herself had succumbed to its snare.

He pitched the lump of concrete at the growing spiderweb in the windshield of an '85 Oldsmobile. The glass shuddered and the rock rebounded to plunge through a rusted hole in the hood, vanishing with a clunk into the remains of the engine. The tires had long since deflated and were inhabited by colonies of warring ants. Small green and yellow leaves poked above the cracks and crevices of the hood and roof where dust and decomposing leaves had accumulated over the years.

"There just wasn't anything me or Gram could do," he thought, kicking at a smashed television set. Everywhere it was the same. Gram had once been convinced at first that the whole affair was a foreign ploy to complete the slow decay of the West, so the U.S. could be won without a fight. But in a dozen years they hadn't seen a new face in the town.

If anyone was actually *behind* it, they'd won a hollow victory. It had been an insidious change. Peace and love and prosperity first; all the flower children causes of another age seemed to prevail; but this fleeting golden age was followed by a complacent decline. The high intellect professions were the first to go. Soon newspapers stopped printing, because people stopped purchasing them and reporters stopped going to work. Nobody cared anymore.

"Pathogenic apathy," Dave termed it. Gram had said at one point there were nail factories producing heads which would never be hammered and auto plants manufacturing vehicles which would never be driven.

"In fact, nothing is being driven," he thought as he passed another decaying car. He stared at the darkening sky. The distant suns seemed to shine with increased clarity every year.

"The only good the plague ever did for us," Gram would say. "It's killing the smog." He noticed the dull glow on the horizon opposite the meager purple remains of the sunset. "Someone's still there at least," he thought grimly.

With a glance around at the countryside he realized how far he had come, and remembered with a twinge of guilt that he didn't want to leave Gram alone long, tonight especially. Reagan had been missing from his side for some time.

"Not paying the old boy enough attention," he realized and shrugged. Cupping his hands to his mouth he called the dog's name, but received no reply. The night remained oppressively silent as he turned to retrace his path. The wind was picking up, blowing his knotted hair into his eyes. He brushed it back with an unconscious reaction, realizing that a storm was blowing in. "I suppose the mutt can fend for himself. Always has." The road wound its way slowly back into the barren village. The only noises were of loose garbage cans rattling and tree branches scraping against old screens, straining and clawing to capture the comatose inhabitants within.

The street lamps stood dark, long since extinguished by hordes of children on guerrilla missions with BB guns. No one had been around to replace them, but through the windows of many houses, the colors of the rainbow emerged in a wrenching spectrum of reflection and projection. There was something intrinsically wrong with that light, and Dave's eyes strove to exclude it from their focus.

It was near the edge of town that he noticed the barking.

"The pack must be excited about something," he thought. Unconsciously he stepped up his pace and realized they were getting closer. He did a quick about face, and scanned the meadowland just as they crested a rise about a hundred yards away. He squinted to see the leader. It was Reagan! And he was leading a pack of snarling hungry dogs straight at him! He knew hunting cries, and that's what was issuing from the anguished vocal cords of the pack. He ran.

The town, which before had seemed small, tame and unpopulated, was suddenly a vicious metropolis. His breath came in short, unnatural rasps, with quick, pained intakes when the soles of his feet met the remnants of human society strewn across the road. He passed abandoned shops, the moonlight jeering off the jagged glass remaining in the storefront windows. They were just three blocks away when he twisted a bloody foot between the railroad tracks. He looked up with renewed hope as he saw the ravaged Crepin car just two houses away. Lurching to his feet, he staggered across the wild, prairie-reclaimed lawns, rubbing against thistles and dandelions, leaving a cloud of white floating seeds to mark his passage. The Crepin's front door was open a crack and he plunged through it just as the dogs crossed the tracks. He bolted the door behind him, and limped his way to the stairs, praying they wouldn't find a broken window on the ground floor to get in.

Upstairs, he chose a room with a window facing the front of the house to observe the pack. "Obviously Jack's mother's room," he thought as he pushed aside the faded pink chintz curtains from the glass and stared into the street below. The dogs were waiting at the door, scratching the mail chute with a grating sound that gave him the chills. Desolation washed over him. "The hounds of hell," he wheezed, disturbing the heavy air around him. "And Reagan their leader. I should have expected it. Nature is directing her vengeance on all men, not just the ones she doesn't like. Why should I escape?" But suddenly a feeling of exhilaration filled him. Reagan stood apart from the other animals, wagging his tail and whining. "Maybe he just came when I called, and they just followed, scenting food."

His eyes had become accustomed to the house's dreary interior, but as he examined the contents of the room, it dawned that something was very wrong with this particular shelter. His gaze swiveled from the shadowy dresser and night table along one wall to the queen size antique four-post bed on the other. The bed was not empty.

Dave stared with a growing lump in his throat at the darkness which divided the mattress in half with its mass. And deduced the source of the room's odor. With the taste of bile in his throat, he quickly exited the room containing the putrifying remains of Mrs. Rhona Crepin.

He darted out the back door, ignoring the shooting pains in his feet and the canine threat, but hadn't gotten far before they were on his trail again. He hopped a couple fences to slow them up, but knew he wasn't going to make it home tonight, one way or the other. He heard their hoarse barking and baying behind him and could feel his blood pumping through his pounding head. His ears felt on fire, his chest burned as his lungs struggled to pull oxygen in through a constricted throat. He would have to get into another house or be chewed to a bloody mess by the maddened hounds.

He spotted Jenny Finner's house on his right and on a whim dashed to the side door. He had once had a deep crush on Jenny before the plague had touched her. "Chased by hungry mutts into dead people's houses," he laughed and choked as he stumbled across the grass. "What a situation! No we don't have rapists or convicts, Gram, we have ravenous pets!"

He threw himself through the door and slammed it behind him with enough force to knock an antique dish from its perch on the kitchen wall. It smashed on the floor, one piece spinning around and around in a circle, toilet bowl effect. Just when he was about to step on the damn thing, it was still. Dave collapsed to his knees, resting his flaming head against the door frame. The sweat ran down his face in tiny rivulets, and his breath came in heaves. Blood from his feet smeared the floor. "Good housekeeper" he observed, glancing with disgust at the litter which covered the tiled floor. The cabinets hung open at crazy angles, and drawers, kitchen implements and empty cans lay everywhere. "This may be beyond even Mr. Clean," he said aloud.

"Dave?" a dreamy voice asked from behind him.

He jumped to his feet, thought better of it, and fell heavily against the wall. She stood a few feet away, holding out a trembling hand. He knew it was Jenny, but a far different Jenny than the one he once idolized. This Jenny was dirty, emaciated, her eyes nearly vacant. She resembled the kitchen – quiescently falling to ruin. But some of her old beauty remained. Her face still betrayed those strong but soft lines leading in a sensuous curve from her high cheekbones to her pink pouting lips. Her breasts poked through a frayed, stained t-shirt.

"Jen," he gulped, dumbfounded at finding her alive – and finding himself still, in spite of everything, attracted to her.

"You don't look very good, Davy," she said, her gaze fixed on the third button of his shirt.

"Me," he laughed. "What about..." He stopped in mid-sentence as the lips he had always longed to touch attached themselves to his own. With that kiss, he knew the Jenny he loved was gone; the replacement was a shallow mockery. Ants skittered out of their way as they sat down at a sticky table.

"Sit a minute. Let me get you a drink," she said, and moved to pick up a bottle from the counter. "Then you can tell me why all those nasty puppies chased you to my door. Zoron must have willed it for me. I've wanted a man for a long time now."

Dave cringed at the childlike fantasy quality of her speech, and longed to leave. In some ways seeing her like this was worse than Becky's trance, or smelling the worm-ridden guts of Mrs. Crepin. This was active psychological devolution, and it made him sicker than any physical decay could. But outside the dogs were still whining, and he could barely walk. For now, escape was impossible.

Jenny poured them each a glass of liquid and returned to the table. Dave drained his in a gulp, and at her insistence recounted his experience with the dogs while she stared at him in admiration.

"You're lucky I was awake, you know. I'm usually farlish by this time." She rose. "C'mon, let's go into the living room."

Dave's knees threatened to give out, but with her support, they staggered dizzily to an ancient couch. He noticed in the back of his mind that the dogs had stopped barking, so it should be safe to go home soon. Gram would be worried sick. His entire body was becoming numb, and his head was spinning. It was as if he'd just downed half a bottle of tequila. She leaned over and kissed him, hard, as a growing suspicion took hold in his mind.

"Jenny," he mumbled, pushing her away. "What was in that drink?"

"Oh, are you ready now?" She chirped happily. "I'll turn on the Cinevox for you."

He wanted to scream, to reach out with his leaded arms and strangle the girl. She only smiled dumbly and moved across the room. He knew he'd never be able to do either. In fact, he'd probably never leave this house again. Unwittingly he had drunk the catalyst of "the last plague" – as had Becky and the rest of the world in an unprecedented lemming-like escape from reality.

When those computer-induced and maintained spectrum shifts met with his optic nerves... Helplessly he watched her walk across the room to the large screen in slow motion, his lips still moist.

"Thy drugs are quick," he recited bitterly. "Thus with a kiss I die."

He felt Jenny slide her body in close to his own. She smelled of stale urine and other odors of neglect.

"I wanted her," he thought.

In slow motion, he turned his head to the screen. "But not like this..."

"Farlish," giggled Jenny, as a thin strand of spittle spun from her lip.

And then the shifting coalescing patterns entered his brain, the heightened awareness of the drug sensitizing every nerve to the touch of the burning computer serials of color. His eyes found heaven – perpetual stimulated happiness, and his consciousness sank into an inescapable sensual oblivion.

Lightning lit the sky, as the storm unleashed its torrential fury on the decaying apparatus of man. The water pounded the asphalt, removing another fleck of concrete here or there. Small victories, but continual ones. And nature wasn't hampered by clocks, or time.

Reagan whined to himself while cowering with the pack in the hills, longing for the touch of his friend. And a mantel clock steadily ticked off the hours, muffled by nature's watery demolition.

And an old woman cried, and was truly alone.

Artists in nearly all media have their favorite "included at the very last minute" stories. Bands always seem to land their biggest hit single from the song that they tucked onto the album just hours before the final CD sleeves were printed. The following story was written specifically for this collection, thanks to the artwork Andrew Shorrock developed for the color illustration. Since he lives in England and I'm near Chicago, we couldn't easily talk in person or on the phone about what I wanted to define the "look" of the book, but after e-mailing back and forth and sharing some of the stories with him, he came up with a visual metaphor for love and sex, pain and beauty, obsessions and relationships that I found immediately powerful and evocative. It was just days later that I felt compelled to write the following story based on his imagery.

Bloodroses

Tanya loved the roses; she only wished she could look at them. Every morning, her husband Mel guided her down the stairs from her bedroom, through the house, and down the rocky steps to the rose garden.

"Let me help you with that," he'd say, and tenderly lift the shirt over her head, undo her brassiere and slide her pants to the ground. With a kiss and a pat he sent her forth, into the tangle of thorns and leaves and sharp, rocky earth.

Tanya loved to run naked through the rose garden. She loved to feel their feathery touches, their sharp bite. Once she had been able to smell the humid sugar of their perfume, and see the vibrant smears of crimson across their petals. But that was long ago. Now Tanya could only experience her rose garden by touch, and so she drew the prickling bushes to her bosom and bled with every kiss of their stingy boughs.

She'd been 16 when it happened. Skin of virgin vanilla, cheeks blushed bright cherry, eyes like sapphires glinting against the stark satin of her raven hair. The boy then had been called Marshall, and she met him late each evening, a mute moon the only spectator to their urgent, exploring gropings.

They whispered and laughed and lay down on the bricks to stare out at the stars. "I wonder who's out there," they said aloud, inside, thinking, "I wonder who's in here."

She had ached for the taste of his tongue as the tickle of fallen rose blossoms caressed her neck. Each night after 10 she would climb down the trellis beneath her bedroom and wait on the brick patio by the fountain. She always heard him before he arrived, heavy shoes clicking like flint strikes against the stone. She was smoking inside; nearly ready to go up. Each night as they kissed and necked, he was tender with her and warm; at first. But as their meetings lengthened, as the moon waxed, his fingers strayed from tremulous sneak attacks beneath her shirt to bolder thrusts beneath her skirts and he grew insistent. One night, as the moon blinded the owls with its full searchlight shine, he pressed for more.

First he stripped her favorite blue t-shirt from her completely, a bold move there just yards from her father's back door. "Wait," she whispered, but not too convincingly. Soon her jeans were gone too, and his own flesh fully exposed to the wan tan of the moon, and open to the massage of her hands. A tremor ran through her belly at this unfamiliar territory, but still, his flesh felt soft and delicate, yet solid as wood. She could feel herself heat and grow with his watering kisses, her tight bud engorging with first passion to unravel in a satin-slick flower of invitation.

But then with the pass of a cloud over the faerie light she shivered and whispered "no."

He seemed not to hear and pressed himself tighter to her. She felt the rose of passion wither and scorch and pushed with tight fists against his shoulders again "no."

"Yes," he answered this time, through gritted teeth. "I can't wait anymore."

A pain shot through her like a thousand barbs of thorn, and Tanya at last opened her mouth to scream, only to have it filled with his tongue, his thick, sour tongue that suddenly tasted not so delicate and fine but fat and base and ashy with the flavor of cigarettes. She panicked then, and struck him in the ear with a fist, but he didn't relent, in fact her struggles only seemed to encourage him. Replacing his mouth with a gritty palm he held her to the brick as he took her, impervious to her cries and wiggles and wide eyes. Finally she bit down on his hand, hard, so that she felt the skin give way. The hand yanked backwards, but rather than nurse his wound, her sweet and gentle Marshall brought that hand back down in a closed fist and struck her fast and ruthless in the mouth.

And again.

With his hands on her neck then, he kissed her, but not with the blending of a lover, rather with the penetrating jabs of a conqueror savoring his bloody victory. Then he pulled back to ride her in animal anxiousness, lifting her head with each thrust and slamming it back to the brick with each release.

Tanya felt the warmth pooling beneath her head, at the same time as it slicked and gathered beneath her buttocks. Her heart was screaming in horror as her flesh screamed in pain. How could this be happening? How could she have been so wrong about this boy, this wicked young man? She swam in a sea of black filth, every light touch and kiss of the past nights re-experienced as a violation, a betrayal. There were stars of hurt in her eyes as the heady scent of roses engulfed her like a savior cloud as Marshall came to climax. She breathed it in and savored it as if to blot out the knowledge of the situation, eyes closed, mind seeking another world. And then its sweet perfume turned sickly in her nose, icy sharp in its character, like rotting candy.

Distantly she felt him remove himself, heard the rustle of his jeans dragged across stone.

Heard him murmur "shit."

She kept her eyes closed as he scurried away into the night.

When she woke next, Tanya strained to see through the blackness, but could not. Her nose felt sniffy, but she could not smell the roses.

"Marshall," she called.

Then, "Mom?"

The nurse's hand on her brow was cool. "You're in the hospital dear. How do you feel?"

"Could you turn on the light?" Tanya asked. "I can't see."

There was no answer at first, and then she heard the nurse talking to someone at the far end of the room. Whispers, and the tongue clicks of pity.

"It may pass," she heard a woman say.

But it didn't.

Her world remained a black void where only sound could enter. Tanya was alone in a room without windows. Her food had no taste, the roses had no smell. And no color.

But she could feel them. It became her only release. To press the world against herself in a smothering embrace. "You're there," she sometimes murmured. "You're there, I can feel you."

Tanya met Mel at a special education class. He was the teacher, and she loved to listen to the mellifluous tones of his voice. It was caramel and chocolate. Molasses and cream. She already loved him when he told her she was pretty one night, as she stood in the foyer, waiting for the familiar step of her mother who came each night to drop her off and pick her up. She felt her skin flush, but at the same time, shrugged away his compliment.

"No," she said softly, "...but thank you."

He took her hand in his – wide, leathery, strong – and pressed it tightly.

"Yes, you are. Do you like coffee?"

"I can't taste it," she deflected.

"You can feel hot and cold, can't you?"

In a month, her mother was no longer driving her to school. In six, Tanya was standing against the wall in their kitchen, listening as piece by piece of her 25 years were carried past, landing with thuds and rattles and grunts in the bed of Mel's van.

"I'll take care of her," he promised her mother. Tanya imagined the wrinkles playing like braille across her mother's falling cheeks.

"Do," was all she said.

Mel fed her ice cream and coffee that she couldn't taste, but could feel. He massaged her feet. Mel read Sylvia Plath and Jackie Collins to her. Mel seemed to smile with his voice at every move she made. But most importantly, Mel took her to the rose garden.

"I can't," she insisted, the first time they drove to the conservatory. "It's where... I... just can't."

"Taste the air with your tongue," he advised. "Feel the scent in the humidity on your skin. It's healthy, even if you can't see them or smell them."

In the end, she gave in, and walked with him tremulously on nearly even flagstone steps. Once she stumbled at the rough rise of a heavy stone and he held her upright by her elbow. She shook with relief and fear. But as they wove deeper into the strange maze of muffled glass houses, she realized he was right. Each house was like a special pressure chamber; the air changed its feel, growing Florida muggy and Phoenix arid and Oregon cool damp with each whoosh of the doors behind them. Its flavor eluded her but she could *feel* its taste. The heat of the sun through the glass panes warmed her head and neck and the clasp of his hand on hers led her to explore the more ethereal aspects of the garden, if not its view.

"Touch this," he commanded, moving her hand by encircling her entire wrist, and placing it in contact with ferns and foliage, buds and stems.

And then.

"Touch this," he said, and laughed when she drew back in pain.

"Every rose has its thorn," he said then, and hugged her to him.

"That wasn't very nice," she pouted, pushing him away. But he kissed her and apologized.

"If you don't feel the pointed things in life, you'll soon take the soft ones for granted," he said. This made sense to her and she found she loved him more.

"Can I feel your pointed thing," she giggled, running a hand up his thigh.

"Yes," he promised, but instead led her to feel the bark of a sequoia tree. It was rough against the back of her hand and she pressed against it, drawing its detail inside herself until her hand was raw. Her blood flowed hot through her arms and she knew that she had crossed a precipice. A divide. She had spent years learning how to avoid bumping into furniture, years hiding from the sharp edges of the world. Years hiding from Marshall.

She wasn't hiding anymore.

"Let's get married," she announced, and in a house filled with unseen armies of roses, she listened as his voice trembled and he said, simply, "yes."

※ ※ ※

"I'm going to grow you a rose garden," Mel said one day, as he lightly ran a knife along the bottom slope of her cleavage. It was a game they had developed. She had taken his message to heart: *every rose has its thorn*. She would not try to savor the rose without first feeling its thorns. It made the end pleasure of the petals so much more intense. Likewise, she would not make love to Mel without first snipping her nerve ends raw.

He would carve sweet nothings in her skin or decorate her with forests of twining, twisting pins. Each sharp prick of her flesh made her face contract, and yet, the rush of the blood through her heart made her beg him not to stop. Each week, they played the game anew, the goal changing with every implement Mel used. The pain made her feel alive, broke her out of her black detachment from everything around.

"Can you stand 40 pins?" he would ask.

"Yes," she answered, in a tiny voice. "45."

If she cried "uncle" before reaching the number, she lost. If she let him go further, she won. Either way, when the game was over and his kisses finally swelled her lips and tightened her nipples, she ended in ecstasy.

"I *would* like a rose garden," she admitted presently. "I could feel their petals against my skin every day, then."

"And their thorns," he added.

"Yes," she said. "And their thorns."

※ ※ ※

The first time they walked together in the garden, the rose bushes had no buds. Tanya ran her hands up their thin stems and winced as the blood ran in rivulets down her arm.

"They're all thorn," she complained.

"Give them time," he said. "First come the thorns, and then the flowers."

And they did come. The garden grew with the breadth of her belly, which Mel had seeded with a child. And in her fifth month, Tanya felt the first perfect, satin-smooth bloom.

"Oh, Mel," she praised. "It feels wonderful. It's softer than a feather, and more velvety than velvet."

He laughed and promised, "Soon, it will all be in bloom. Just like you."

\\\//\\/\\\/\/

When the contractions racked her body with feral bites of pain in her sixth month, Tanya cried for her baby, and for herself. She felt alive with the fire, and yet shredded near death at its kiss. It was over quickly; Tanya writhed and sobbed in the endless darkness and her pregnancy rushed out of her in a flood of bitter, heated acid. The bed was sodden, soaked in an empty broken promise.

She didn't blame Mel, and yet... His knives seemed sharper of late, his games more intense. She wondered, as her wracking pains slowed, could his long needled probes have killed their child? Just yesterday, he had brought her to screams with his penetrations.

No, unfair, her mind railed. That was her fault, as much as his. She craved the blades, encouraged their attacks. The pain made her *feel*. Its intensity almost made up for the senses long lost, but still imagined. Sometimes the ghost of a peppermint stick washed painfully across her tongue making her mouth water, or the scent of her father's aftershave before church on a Sunday smothered her to coughing for a second before disappearing, leaving behind an emptiness deeper than the black sea her eyes swam in, day after night. She wished more than anything that she could part that cruel curtain, and see the man who kissed her and held her and kept her safe, as he indulged her twisted needs.

She wept then with guilt at her lack of trust in him. Guilt at her own inadequacy. She had lost their baby. Even in this she was only half a woman.

Mel only made her feel worse as he waited on her carefully, patiently, over the next few days, bringing her soup and toast and helping her to the bathroom, watching to make sure her bleeding didn't continue.

"I love you," she told him, "I'm sorry." And he hugged her tightly.

\\/\\/\\\\/\\/\\/\\/\\/\\/\\/\\\\/\\/\\/\\/\\

Two weeks after her miscarriage, Mel came into their bedroom and announced, "The roses are in full bloom. Do you want to go?"

"Yes," she answered, and he took her hand dramatically, like a knight come to escort the princess to the ball.

The stairs seemed endless, her legs weak and trembly; it had been almost two weeks since she'd left her bed.

"Are you sure you're ready?" he asked, as they walked through the kitchen.

She nodded and took a breath.

"I'll be fine. I need to walk."

Step by step they descended to the garden, the air teasing Tanya's hair in a ghostly kiss that made her sigh.

"I've missed it out here. Show me the prettiest ones."

He took her hand and guided her to a bush of thick cushiony buds. Tanya held the thorns to her palm and brushed the petals across her cheek to tickle her nose.

"Tell me how it smells," she begged.

He laughed. "Like life," he said, his voice heavy and delicious. "It smells like the breath of the sun and the kiss of life."

She left his guiding hand then and twirled her way through the garden, stopping at each scratch of thorn across her flesh to kiss and rub the buoyant flowers on top, laughing with a giddiness that had seemed lost to her just an hour before.

"My roses are beautiful," she laughed. "Thank you."

"There's just one thing," he said, his voice close in her ear, startling her. She'd thought he remained by the stairs.

"What's the matter?" he said when she jumped at his voice. "Did I scare you?"

"No," she said, steadying herself against his shoulder. "I just didn't hear you there."

"I can be very quiet," he agreed.

"What one thing?" she asked.

"The garden is not quite complete."

Something stabbed at Tanya's back and he yelled "wait, stand still," as she shrieked, backpedaling into a razor sharp tangle of thorn and flower.

"Something bit me," she cried out. "Mel?"

His hand reached out to her elbow to steady her. But she was still off balance; she felt the blood running down her back and she twisted, lashing out at the bite, finding her hands punching, not some stray dog at her feet, but hitting Mel's face.

"Take it easy," he soothed, voice of chocolate tinged with bitter lemon, but she was tumbling away from him, tripped by the slash of a rose stem and sudden vertigo.

The world exploded in a rainbow of fireworks across Tanya's black horizon, and with the light, her thoughts blinked out.

Her first thought was that her right leg was broken. A stabbing, red-hot scald ran up and down its length.

Her next was that something had died.

"My god, what is that smell?" she exclaimed, not realizing what she had said until she opened her eyes and saw the man bending over her leg, using an instrument resembling a cheese grater to peel slices of skin from her thigh.

Without thinking she kneed him in the face and pulled herself backwards, crablike.

"What..." she began to ask, ignoring the blood running in slow dribbles from her leg and looking around her.

"...is this?"

The man was rubbing his chin with his hand. He was the ugliest man Tanya had ever seen. His left eye was glazed over with white, his cheeks were sunken and gray. Her hands had always known that his arms were somehow misshapen, but now she could see the breadth of his deformity; odd tufts of hair matched with twisted cords of muscle to produce a manged and mangled appearance. His chin jutted sideways and his nose was just a blob of wide-pored clay. His face and arms were covered with a network of discolored scars, a pink and white cross work of snip and stitch.

"You can see!" he exclaimed. His grin grew wider, dragging his cheeks into eclipse with his eyes. He scrambled to his feet, and lifted his arms.

"I've built it all for you," he said, gesturing around them at the low ceilinged heat lamps beating down orange and bare between the wooden beams just a couple feet above them, and the quiet, slowly oscillating wall fan. There were no windows, only four concrete walls. All this time, she'd thought it was a spacious garden of open breezy air beneath the warmth of the sun.

"It's your very own private garden," Mel bragged. "It will never fade or wilt. It will always be here for you to touch."

Tanya stared at the basement maze of winding paths amid twined branches of barbed wire. She was surrounded by the glint of metal, some barbs rusted, no doubt from the spray of her own blood.

At the top of most of the barbed wire bushes were the pale flowers she had brushed her face against so many times these past months. Intricate blooms of layered petals, painstakingly pieced together by her husband and mounted, somehow, on these bushes of unforgiving cruel steel.

"I started with my skin," he explained, pointing to a misshapen rose of brownish black. A strip of Tanya's own bleeding flesh still hung, seemingly forgotten, from his clenched hand.

"It took me a few tries to learn the best way to cure it without it rotting or turning hard. After that, it was easy. Just harvest and cure, assemble and mount. Your mother gave us this whole section here," he gestured to a group of pasty bloomed bushes, adding, "And I did this whole bush here just last week."

He pointed to the devilish twinings of barb and peach-fuzz fine flower next to her.

"That's the culmination of our love, honey."

She looked at the pinkish buds, tightly woven petals seemingly bursting with the need to open and shower their scent to the world.

"That's our baby," he said, nodding, white eye glinting like the moon on a gray day. "Isn't she beautiful? She was delicate to peel, but I think she's the most beautiful rose here."

The tears coursed in heated rivers down her face as she touched the baby soft skin of the rose crafted from her lost child. Then she kissed it and breathed in the scent of her daughter.

"How could you?" she whispered, stomach contracting in horror and despair. Her senses attacked with an intensity sharper than any knife Mel had ever wielded. She could smell the gagging stench of decay of her mother and baby all around her like a palpable thing, a blanket of death. And the everywhere glint of steel and skin made her want to close her eyes again forever.

She looked down, unable to face the remains of her baby. Or her husband.

She saw the sheen of electric red blood slicking her leg, and saw the scars that pitted and poked their way up her thighs, turning to criss-cross trails of a city road map gone mad on her belly.

Her once taut and beautifully creamy skin was a wrinkled mess of tears and mends, slices and stitches. There was no more beauty there; her youth was carved away, one pore at a time. Left behind on the points of Mel's pins and knives and barbed wire roses.

There were spots discolored, like the stretched skin of a wax figure that was slowly melting and stretching, taffy in the ghastly machine. Idly, she wondered which of the roses here was made of her own tortured flesh. Surely some of the gouges she'd thought to be innocent wounds of passion at the time had been meant to make harvests for Mel's twisted garden.

"Are you OK, honey?" he asked softly. "I know it's probably a lot to take all at once."

She nodded, unable to answer, eyes drawn again and again from her own ruined torso to the tender sculpting of her baby before her, every petal paper thin, yet still a rose grown thicker than most in life. There were bare stems next to it still, barbed branches waiting patiently for their own bloodroses to bloom, and Tanya closed her eyes and said, "it was better to be blind."

She closed her hands around the barren stems until blood dripped brightly to the ground below. She brought her face down as if to sniff the sharpened barbs and then with a wrench screamed as their tips scraped out her sight, a violent abortion, fake thorns carving new scars in the broken pits of her eyes.

Dimly she heard Mel's usually honeyed voice turn to broken glass as he screamed "no," but it didn't stop her from twisting the rose stems this way and that, twirling them deliberately all around until the red fire of pain and betrayal slipped from nausea, to numbness, to final, freeing black.

Tanya loved the roses, but she couldn't bear to look at them anymore.

Afterword

The year 2013 marks the 20th anniversary of my first short story sale to a magazine ("Tomorrow," which was eventually reprinted in this, my first book-length collection). Just a few months from the time of this writing will mark the 15th anniversary of me signing the contract for my first book, *Cage of Bones & Other Deadly Obsessions*. I've published a lot of work since then, including seven novels, but *Cage of Bones* will always hold a very special place in my heart.

Back in 1999, when Delirium Books contracted to publish this collection, I had been sending submissions out to magazines for six years, and had published dozens of short stories, in a lot of very tiny magazines. But as the '90s were winding to a close, I'd finally started "cracking" some markets that were a little more well-known (in the horror community, anyway). "Cage of Bones" had appeared in *Into The Darkness* (the editor would shortly thereafter found Necro Publications), "Pumpkin Head" had appeared in *Grue*, "Anniversary" in *Dead of Night* and "Remember Me, My Husband" in *Terminal Fright*. These were important magazines to me; they were the places I really worked to "crack" and have my stories appear in. Plus, "Tomorrow," my very first sale, had been accepted by *2 A.M.*, and "When Barrettes Brought Justice..." by *Haunts*, both of those holy grail magazines for me at the time, though both publications folded before printing those stories.

So when the fledgling *Delirium Magazine* accepted both "Pumpkin Head" as a reprint and "The Mouth" for first-time publication, I figured I had a lot of published work and I decided to pitch the editor, Shane Ryan Staley, on putting together a collection of my stories. He had just announced that in addition to publishing the magazine, his new imprint Delirium Books would be publishing a line of soft and hardcover fiction collections, and I figured I might have a shot at a softcover book.

Turned out, Shane really loved my work and slotted me for a hardcover release.

I had hit the big time!

At least, it felt like it back then.

I spent the next few months suggesting new pieces and re-editing older stories, and looking for artists I liked on the Internet to solicit for the cover art (I found Andrew Shorrock's work and he did an amazing cover). I asked P.D. Cacek, who I had met at the World Fantasy Convention in 1997, and whose work had appeared in the *Hot Blood* anthology series, if she would consider introducing the collection. Both she and Andrew agreed, and slowly, the book took shape. At the time he was creating the art, roses were out of season in the part of the UK that Andrew lived in, so I actually bought, scanned in and emailed him the rose that appears on the cover so that he could use as part of the art… and later, after his initial collage inspired the book's final story, "Bloodroses," I sent him some handwritten prose from the story which ended up being included at the bottom of the final cover treatment.

Cage of Bones & Other Deadly Obsessions originally was released as a signed, limited-to-300-copies edition in October, 2000. It was a black-bound hardcover with a gold foil stamp design created by Colleen Crary. Andrew Shorrock's cover art illustration was printed on the inside, because Delirium didn't print dustjackets. However, I had suggested to Shane on a couple occasions that he might get more bookstore distribution if his releases had normal dustjacket book covers, and so a month after *Cage of Bones* was released, he decided to dive into that market, and retroactively issued a dustjacket for *Cage of Bones*, which was shipped to anyone

Afterword

who had ordered the collection. From that point on, most of Delirium's releases had dustjackets.

Cage of Bones received good reviews (including one in *Asimov's Science Fiction Magazine* – which was a coup for me, since that was a magazine I had read religiously as a teen!) but since Delirium's business model was "limited editions," ultimately it disappeared from easy access for many years. I saw copies pop up and sell on eBay for as much as $150 at one point in the mid-2000s.

In 2010, at the dawn of the e-book revolution, Shane reissued the title as an e-book on his Darkside Digital imprint, but that edition was lacking P.D. Cacek's introduction, as well as the short introductions I had written to all of the stories. It also had a slightly different cover text treatment. When I got the rights back to the book in 2013, I reinstated the introductions and original cover art for this Dark Arts Books re-release – which also will make the book available in trade paperback for the first time ever.

It's been 13 years since its original publication, and I still think some of these tales are the best – and most daring – things I've written. I hope you found some fun in them – because they were definitely a lot of twisted fun to write.

Dark Dreams, indeed!

– John Everson
Naperville, IL
July, 2013

About The Author

John Everson has developed a deep fascination with the culinary joys of jalapenos and New Mexican chiles over the past 13 years since the original edition of *Cage of Bones*, his first book, was published. His favorite band remains The Cure, but he was first in line to buy the new Ke$ha CD. Over the past decade, he has authored seven horror novels and dozens of short stories.

His short work, ranging from light fantasy to erotic horror, has appeared in anthologies like *Best New Zombie Tales (Vol. II)*, *Best New Werewolf Tales (Vol. I) The Necro Files: Two Decades of Extreme Horror*, *The Green Hornet Case Files* and many more. His fiction has also appeared in a variety of magazines, including *Dark Discoveries, Grue, Literary Mayhem, Doorways, Bloodsongs, Dead of Night, Terminal Fright* and *Sirius Visions*.

In October of 2000, many of his erotic horror tales were collected and published in hardcover by Delirium Books as *Cage of Bones and Other Deadly Obsessions*. A second collection, *Vigilantes of Love* (originally published by Twilight Tales), followed three years later. His more recent fiction collections include *Needles & Sins*, *Creeptych* and *Deadly Nightlusts: A Collection of Forbidden Magic*.

Over the past decade, Everson has written seven novels – *Covenant, Sacrifice, The 13th, Siren, The Pumpkin Man, NightWhere* and *Violet Eyes*. His first novel, *Covenant*, won a Bram Stoker Award upon its original limited edition release through Delirium Books in 2004. It was later reissued in mass market paperback. *NightWhere* was a 2012 Bram Stoker Award Finalist.

Everson is the publisher of Dark Arts Books and a member of the Horror Writers Association (HWA). He has served as a longtime copyeditor for Necro Publications and Cemetery Dance, and in the early 2000s, was the publications director for Twilight Tales, as well as a fiction editor for *Dark Regions* magazine and the music columnist for *Wetbones* and *Talebones*.

Despite an omnipresent nagging dream of relocating to warmer climes, John still lives in the west 'burbs of Chicago with his wife Geri, his son Shaun, and three petulant birds.

Read his blog, join the e-newsletter and find out more about his fiction, art and music at www.johneverson.com.